When Comes Forever

by

Loretta C. Rogers

When Comes Forever

Cover Art by *Debbie Taylor*

The Wild Rose Press, Inc.
PO Box 708
Adams Basin, NY 14410-0708
Visit us at www.thewildrosepress.com

Publishing History
First Tea Rose Edition, 2018
Print ISBN 978-1-5092-2017-5
Digital ISBN 978-1-5092-2018-2

Published in the United States of America

As if it gave her comfort, she once again dipped the pen and, careful not to mar the page of her journal with ink splatters, continued to write.

The wind claws at the door and rattles the shutters as if it were a monster wanting to get inside. And when all is quiet, I hear them snuffling outside, see their sharp toenails as they scratch between the floor and the bottom of the door. I dare not cook for fear the scent of food will drive the wolves mad and somehow they will figure a way to get inside the cabin. Who would rescue me?

Her stomach rumbled, reminding her she hadn't eaten since noon. Reaching across the table, she pulled a plate of day-old cornbread toward her. It would suit her just fine if she had a glass of fresh milk to wash down the meager meal. Instead, she finished the tea that had grown tepid.

She rubbed the small of her back as she pushed from the cane-ribbed chair and walked to the basin. Leaning forward and balancing on her tiptoes, she peered through the peephole in the shutter that covered the window and closed out the world. Darkness stared back at her. She longed for the noise of Chicago's streets, the comfort of her parents' home, and the inane chatter of her two sisters.

The baby stirred again. Rebecca walked back to the chair and sat. Before closing the journal, she penned a last line.

Dedication

To all my readers,
who energize my writing with your glowing reviews

Chapter 1

Rebecca Donnelly struggled to keep her hand from trembling as she dipped the pen into the inkwell. Alone and pregnant, she had little reassurance of safety from the rifle cradled across her lap. Sitting at the rough-hewn table in front of the stone fireplace, she leaned toward the open journal.

I pray God forgive me for being a coward. Yet I must confess, I am truly afraid. Where is Frank? I expected him to arrive with the doctor a week ago. I fear he has abandoned me, or worse is lying dead somewhere on the prairie.

Drawing the heavy woolen shawl closer around her shoulders, she dreaded the nights when the wind moaned like an unseen specter around the outside of the two-room cabin. She shivered against the chill that invaded the small room. Riveting her gaze on the sturdy crossbar that solidly braced the planked door against intruders, she rose to place a single log on the fire. With the rifle's barrel in one hand, she used the other to grip the iron poker and stoked more life into the embers.

A new worry filled Rebecca when she eyed the dwindling stack of wood. Frank had warned her not to leave the cabin. "I've laid in enough kindling and logs to last you until I get back with the doctor," he'd said. "There's no need for you to go outside while I'm gone. It's dangerous, Rebecca. Heed what I say."

She fought down the hysteria building inside her. Taking stock of the furniture, if worse came to worst, she would burn the table, then the chairs. No, no, she reasoned. That wouldn't do. How dangerous could it be outside and in the broad daylight?

Placing the rifle within easy reach, and then standing on tiptoes, she removed the tin of tea leaves from a shelf and spooned enough for one mugful. Careful not to burn her hands, she used the hem of her skirt to lift the kettle from the iron crane and poured hot water into a green ceramic teapot—her only wedding gift from her new husband.

She knew her actions were measured and deliberate. Fifty miles from town and only God knew how many miles from another woman, what else did she have to do besides measuring time?

For a long moment she lost herself to meandering thoughts while savoring sips of hot tea. She closed her eyes and cocked her head to one side to daydream about the laughter she had shared with her two sisters as they sat in front of the fireplace in the upstairs parlor adjacent to their bedrooms. They had shared secrets, hopes, and dreams. Foolish dreams that only young girls imagined. Her thoughts turned sour. Her sisters had married men of substance and each lived in grand houses within a few blocks of her parents. While she—

The baby inside her womb kicked, interrupting her musings. Rebecca smiled as she gently massaged the tiny protrusion that seemed to stretch and press against the area beneath her ribs. The smile faded, and she was left with a profound sadness.

The youngest, she had been dubbed by her father as the most intelligent of his three daughters. But then, the day before her sixteenth birthday, Frank H. Donnelly, Esquire, had bumped into her, nearly knocking her off the boardwalk and causing her to dump all her parcels into the street. She'd looked into a face more handsome than any of the characters in her favorite dime novels. He'd had an angel's smile and the devil's eyes, and his touch had made her shiver with a yearning she had been too young to understand. Her father had warned her about Frank's "idealistic nonsense." He had also denied Frank's request to formally court her.

"My God, man, you are twenty years my daughter's senior." Her father had shaken his fist at Frank. "Get off my porch before I grab you by the scruff of your scrawny neck and throw you into the street."

Recalling the argument that had ensued between her father and herself, Rebecca now swiped the tears threatening to spill from her lashes as she released a despondent sigh. She had spent a thousand lonely nights since haughtily announcing she was her own woman and would accept Frank's calls and no one could stop her.

There was no fancy wedding. No beautiful gown. No father to walk her down the aisle. Frank had convinced her to elope, and they had spent their honeymoon in a passenger car on a train bound for Oklahoma Territory. And, of course, there was the little matter of the five thousand dollars he had convinced her to take from her father's safe. The money was rightfully hers. Well, almost. A gift from her grandmother, she was expected to wait until her eighteenth birthday to claim the money, and then it was to be partially used for a coming-out trip to Europe, with the rest set aside for her attendance at Mrs. Dubois' Finishing School for Young Ladies.

Her mother had always said that once you chose your bed, no matter how uncomfortable, it was yours to lie in—forever.

With that thought in mind, another tear dripped from Rebecca's chin, landing on the wet ink and causing it to spread in a macabre shape across the page. She quickly blew on it to dry the spot before it widened and ruined the rest of her writing. Lifting a corner of the shawl, she wiped her eyes, and as she reread her entry she asked herself the same question she'd asked a hundred times since coming to this piece of dirt that Frank called a ranch—did she love her husband, or had she been in love with a fantasy?

The wind rattled the door. Her heart pattered wildly against her chest. Even her whisper sounded overly loud in the forlorn room. "Look where my stubbornness got me. How could Father ever think I was smarter than Melinda and Beth?" As she drew a breath against fresh tears, her lower lip quivered anew.

As if it gave her comfort, she once again dipped the pen and, careful not to mar the page of her journal with ink splatters, continued to write.

The wind claws at the door and rattles the shutters as if it were a monster wanting to get inside. And when all is quiet, I hear them snuffling outside, see their sharp toenails as they scratch between the floor and the bottom of the door. I dare not cook for fear the scent of food will drive the wolves mad and somehow they will figure a way to get inside the cabin. Who would rescue me?

Her stomach rumbled, reminding her she hadn't eaten since noon. Reaching across the table, she pulled a plate of day-old cornbread toward her. It would suit her just fine if she had a glass of fresh milk to wash down the meager meal. Instead, she finished the tea that had grown tepid.

She rubbed the small of her back as she pushed from the cane-ribbed chair and walked to the basin. Leaning forward and balancing on her tiptoes, she peered through the peephole in the shutter that covered the window and closed out the world. Darkness stared back at her. She longed for the noise of Chicago's streets, the comfort of her parents' home, and the inane chatter of her two sisters.

The baby stirred again. Rebecca walked back to the chair and sat. Before closing the journal, she penned a last line.

Christmas draws near, and the baby grows anxious to make its grand entrance into the world. I am afraid. I am alone.

She whispered a silent prayer. "Please, send Frank home soon." She placed her hands against her face and wept. Drawing a breath between sobs, she laid another log in the fireplace and then snuffing out the candle, she used the moonlight to trundle to the bedroom. Not bothering to undress, she unlaced her high-top boots. Setting them neatly aside, she climbed beneath the quilts. While lying in the dark, she thought of all the ultimatums she would present to her husband—give up this foolish notion of his and return to Chicago, or…or what? And what was his plan? She wasn't certain he had made it clear.

She thumbed an imaginary gold band. Though she

hadn't spoken the words, her thoughts seemed to echo in the small two-room cabin: "or I'll go back to Chicago without him."

There. She'd said it. "Let him have his dream. I'd rather die than continue to live out here, miles from nowhere, with no one to talk to except tumbleweeds."

She wrapped her hands around her extended abdomen. "Don't worry, baby. I won't have you growing up in a heathen land."

The realization that Frank had wooed her for the money was a bitter pill. It hadn't taken long for him to treat her like a child, even like a nuisance sometimes. It had been as if the blissful dreams she had sustained turned into a hellish nightmare. The exact opposite of the romantic novels she had surreptitiously read.

He'd said she was like a lovely rosebud and that he wanted to be the lucky man who helped her blossom into a beautiful flower. It had all sounded so poetic.

She chastised herself for falling victim to her husband's infectious enthusiasm, and to her own whimsical, immature daydreams of moonlit rides under skies littered with stars. She'd imagined Frank as a gentle lover lifting her to soaring heights of climatic ecstasy. Instead he was a rutting animal, taking his pleasure and leaving her unfulfilled while he finished the night snoring.

As if in protest at being hugged too tightly, the baby gave another round of solid kicks. Unable to find a comfortable position, Rebecca clumsily rolled from the bed, and padding in stocking feet, returned to the main room. Lifting the lid to her sewing basket, she removed the white christening gown and set her embroidery needle to stitching tiny rosebuds on the collar.

She worked until her eyes grew tired. Setting the sewing aside, she yawned and stretched. This time she would sleep.

****

Rebecca awoke with sharp pains in the small of her back. A persistent ache tugged at her girth. Rolling to her side, she used a pillow to support her belly.

Closing her eyes, she drifted back to sleep. Her dream was interrupted by the pains in her abdomen as they grew sharper, causing her to suck in a deep breath in order to keep from crying out when the discomfort intensified. She counted on her fingers. It wasn't time for the baby to be born. By her calculations she still had two weeks.

"Not yet. Please, baby. Don't come. Not yet. Be patient. Wait until your daddy arrives with the doctor."

She shifted against the mattress, seeking a more comfortable position. Instinctively she rubbed her burgeoning middle as she recalled her father's harsh words.

"Not one cent of inheritance will you receive if you insist on marrying this…this fiddle-footed no-account. And once you come to your senses and see Frank Donnelly for the shiftless wastrel he is, don't think you can come running home. You'll not be welcomed."

He'd ordered her to her room and had ordered Frank out of the house with a threat of having him arrested if ever stepping foot on the premises again.

Without his knowing, her father had fueled her romantic fire that night, and Frank had fanned the embers into full-blown flames when, hours later, he had tossed pebbles at her window. Slipping from her room, she had sneaked down the backstairs, and together she and Frank had planned their elopement.

The ache in her back grew more intense. "Oh, Mother, you were right. I've made my bed and now I must lie in it. Thorns and all."

Knowing her father was a man of his word caused her melancholy to intensify. She could never go home again.

Rebecca woke before dawn. For a moment she couldn't remember where she was. Sun flooded through the crack between the shutters, revealing an area much different from her bedroom in Chicago. This room consisted of a bed with a mattress thin enough for the rope slats to cause discomfort, her brown leather valise, a cracked mirror, and several pegs on the door to serve as an armoire. A crude shelf nailed on the wall housed the stack of dime novels she'd packed as an afterthought on the night of her elopement. Beyond what she saw, the room was void of the creature comforts she longed for. Definitely a man's room—sterile, impersonal, and cold enough to cause chills to ripple through her body.

She crawled from the bed and, wrapping the natty quilt around her shoulders, walked to the main room, ladled water into the kettle, and set it on the iron crane.

The baby moved, and whether from motherly instincts or from loneliness, Rebecca smoothed her hand over the area as she spoke to the child. "I never realized how spoiled I was until not having the comforts of a modern kitchen with a stove and a baking oven. Not that I cooked all that much. And a tub. Oh, how I yearn for a true bath, with lilac soap and rosewater."

She leaned toward the fireplace and blew tiny breaths, hoping to find a few live embers, while using the poker to sift through the ash. When several timid red sparks appeared, she stacked pieces of kindling the way Frank had taught her. Once the small sticks of wood ignited, she carefully laid a log and then another until lively flames danced in the hearth.

Busying herself, she cut a thin slice from the diminishing side of bacon. She longed for eggs to complete her breakfast. Unfortunately, the wire pen Frank built had proved no match for the varmints that killed the chickens. He'd promised to buy a dog the next time he went to town.

"Frank promised a lot of things." She harrumphed aloud at the thought. Finishing her meager meal of bacon, stale cornbread, and weak tea, she washed the dishes and set them to drain. Staring at the stack of cordwood, she counted.

Ten.

Ten pieces of wood to last until Frank could chop more. Removing the quilt, she slipped the woolen shawl around her shoulders, then draped the quilt over the shawl. She was cold. The cabin was cold.

"He'll be home today. He wouldn't dare miss Christmas." The thought of her favorite holiday cheered her. Ignoring her husband's warning to keep the shutters barred, she walked to the window over the kitchen's basin stand, and removed the bar. When she folded the shutters against the wall, the dimly lit room flooded with sunlight. Outside, the world was bright and blanketed in white.

Laying another log on the fire, she decided to treat herself to one more cup of tea. This time she'd brew it a little stronger. She rubbed her hands over her midsection. "He's coming home, baby. You'll see. Christmas is only fifteen days away. We'll have a fine celebration. Yes, I'll go to the root cellar and see if there's a bottle of jam. I'll bring up enough flour and sugar to bake a cake." She tapped a finger against her cheek. "Maybe there are a few apples left."

And then a thought struck. She'd have to venture outside to get to the root cellar. Frank had warned her about not leaving the cabin. He'd said there were enough supplies inside to last until he returned. Except that was ten days ago.

Pouring hot water over the tea leaves inside her small green ceramic teapot, she decided to write while the leaves steeped. She opened her journal and dipped the pen into the inkwell.

December 10, 1881

I am seventeen years old. A woman about to bear a child. I don't feel fully grown, and

becoming a mother frightens me. I've never held a baby. I don't know what to do

if it cries. Christmas is fifteen days off. If I close my eyes, I can see the beautifully

decorated tree in our salon, its top reaching to the ceiling. Father always admired a tall

tree. I wonder if my sisters think of me. I wonder if Mother thinks of me. I miss them sorely.

She stopped long enough to sip her tea and let the liquid warm her insides. She dipped the pen again, careful to wipe the excess ink against the lip of the bottle.

If I am to be a woman, then I must act like one. I am here, alone, in this wasteland of white. The water bucket needs filling, and the slops need emptying. I am reviled

by the odor. The kindling box is near empty, and though I have never swung an

axe, surely chopping wood isn't that difficult. I will bundle against the cold

and brave my way to the root cellar. While I must remind myself that I am the size

of a fatted calf, it is with great care that I will climb down the ladder and back

up again. Perhaps I will find a ham and a few potatoes. Frank will be surprised

when he comes home. I'll prepare a Christmas dinner fit for a king. I wonder if Frank found a suitable dog? A puppy for the baby would be nice.

She glanced around the stark room and bent once more to the lined pages.

What is Christmas without a decorated tree and gifts underneath wrapped in colorful paper? I hope Frank remembers that it is Christmas. I fear he has squandered my money.

Rebecca placed her hands against her cheeks. It was depressing to think about her future and the future of her child.

I have come to the painful realization that I allowed myself to be played for a fool.

Chapter 2

Home.

The word appealed to him. Jesse Starr vaguely remembered being pulled from his sobbing mother's arms. He'd been two years old when his father had left the Kiowa village and returned to England, taking Jesse with him. He'd never expected to travel this way again, except now that he was headed toward the village of his mother's people, he was damned anxious to get there.

Was his mother alive? Would she remember the son she'd borne to an Englishman who'd come to hunt buffalo and stayed for two winters? Her Kiowa name was Leotie, Rose of the Prairie, but Viscount Addison Starr Fitzroy had called her Starr's Woman.

The bay gelding huffed a grunt as if warning Jesse. "I see it, Chief." Puffs of white vapor formed from his breath when he spoke to the horse.

Jesse fisted his gloved hands and blew, his breath doing little to warm his numbed fingers. He was used to seeing horses on the prairie, just not one with a saddle hanging from its side. He stood in the stirrups and scanned the wide snowy expanse. Seeing no breaks in the drifts, he nudged the bay forward.

"Reckon some pilgrim's gone and got himself into a peck of trouble." Snow scrunched beneath the horse's hooves. "Slow and easy, Chief. Don't want to spook him." The animal flicked its ears as if understanding the man's words.

Being a man who'd experienced his share of trouble, Jesse had a gut instinct that told him to ride on—to mind his own business. By nature, he prided himself on needing no one. His only purpose was to locate the Kiowa village and hopefully find the woman who'd given birth to him.

He rode the few hundred yards to where the roan gelding stood pawing the snow. Jesse reached down and grabbed the dangling reins before the animal decided to spook and take flight. Dismounting, he ground-tied his own horse. Then, crooning soft words, Jesse ran a hand over the roan's withers. He spoke reassuring words to the animal who had now tensed its muscles.

"Ain't no call in getting yourself all riled up, horse. We Kiowa value a good pony, and you look like a keeper. Where's your master?" Jesse rubbed his hand down the animal's neck and shoulders.

Shoving the saddle into place on top of the horse's back, he unbuckled the saddlebag and reached inside, hoping to find a clue to the missing owner. He removed a leather secretary wallet. "Humph. Pilgrim's flat broke." Instead of money, Jesse found a slip of paper. He read aloud. "Franklin Horatio Donnelly, Esquire, owes Ralph Wittier a sum of no less than five thousand dollars due and payable in full on December 25, 1881." Scrawled across the bottom, and in a different handwriting, "Pay up or die" and the initials RW.

Jesse folded the paper and slipped it back into the case. He'd emitted a low whistle when he read the amount. Then he spoke the name aloud. "Franklin Horatio Donnelly, Esquire. Mighty fancy moniker for a greenhorn." Returning the case to the saddlebag, he gathered the reins to his horse and in a single fluid motion swung into the saddle.

"Well, Chief, reckon we're obligated to find out if the pilgrim has gone and got himself killed or is laying somewhere all busted up."

Gathering the stray horse's reins, Jesse kneed the gelding beneath him, and gave a violent jerk to signal the reluctant roan to follow. Using his skills as a tracker, Jesse searched for signs that would lead him to the missing rider. He figured the horse hadn't traveled far. He was wrong.

An hour later, he hauled up on the reins and unwound the canteen's strap from the saddle horn. Removing the cap, Jesse lifted the container to his lips. It didn't surprise him that the water inside had frozen solid. He sighed, his breath creating vapor in the frigid air that stung when drawn into his lungs. "Damn, sure wanted to wet my whistle."

While looking skyward, he squinted to bring the dipping and soaring black dots into focus. "Buzzards. Unless I miss my guess, Chief, reckon we found our pilgrim."

He replaced the canteen and urged the horses forward, riding slow and allowing the gelding to pick its way until reaching the precipice of Devil's Canyon. In a world where white meets white, the sharp drop off was misleading. Jesse figured the stranger, being unfamiliar with the territory, galloped right up to the ledge; the horse must have balked and sent his unsuspecting rider head over heels out of the saddle and fifty feet below.

Dismounting, he tied the roan's reins around his

own saddle horn. Careful of his footing, Jesse edged his way to the sharp shelf and, squinting against the snow's white glare, peered over. The body of a man lay sprawled on the canyon floor. Dropping to one knee, Jesse called out, "Hey, mister. How bad are you hurt?" Not that he expected an answer. Experience told him by the way the vultures waited there was still life in the man, even though the carrion eaters edged forward bravely, daring a peck or two.

Jesse's voice echoed across the wide expanse when he yelled, "Hi-yaw! Get outta there, bloody buzzards."

Life had taught him how to go days surviving on meager meals and little potable water, and how to see what was before you yet hidden in plain sight. In this blanket of white, his instincts said there had to be a way to the bottom of the valley.

His instincts were rarely wrong. Inside his head, a quiet voice seemed to say, *Trust your horse. He'll know the way.*

It wasn't the first time this little voice had given him sage advice. It was as if he had his own invisible mystic.

Setting a toe in the stirrup, and in spite of the heavy buffalo coat he wore, Jesse swung into the saddle with little effort. He guided the horses toward the west side of the shelf and down the dangerous snow-covered slope. He trusted the well-muscled bay horse to plant its hooves to keep from sliding out of control. The ten-minute descent seemed an eternity. Once at the bottom, Jesse didn't hesitate. His only regret was the frozen water inside the canteen. The injured man would surely need a drink.

Squatting, he removed a glove and placed two

fingers against the man's neck. The pulse was there, faint, but beating nonetheless. "Mister, can you hear me?" He gathered snow to moisten the man's chapped lips.

The man's eyes fluttered open. His tongue flickered over his wind-cracked lips to catch the moisture. Jesse bent close and listened to a voice barely audible. "My wife…" The man's eyes fluttered. "I'm all busted up inside. My wife…" He moaned, his pain obvious.

"You Franklin Donnelly?"

A slight blinking was his answer.

The ashen pallor of the injured man's face was enough for Jesse to know death was this man's destiny. He wrestled with his conscience. One part wanted to climb in the saddle and ride on. This was none of his business. The man was a goner anyways. But he'd spoken of a wife. Jesse thought about his mother and the hardships she had surely endured. A white woman alone and this far from town had little chance of surviving.

He heaved a sigh. "Don't worry, pilgrim, just point in the right direction, and I'll get you home."

The man closed his eyes. Jesse used snow to rouse him back to consciousness. "If I'm to get you home, you need to stay conscious long enough to tell me where to find your ranch."

Jesse knew from the red sputum that dribbled from the side of the man's mouth when he spoke that this tenderfoot wasn't long for this earth.

Donnelly lifted a feeble hand and pointed eastward. "Old…Hawthorne…place."

Jesse followed the direction. "How far?"

"N-not sure. Twenty miles, maybe."

"'You hang on, mister. I'll build a travois. Won't be the most comfortable ride; I'll do my best to get you home."

"H-how long?"

"Two days. Three at the most."

"No time. The doctor, n-not there. Waited. Didn't come. My wife, she's…" He reached up and with only the strength that a dying man could muster gripped the lapels of Jesse's coat. "Take care of my wife."

"Yeah, sure. Okay."

"Poker. Lost all the m-money. I've done wrong by her. Don't let them hurt her." He coughed, a hacking rattle. "Swear it before God. Swear to take care of…" The breath sighed out of the man's throat like air escaping a balloon.

Jesse pried the hands locked in a death grip from the lapels of his coat as he stared down at the lifeless body. "Damn. Bad enough the pilgrim got himself killed, plus he has a sick wife to boot."

Glancing up at the billowing clouds, Jesse pulled the jacket closer as a shiver wracked through him. A fat white flake landed on the dead man's face as Jesse closed the staring eyes. Brushing the snow from his knees, Jesse walked to the horses. He untied the rain slicker from the roan's saddle. Grumbling to himself, he wrapped the yellow raincoat around Donnelly's body, then hefted him across the saddle.

"Ought to leave him here for the buzzards to pick clean. Who's to know I found him? Nobody, that's who." Jesse used pigging string to secure the body's hands and feet to the stirrups. "Don't need to go getting involved with a sick woman. What if she's got cholera?

17

Besides, I've got to find my mother."

Jesse mounted the bay gelding and gigged him forward. The horse didn't move. "C'mon, Chief. It's damned cold. The roan will find his way home." He gigged the gelding a little harder. The horse squealed and kicked forward with its hind leg.

"Hellfire, horse. What's got into you?"

The bay turned its head and looked at the man in the saddle. Jesse frowned as he snugged the sweat-stained Stetson tighter on his head. "Sometimes, Chief, I swear you're part human. I only promised so the pilgrim could die in peace. Didn't mean nothing by it."

He gigged the bay again. This time the horse bucked, toppling his unwary rider into the mound of white cold. Jesse stood, spitting snow from his mouth. "Oh, hell. All right. I'll keep my promise." He walked over and gathered the reins of the dead man's roan. He led the horse next to the bay and hefted into the saddle. "You satisfied?"

The bay gelding snorted and walked forward. Jesse spoke only to the wilderness. "Donnelly should've been home hugging his wife and sitting down to a hot meal. Instead he'll be pushing up daisies when spring comes."

Like earlier, he wished he'd minded his own business and kept on riding. Now he was obliged to take a dead man home, see to his burying, and deal with a sick woman. And worse, the pilgrim had said somebody wanted to hurt her.

"Bloody hellfire and damnation. C'mon, Chief. Maybe the bereaved widow will offer us a place in the barn and a blanket or two. Storm's coming. We'll need a place to ride out the winter."

The cold nipped his ears, and the wind found every

open place in his coat. The chill closed in on him as he rode toward an old trapper's cabin with the frozen body of a dead man in tow.

Chapter 3

Rebecca sat on the edge of the cot, brushing her hair forward, and suddenly straightened, sending a tumbled cloud of corn-silk blonde strands flying backward as she stiffened at the sound of a horse nickering outside the cabin door.

"Frank!"

In that one instant she forgot every stricture with which her husband had warned her. Oblivious of the cold against her stocking-covered feet, she skipped across the wooden floor. With some effort, she managed to lift the crossbar and pulled the door wide. For a moment, she squinted against the blinding sun.

Panic lanced through her. The face that greeted her was unfamiliar, and frightening. She felt the need to protect herself and grabbed the door, fumbling to slam it shut, and was stopped short by a gloved hand grasping her wrist.

Rebecca stilled, and then she drew in a deep breath to prepare herself for the worst before she turned her head in the direction of the man's piercing gaze. And exhaled in a kind of helpless gasp as she tried to wrestle from his grip.

"Settle down, little girl. I mean you no harm."

Be strong, Rebecca, be strong, she cautioned herself. "Who are you?"

"Jesse Starr. Is your ma or pa home?" Jesse

glanced over his shoulder. "I found this poor soul at the bottom of Devil's Canyon. Before he died, he made me promise to get him to his wife. He said she was sick. Would you be knowing where I might find Frank Donnelly's cabin?"

An involuntary shiver of pure terror ran up her spine. Her heart pounded so hard it thundered inside her ears. Her worst fear had happened. She was near her birthing time, stuck in the middle of nowhere with no money, and now a widow.

"Oh, no…oh, no!" Her hands flew to her mouth as her gaze shifted to the body wrapped in a yellow raincoat and draped over a horse.

Frank's horse.

"Oh, no…oooh." She made a giant effort to maintain her composure. "I-I'm Rebecca Donnelly. Frank is…was…my husband."

Jesse let loose her arm and stepped back. "Why, you're just a mere slip of a girl."

Rebecca watched the disquiet in his eyes intensify as they wafted over her to settle on her midsection. "How old are you…twelve…thirteen?"

"Seventeen," Rebecca answered as she grappled with the sensation of the world spinning out of control as she fainted dead away.

****

Jesse carefully laid the inert Mrs. Donnelly on the cot and covered her with the quilt. He looked down at her ethereal beauty and didn't know what annoyed him more—the fact that this was an innocent child in a woman's body, probably unschooled in the ways of the world, and he'd promised to take care of her, or that he wanted to bury Frank Donnelly and get on his horse, ride out, and never come back. Rebecca Donnelly was not his responsibility.

Her eyes fluttered open. She gasped and gripped the quilt close to her chin. The way her eyes riveted back and forth reminded him of a frightened animal. He backed away from the bed, and spoke in soft, even tones. "I'm not here to harm you, Mrs. Donnelly. Once I've given my word, I never go back on it."

Bloody hell, that's a whopping lie. Soon as the burying's done, I'm on my way. He cleared the rasp from his throat. "Is there a particular place you'd like me to bury your husband?"

Her chin quivered and tears filled her eyes. "Are you sure the man is my husband? I mean, it could be someone posing as him."

Jesse had removed the heavy buffalo hide coat. He reached between the buttons of his Lindsey-wool shirt and removed the leather secretary. "This was in his saddlebags. When I found him, he said his name was Frank Donnelly and asked me to get him home to his wife." He handed her the wallet.

She didn't immediately open it. "I don't mean to question your account, Mr. Starr, but..." Her voice drifted off. She heaved a soulful sigh as she tossed back the quilt and slid from the bed. "If you don't mind, I'd like to make sure the man we're burying is really Frank."

"Yes, ma'am, if you insist."

She grabbed the shawl and wrapped it close to her body as she followed Jesse outside.

"Sure you're up to this, Mrs. Donnelly?"

She nodded.

Outside and standing next to the roan gelding,

Jesse hesitated before motioning her forward, offering her the opportunity to return to the house. She just stood there, shivering, whether from the cold or from jitters he couldn't tell.

Either way, he pulled back the raincoat and lifted the dead man's head.

She cried out, gripped the sides of her stomach, and sank to her knees.

Jesse lifted her into his arms. Even heavy with child, he'd hefted kegs of rum heavier than she was. He sprinted up the steps and to the small bedroom. "You're not fixing to have the baby, are you?"

She moaned. "Yes, no, maybe." She moaned again. "I don't know. I've never had a baby before."

He mumbled, "I think we're in trouble. I've never delivered a baby. I've stitched up men with cuts and wounds, treated a few stomach ailments, even amputated a leg once."

Hope shone in her eyes. "Are you a doctor, Mr. Starr?"

Jesse cautioned himself. His past was his to know and no one else. "'Fraid not, Mrs. Donnelly. Just seem to have a knack for doing such things."

Her face seemed to crumple in disappointment and perhaps a hint of panic as she expelled a deep sigh.

"If it gives you a bit of comfort, I once helped deliver a litter of kittens, and a foal." *Well, damn, that was a stupid thing to say.*

She lay with her eyes closed, biting down on her bottom lip—to keep from screaming out loud, he supposed. He chastised himself for his rough manner with the girl. She was not a horse or a cow. She was not a *thing.*

"It's okay, Mr. Starr. The pain has passed." She sat up abruptly and wiped away her tears. "There is a lone tree out behind the barn. I suppose that's as good a place as any to lay Frank to rest." She swung her feet over the edge of the cot. "Will it take long to...to dig the grave?"

He wanted to touch her on the shoulder. To reassure her. Reassure her for what? That he'd dig a good hole, that he'd return to the house once he'd finished? "Fortunately, we've had a mild autumn and the ground isn't completely frozen. Couple of hours. To dig the hole, that is. You want me to come get you before I lay him in it?"

"No...afterwards. I think saying a few words over him would be proper."

"Yes, ma'am."

Jesse reached out and touched her lightly. "You should rest." He dropped his hand.

Rebecca opened her mouth to protest and then, seeing the slight subtle set of his jaw, returned to the cot.

Jesse left the bedroom. The door creaked as he opened it and then again as he shoved it shut.

****

In the hours that followed, Rebecca felt as if her whole world had turned topsy-turvy. Overwhelmed, torn between sorrow and apprehension, wanting desperately to leave this god-forsaken wasteland and yet fearful that she had no place to go, all she wanted was to return to Chicago, to resume her old life.

She laughed at the thought.

She used the time to busy herself making coffee. Men liked coffee. At least Frank certainly did.

A light rap sounded, and then the door creaked open. "Mrs. Donnelly, it's time."

Rebecca had changed into a dark brown traveling suit. With her enlarged girth, she was forced to leave the waistband unbuttoned. No matter, as the heavy shawl draped over her shoulders hid the indiscretion.

Once outside, she lifted her face to catch the sun, and then breathed in the sharp cold air that caused her to cough. Her advanced pregnancy made her body feel heavy and awkward as she followed the stranger through the snow-cleared path he had created. Her heart thumped at the sight of the freshly mounded dirt beneath a tree barren of its leaves.

An instant grief washed over her, followed by a horrible feeling of resentment. Had Frank loved her? Why did she always have thoughts and questions tormenting her about why he had insisted on an elopement? Was he really only after her money? Had he done this to other young and unsuspecting girls? There was no one with whom she could share her doubts and uncertainties. Even her fears seemed to be channeled into strange occasional nightmares that she never remembered when she woke up crying and drenched in a cold sweat.

She would just write all of this down in her diary; her diary was her best friend, her diary never betrayed her, and once the words were down in black and white, she would feel strengthened enough to face the next obstacle with some degree of self-possession, and hope the searing disappointments would eventually go away.

Mr. Starr's polite cough interrupted her reflections. She opened the small Bible clutched in her hand. The words blurred on the page. It was all so hypocritical.

Frank hadn't loved her, and she had come to realize that she had fallen in love with the idea of being in love. Standing here, under a dead tree, and shivering with cold while staring down at a mound of muddy slush, she was free. It worried her that this should be a comforting thought. Wasn't she supposed to grieve, to be wracked with sorrow?

"Would you like me to read the passage?"

Rebecca looked at the man, startled that he had somehow read her thoughts. Her voice barely a whisper, she said, "May God have mercy on Frank Donnelly's miserable soul."

She turned, and in her haste to escape, almost tripped on the hem of her dress.

Chapter 4

When he returned to the house, Jesse found her lying on the cot, curled in a tight knot. From the puffiness of her eyes, it appeared she had sobbed herself to sleep. Mauve crescents of exhaustion lay like dark shadows beneath her eyelashes.

He reached down and smoothed back a wisp of hair that had fallen across her forehead. He hesitated for a fraction of a second. This child-woman wasn't his responsibility. He'd kept his promise to a dying man. Now it was time for him to move on. With that thought, Jesse eased from the room and closed the door slowly behind him. The window over the sink was shuttered as if to shut out the world. Only a soft light filtered through, and nothing else. He stepped to the window and quietly removed the safety bar and swung back the wooden flaps. Light flooded in, adding a welcoming glow to the small space.

Jesse glanced back at the closed bedroom door. Near as he could figure, he and Frank Donnelly had been about the same age. What circumstance had caused a young girl to wed a man so much older than her?

The rich aroma of coffee reached out to tantalize him. The earthy fragrance brought long-forgotten memories of home. A stable of horses with regal bloodlines, a father who loved him, servants, and events best forgotten. Events that haunted him. Events that had taught him how to empty his heart and close off his emotions. Still, his taste buds yearned to savor a cup of something that didn't taste like yesterday's dishwater.

As he laid his gloves on the scarred plank table, a stench reached his nostrils. Beyond his own unwashed body's stink, he couldn't ignore the odious odor that seeped beneath the bedroom door. As badly as he wanted to quench his thirst with a good cup of java, he knew what he had to do.

Removing the bandana from around his neck, he tied it over his nose and mouth, then eased into the bedroom, careful to tiptoe past the sleeping girl; he grabbed the wooden pail's rope handle. It took a second for him to swallow back the retch that traveled from the pit of his stomach and demanded to be loosed. Not wanting to spill the pail's repulsive contents, or to splash himself, he held the bucket out in front of him with both hands.

Like a man on an urgent mission, he opened the front door and carefully stepped from the porch, hotfooting it to the rear of the cabin. The outhouse's rotting door hung askew by one leather hinge. Jesse used the tip of his boot to swing back the door. Inside, he emptied the slops into the depths below the hole. This time the gagging nearly doubled him to his knees.

He sprinted some distance, then scooped a handful of snow over his face and sucked in great gulps of lung-freezing air.

Huddled against the bitter cold, he raced to the well and drew a pail of water, rinsed the bucket, and then with the clean bucket and another pail of fresh water hurried back to the cabin's meager warmth.

One cup. Just one cup of earthy richness to fortify him against the wintery chill, and he'd be on his way. When Jesse reached to pour the simmering liquid into a mug, he noticed the dwindling woodpile. Looking farther, he took stock of shelves barren of canned goods. He lifted the dishtowel that covered a plate to find a mere sliver of cornbread.

His stomach rumbled a reminder that it'd been a while since he'd last eaten. He settled at the table and stretched his long legs toward the fireplace, then lifted the mug to his lips and blew to cool the amber brew enough to take a sip. He leaned back, and as he looked up spotted the corner of a book. Always a reader, he stood and lifted the leather-bound tome. Taking another sip of coffee, then setting the cup aside, he opened the front cover only to discover this was the private journal of Rebecca Anne Throckmorton. She had drawn a careful line through "Throckmorton" and added "Donnelly."

He didn't mean to invade her privacy, yet he found himself unable to stop reading the neatly penned words, and the more he read, the more he understood Rebecca's quiet indifference at the grave. Frank Donnelly had clearly duped her into thinking he loved her. He had not only stolen and squandered her money, he'd also treated his young wife no better than a ten-cent whore.

While reading, Jesse surmised that her beauty and youthful naivety, not to mention her obvious wealth, were all against her. She had for all practical purposes been sheltered from the harsh realities of life and taught to trust and believe in the innate honesty, goodness and kindness of her fellowman, which made her an easy mark for a con man like Donnelly.

Jesse's shoulders tensed with irritation. The bastard had dragged this innocent girl to the ends of nowhere, then left her to fend for herself while he sat in a warm saloon and gambled away all the money and the deed to a dilapidated shack, a barn with a crumbling roof, and land not fit for raising jackrabbits.

He turned the page and continued to read. Her next words caused a knot to fist inside his gut. Rebecca's father had not only cut her off financially, he had also forbade her to return home.

He closed the journal and set it back in its resting place, then poured the remains of the coffee into his mug. He eased the bedroom door open. What the bloody hell was he supposed to do with a pregnant girl that had no place to go and no money to get there even if she did?

He prowled the room like a caged animal, hungry, edgy, but also angry and spoiling for a fight—and he did not know why.

To quell his emotions, he decided to chop enough wood to last her through the winter. Then he'd go to the root cellar and bring up all the food, and then he'd…do what? Ride out, leaving her to birth a baby all alone? Yeah, that rated him right down there with Frank Donnelly, or worse.

Grabbing his heavy coat, he figured the least he could do was replenish the woodbox and scour up enough food for supper. From the entries in her diary, it had been nigh on two weeks since she'd eaten a decent meal.

****

A delectable aroma caused Rebecca's stomach to

make small squeezing sounds. Her eyes fluttered open. For a moment she lay dazed, trying to recall whether Frank's death and burial were a bad dream, or if she had actually stood at his grave. The baby was restless. Rebecca made small cooing sounds as she gently smoothed the area where the infant kicked.

She bolstered her energy and rolled from the bed to stand in front of the small round mirror that hung from a nail on the wall. She adjusted the few strands of wayward hair back into place, efforts that did little to improve her weary image, and when she turned from the mirror, she was biting her lower lip hard to still its sudden trembling.

Yet, the task of continuing to reinforce her courage seemed insurmountable. Her stomach rumbled again. She was weak with hunger. Almost too weak. The delicious smell drew her to open the bedroom door.

Stripped to the waist, his back was to her.

Involuntarily, her breath caught in her throat at the myriad of puckered scars that crisscrossed from his shoulders to his waist. What had he done to warrant such vile abuse?

He turned.

Her thoughts shifted. Why had she not noticed before? He was undoubtedly the most handsome man she had ever seen, tall—inches over six feet, much taller than Frank. Lithe and powerfully built, his body rippled with supple grace. His broad shoulders tapered to a firm, flat belly. His wet hair was as black and gleaming as obsidian, swept back in shaggy waves from his bronze, hawkish visage that was as hard and impassive as chiseled stone. Not only the color of his skin but also his fine aquiline nose, with its flaring nostrils, revealed what must be either a Mexican or an Indian bloodline.

In her initial distraught state, she hadn't noticed that his eyes shone like two lustrous sapphires deep-set beneath swooping black brows and spiked with thick black lashes. His aristocratic bearing and blue eyes belied European ancestry.

In a handsome sort of way, his face was worn and rough. It was a face that seemed as if it had seen hardships and been places beyond her knowledge.

He was eyeing her now. Looking her up and down.

A spark of emotion lit every inch of her as those bright blue eyes concentrated on her. Something in the way he looked at her made Rebecca draw in a very deep breath to quiet the tumult of emotions inside her.

A few short months ago, she had never been kissed, had never seen a fully naked body, not even her sisters', and had been a silly girl with romantic notions about having a man make love to her. In reality, the sexual part had been rough, painful, and unpleasant, leaving her disillusioned about what went on between a man and a woman.

Here she was, heavy with child, feeling fat and ugly, and it was as if her body had a mind of its own. *What is wrong with me? I want him to hold me, touch me. Dear God, why am I thinking this?*

She put her hand to her mouth. "I-I'm sorry, it's just that…well…ah, forgive me for intruding on your bath."

Jesse reached for the clean long-sleeved undershirt and quickly pulled it over his head. A mocking smile curved his lips as though he had read her thoughts. To her humiliation, Rebecca's cheeks grew hot, and not from the fire smoldering in the hearth.

"No apologies, ma'am. I should've been quicker getting finished."

She swayed a little and gripped the edge of the table. He rushed to her side and steadied her while she sat in a chair. She passed a hand over her eyes. "With all that's happened today, I forgot to eat."

Jesse immediately grabbed a bowl and ladled it with bubbling soup made of three potatoes, one yam, and two onions. He'd added bits of a canned ham from his own dwindling supply.

Her hand trembled as she lifted the spoon to her mouth. "It smells heavenly."

His voice was soft when he spoke. "Ma'am, when was the last time you went to town to replenish your food stock?"

He filled a bowl for himself, along with a cup of coffee. He had also found the tin of tea leaves and now poured a cup for Rebecca.

She blew to cool the portion before downing another spoonful of the hearty broth. "Frank said he'd bought enough salted meat and fresh vegetables to last us through the winter. Why do you ask?"

"Did you bring all those supplies in a wagon?"

She downed another mouthful, closed her eyes and savored every morsel. "Oh, no, Frank had two laden sacks draped over his horse, and two over mine. He said we didn't need a wagon because he'd made a bargain with the man he bought the ranch from to leave everything for us." She laid the spoon aside, and lifted the cup to her lips. "It was thoughtful of you to make tea for me."

She peered over the rim of the cup. An unexpected

anguish rose inside her. "Why do you ask about the supplies?"

When he didn't immediately answer, she said, "Mr. Starr, I know you must think I'm the stupidest person you've ever met. I'm barely a woman, about to become a mother, stuck out in the middle of nowhere, and without warning, I've suddenly become a widow." Her voice rose an octave. "It's a lot to take in, so…so I'd appreciate it very much if you wouldn't treat me like a child. Whatever it is you have to say, please just tell me."

He offered an apologetic smile. "Fair enough. Tomorrow, I'll go hunting. There is no meat; and since you want honesty, there might be enough potatoes for two more meals. I have a little flour, cornmeal, and salt in my saddlebag. Coffee's about gone, and so are the tea leaves."

A long silence passed. Worry laced Rebecca's face. "What's to happen to me, Mr. Starr? I'm afraid. Really afraid."

Chapter 5

Jesse took his time mulling over how best to answer Rebecca's question without divulging that he'd read her journal. Everyone was entitled to their private thoughts and secrets. Even he kept his own secrets close to his vest. Still he fretted about her present condition and what to do about it.

Pushing back from the table, he cleared the empty dishes and placed them in a pan of hot water. He'd wash them later.

Her voice reminded him of a small frightened child. "Mr. Starr, you haven't answered my question."

He cleared his throat as he stood next to the fireplace. "What about your folks? Maybe I could get word to them to come get you."

He watched the way she laced and unlaced her fingers, the way she bit her bottom lip to keep it from trembling. And while he waited for her answer, he took stock of her disheveled beauty—the rose-petal-and-cream coloring and the widened brown eyes that reminded him of a frightened doe.

She gazed around the room as if searching for some kind of answer. Her voice wobbled as she spoke. "The truth is my father has disowned me. He didn't approve of Frank." Rebecca shrugged her shoulders. "Although Father is a wealthy man, he will never send money for me to return home."

Jesse's mouth thinned with annoyance. "What about your mother, or maybe a brother, or grandmother?"

Rebecca shook her head. "There isn't anyone. Mother would never go against my father. I have two sisters. Both are married." Her eyes brightened for a brief moment only to dim again. "I'm not sure if they would send money or not. Both are married to men who respect my father's dictates."

"You mean your brothers-in-law have limp backbones?"

"If that means are they cowards, all I know is that Arthur and Reginald both work at my father's bank, and in order to keep my sisters in the lifestyle to which they are accustomed, Arty and Reggie do whatever my father says."

"Where is home, Mrs. Donnelly?"

"Chicago."

He blew a low whistle. "Long way from Oklahoma." Jesse continued to press. "I can't imagine someone of your age and innocence doing anything to justify being disowned for merely marrying a man your father disliked."

Rebecca stilled. A dead silence hung in the air. When she spoke, it was slow and deliberate. "It's true that father saw Frank for the charlatan that he was. If eloping were my only sin, I think father might be willing to forgive me."

She looked at Jesse and heaved a huge sigh. "I stole five thousand dollars from my father's safe. Well, s*tealing* might be a bit strong. You see, the money was rightfully mine." She gave a sort of snort. "Oh, that's not exactly the truth. The money was to be mine on my eighteenth birthday. In my father's eyes, I'm not only a thief; I'm also a rotten little tramp…a fallen woman. Even if I did return home and show him my marriage certificate, he'd consider my child a bastard. The Throckmortons are a pillar of society. The newspaper gossip columnists most likely had a high-oh time with their articles. There's probably no end to the unforgivable embarrassment I've caused my family. It's for these reasons that I have no place to go."

Before Jesse could comment, Rebecca's eyes brightened. The wooden chair scraped against the floor when she scooted it from the table. "The money. Mr. Starr, the money. I'm saved!"

She hastened to the bedroom, drew the leather case from beneath the thin mattress, and returned to the main room. "I completely forgot that you'd given me Frank's wallet."

"Mrs. Donnelly…ma'am…there isn't any—"

Before he managed to say there wasn't any cash, she upended the wallet as if hoping money would magically flutter from the pockets.

He watched the girl weep quietly. He didn't need to see the frustrated fury and fear in her face as she read the IOU and the threat written at the bottom by one Ralph Wittier.

Her eyes were filled with sadness and remorse. "You must be thinking that I really am a dunderhead."

Clearly Rebecca thought she was a great sinner. Part of him wanted to gather her in his arms and give her the comfort she needed. Instead he stayed seated. He'd learned a long time ago to suppress his emotions.

Jesse calmly folded his hands together. "What I think isn't important. What I know is that your birthing time is near, and that you need a woman with you."

He hesitated for a moment, running his fingers through his dark hair. "I was on my way to the Kiowa village when I happened to spot your husband's horse." He wanted to say that he should have minded his own business and kept on riding. "My mother is Kiowa. I haven't seen her since I was a wee tot. Even though she might not remember me, I'm thinking even if she doesn't, she or some of the other women will know about birthing a child. My only dilemma is that it's a day's ride there and a day's ride back here. You stayed here alone for ten days. Are you willing to trust me to fetch my mother or another woman and bring them back to help you?"

"I'm not brave, Mr. Starr. Besides being incredibly foolish, I am a coward." She gathered the shawl around her as if warding off a chill. "What if you hadn't happened along and found Frank? What if you don't come back? No, I won't stay here. I won't."

"You trusted Frank Donnelly." He refrained from reminding her that she'd trusted this scoundrel enough to steal money from her father's safe, run off, and travel hundreds of miles with someone she'd barely known.

"Humph. Frank was handsome, glib-tongued, and remorseless. He ruined me, and because of that I've ruined my family."

Jesse stood to place a fresh log on the fire. He stirred the embers until timid flames sprang to life to lap the wood with fiery tongues. Rebecca looked pale. There was just enough light to illuminate her, while the rest of the room was cast in shadows. The eerie sound of coyotes yodeling and answering each other was the only reminder that there was a whole world beyond them and their little patch of light from the flickering fireplace.

"Mrs. Donnelly—"

Rebecca interrupted with, "How far to your mother's village, Mr. Starr?"

"Fifteen miles. Maybe more."

"I can ride a horse that far."

"No, ma'am, not in your condition!"

"If you won't saddle the horse, then I'll walk. I'll follow you."

"Bloody hellfire and damnation, girl."

As if the conversation was over, she rose from the chair. Her back was to him as she was on her way out of the room. At the bedroom door, she turned. "Realizing what a foolish person I am is defeating. I'd like to think Frank cared enough about me to come home. The truth is, he was probably running from another bad debt and needed this as a place to hide out. I'm not even certain we were legally married. There was no minister, no church, just some drunken sot who said he was a judge." She held up her ringless left hand. "Frank said he'd buy me a ring, a beautiful diamond ring, once we were settled." She huffed a sigh. "Frank said a lot of things."

Without another word, she disappeared behind the door, only to open it again. "If you leave without me, I *will* follow the hoofprints. G'night, Mr. Starr."

****

Rebecca absently caressed the little bulge on the side of her abdomen as she lay in the dark thinking about Jesse Starr. So much had happened in the past twenty-four hours that she had hardly taken notice of him—except when she'd walked in on his bath. She had been acutely aware of his maleness and the scent of soap—a touch of sandalwood, she thought. She placed her chilled hands to cool her cheeks as the memory of his near-naked body heated her face.

There was an air of mystery about Jesse Starr. Everything about him exuded upper class, though a little tarnished around the edges, perhaps. He was certainly no ordinary drifter. His accent was soothing and mesmerizing. Definitely British. She knew this because her father and mother had once entertained a duke and duchess from England. Yet Jesse had said his mother was Kiowa. He'd said he hadn't seen her since he was a wee tot. How, she wondered, did someone with a British accent come to have an Indian mother?

Jesse's hands were rough and calloused—from long days of hard work, she imagined. He was tanned, so that meant he spent a lot of time outdoors. His body was taut and muscular, like the build of a common laborer. His nose was a bit crooked, as if it had been broken and healed the wrong way. His brow, his cheekbones, the line of his jaw, though partially obscured by a few days' growth of whiskers, were all finely chiseled.

The scar above his right eye and the rough, roped welts from long past wounds on his back indicated that Mr. Starr was a man with a brutal past.

So different from Frank's reedy body. Until comparing her late husband with Jesse Starr, she hadn't realized that Frank's good looks were almost feminine and the pallor she remembered would suggest he'd spent most of his time indoors. And his hands with their long fingers were soft, indicating he'd never done a day of menial labor in his entire life.

The loss of her maidenhead was the least of her worries. It was the loss of her family that grieved her the most, that and having no idea how she was supposed to take care of her baby once it was born. She had lost faith in her own feelings, her own actions. She had lost faith in love. She had lost faith in just about everything.

Rebecca wiped the flow of tears from her cheeks. She'd had a choice when it came to trusting Frank. She'd made the wrong choice. Now she must trust a man she'd known little more than twenty-four hours. Her unborn child's life depended on it.

Once again smoothing her hands over her stomach, she prayed God's forgiveness for not wanting a boy. She was afraid resentment would keep her from loving a son, especially if he was the image of Frank. *Please let my child be a little girl.*

Fortified by the nourishing soup and the cabin's warmth, she struggled to roll from the bed. With nothing more than the moon's dim light, she lifted her leather valise onto the space where she'd been lying and, with quick measured movements, packed her meager belongings. The one thing she did not care to keep was the green ceramic teapot. Other than her child, she wanted no reminders of Frank Donnelly.

Rebecca set the filled valise on the floor at the foot of the bed and lay down again, closed her eyes, and willed herself to sleep, if only to avoid thinking about her future.

Chapter 6

An icy chill hung cold and sharp in the morning air with no sign of a thaw. Rebecca might as well have been living in limbo. The world of Chicago seemed a million miles away, and her new life in the frontier didn't seem any more real.

The wind stung her cheeks, the bare branches of trees starkly outlined against a gray sky that threatened more snow. There was nothing beautiful about this place.

She stood at the edge of the rotting wooden porch and watched as Jesse walked toward her leading the two horses.

"Mrs. Donnelly, where is the other horse? With your two and mine, that makes three."

She sighed. "Frank wasn't a very good hand with livestock. He left the stall door open and the horse got out. Every time he tried to catch the animal, it would run, so Frank gave up, and it never came back."

She'd come to realize that Frank wasn't good at anything. Not even gambling.

Jesse snorted his disgust. "I really wish you'd stay here where you'll be warm. I'll come back, Mrs. Donnelly. I am a man of my word."

Determination ate away at her. "I've no doubt, Mr. Starr." She stepped closer to the roan gelding. "If you will please help me up, I promise not to lag behind."

Jesse thinned his lips and shook his head at her stubbornness.

Even in her advanced pregnancy, he lifted her with ease and set her as gently as possible astride the saddle. He took the quilt she was holding and wrapped it around her.

"I have one last request before we leave, Mr. Starr."

"Yes, ma'am?"

"Burn down the barn, the outhouse, and the cabin. It was worthless when Frank bought it, it was worthless when he lost it in a poker game, and it'll be even more worthless when the new owner comes to claim it."

He shot Rebecca an amused glance, and tipped the brim of his hat. "Yes, ma'am."

Handing her the reins to his horse, Jesse went inside the cabin. It didn't take long for the old tick mattress and the rotted burlap curtains to catch fire. Flames soon billowed from the front and rear windows. Jesse sprinted to the barn. The dry moldy hay quickly ignited, as did the outhouse.

The air filled with snaps and crackles as fire lapped up the sides of the weather-decayed buildings.

Rebecca watched the gray smoke spiraling toward the sky. Somehow it was hypnotically soothing. Past and present fused into one. She didn't realize she had drifted away until Jesse's voice interrupted her thoughts.

"We'll go slow and easy, Mrs. Donnelly."

She urged the horse forward. "I don't expect to be pampered, Mr. Starr. Shouldn't we go a little faster than slow and easy?"

He glanced at her, his expression solemn. "The

snow is deep. There are places where the horses may have to lunge to get through it. Slow and easy is to keep from risking injury to the horses."

Wanting to crawl under a rock, Rebecca could think of no reply and silently chastised herself for once again not thinking before taking action.

She looked at him looking at her. She was reminded anew of what a handsome man he was, the bones of his bronze face finely chiseled, his mouth strong, and…and kissable. Then with a growing sense of horror at the last thought, she swallowed hard and said, "Of course. I wasn't thinking."

Jesse turned his gelding, urging it forward. Rebecca followed.

The hours marched by, all drifting into one another, all the same without any sign of respite from the tedium. Her inner thighs were chafed, her backside ached, the baby protested the jostling, and she was cold and generally out of sorts.

She would rather die than complain, or even ask Jesse to stop for a short rest. Stopping wasn't a good idea. She feared that if she got off the horse she might not be able to get back on. Besides, she didn't want to hear his "I told you so."

To take her mind off her misery, she allowed her thoughts to drift away into nothing, like wind-blown clouds scudding across the sky. Peace. Heavenly peace that she longed for. A balm for her bruised soul.

Dogs barking and people shouting, with the sounds of horses coming toward them, shook her loose from the tranquility, realizing the riders coming toward them looked none too friendly.

"Mr. Starr, are we in danger?" Her heart thumped

wildly against her chest. She sidled her horse next to his.

He reached out and touched her arm. "It's the welcoming party. Nothing to fear."

****

Except for his slightly slanted eyes and somewhat darker complexion, few people recognized Jesse's Indian bloodlines. This was one time he hoped his Kiowa heritage was evident.

A group of riders encircled him and Rebecca.

"I'm afraid, Mr. Starr."

"Stay calm, Mrs. Donnelly. They're merely testing us."

Jesse had seen fierceness, had stood in the face of mortal enemies in many foreign lands. If these warriors meant to harm them, he would already be dead, and pregnant or not, Rebecca's fate much worse.

In a show of peace, he held both hands forward. His deep baritone voice resonated with authority when he said, "We mean no harm. I seek the one named Leotie."

The circle of horses opened to make way for a regal rider. Even bundled in heavy robes, it was obvious from his stature and the way he sat the prancing pinto stallion that this man was no ordinary warrior.

The man stopped a distance from Jesse. He lifted the lance and thrust it forward so that the sharp tip pressed against Jesse's heart. There was no immediate danger. First the heavy buffalo coat with its thick tanned inner hide acted as a safety shield, and second, he knew from other aborigine encounters that this was a show of power.

A face lined with wrinkles made it difficult to estimate the man's age. Harsh and often cruel living conditions aged everyone before their time. Jesse observed the black hair lined with threads of silver. Obsidian eyes that revealed cunning, wisdom, and still a hint of youth.

Jesse matched the man's stern gaze. Just as he was taking the warrior's measure, he, too, was being sized up. Foe or friend?

All waited. The stamping of hooves against the snow was the only sound. Jesse hoped Rebecca kept quiet. Now wouldn't be the time for one of her silly outbursts.

Just when he thought he'd have to blink and lose the staring match, the warrior lowered the lance. To Jesse's surprise, the man spoke English. "I am Setimika. Some call me Charging Bear. Why do you ask for my sister Leotie?"

Jesse's heart skipped a beat. This man, this chief of the Kiowa, was his uncle. His father had spoken little of his time spent with these people, only that he had loved Leotie with all his being and it broke his heart that she had refused to return to England with him. This was like a page of ancestry unfolding before him.

Jesse's throat was thick with emotion. He cleared the rasp in order to speak. "Leotie is my mother. My father called her Starr's Woman."

A resounding groan caused the Kiowa chief to shift his attention toward Rebecca. She sat hunched forward over the saddle horn. "Mr. Starr…" she gasped, "help me…"

And then Jesse saw the sheen of unshed tears in her eyes, making them squint, and her lips, trembling as she clamped her small, white teeth over her lower lip to control her pain.

She screamed, her agony echoing through the village, and the warriors fought to control their frightened horses. Women spilled from their tipis, fright and curiosity written on their faces.

The chief raised his spear and drew back his arm. "You dare bring a sick woman here? For this you both shall die."

Jesse spurred his gelding forward, ramming the pinto stallion, and nearly upending its rider. "No!" Jesse shouted. "She's with child. I brought her here to get help."

In the melee of whinnying horses, barking dogs, and shouting women, Jesse managed to grab the reins of Rebecca's roan before it broke through the circle. He dismounted and reached up to lift Rebecca from the saddle.

A woman's sharp voice commanded, "Charging Bear, order these foolish men back to their tipis." Without an upward glance at the chief, she said to Jesse, "Bring this child and follow me."

On fleet feet, the woman spoke to several other women in their native language. Whatever she'd said, the women were quick to obey.

Rebecca moaned against Jesse's chest. A hundred concerns raced through his mind as he followed the woman inside a cone-shaped structure.

"Lay her there." The woman pointed to a bed of animal pelts.

Jesse obeyed.

Her eyes wild with panic, Rebecca reached up and grabbed his hand. "Don't leave me."

The woman knelt next to Rebecca. She smoothed a hand over the girl's forehead. "There is nothing to fear. What is your name?"

"Rebecca Donnelly."

"I am called 'Grandmother' because I am a medicine woman. Everything will be all right. You will see."

Rebecca wiped her eyes. "I hope so."

"I must remove your clothing to see if your child is ready to greet the world."

Rebecca pushed the woman's hands away, then gripped the buttoned edge on her coat. "No. It's not time. The pain will pass. It always does."

"The first child is sometimes slow to round the belly," the medicine woman said as she looked at Jesse as if asking for help.

By this time two other women had entered the lodge, setting tortoise shells filled with water on small round stones over the fire. He nodded his understanding, and lifted Rebecca's hand into his. "Mrs. Donnelly, these women are here to help you. You have to trust them."

Her bottom lips quivered. "B-but the pain always passes. It's not time. I'm certain of it."

He released Rebecca's hand and laid it on her stomach. He looked at the Indian woman. "She's little more than a child herself, and her husband died a few days ago." Then back to Rebecca. "I'm not a doctor, ma'am. These women know a lot more about these things than I do."

He hated the commitment he was about to make. In the most soothing voice he could muster, he said, "I'll stay right over there…right where you can see me, if you'll let these ladies tend to you."

She grimaced against another round of pains. "Okay."

Jesse took his leave and settled in a cross-legged position on the other side of the tent. His stomach twisted in turmoil. In his lifetime, he'd helped birth one baby. He could still hear the mother's screams as the child ripped through her body. In the end, it was two burials he had attended. He wasn't looking forward to this experience.

He kept his eyes averted as the women undressed Rebecca and then laid a doeskin blanket over her nude body. One woman placed warm stones in a single row down her extended belly. Another lifted Rebecca's head and encouraged her to sip a white liquid from a small cup.

"Be strong," the medicine woman murmured. "For the baby's sake, you must be strong. Everything will be all right. You will see."

She pushed damp hair out of Rebecca's eyes and then lifted the bottom of the doeskin cover to see if there was any sign of the baby coming. She talked all the while. "The heated stones will help ease your pain and will soothe the baby. The white liquid is from the valerian plant. It will help you sleep."

"What if I die while I'm asleep?" Rebecca rolled her head toward the dim corner where Jesse sat. "Mr. Starr, if I die, promise that you will take my baby to my mother. Her name is Matilda Throckmorton. She and my father live in Wicker Park. Anyone can direct you. Surely she wouldn't refuse to take her grandchild because of my sins."

An unsettled feeling stole over Jesse. His heart

quickened. He had never wanted the responsibility of anyone other than himself. He'd known this girl all of three days, and somehow she had found a soft spot in his heart.

"Mr. Starr?"

"I don't expect you're going to die, Mrs. Donnelly. If it will help you rest easy, I will contact your parents." There, he hadn't fully committed. Because what if he became attached to the child?

In the darkened corner, Jesse thought about Rebecca. Her father was a wealthy banker. She had grown up wrapped in the protection of her family, enjoying all the innocent games and interests of a young girl facing womanhood. And then along came Frank Donnelly, a real snake charmer, who had stolen her innocence and made her an outcast. It was hard not to compare his own life to hers. Except his had been steeped in violence and danger.

His eyelids drooped. His chin settled against his chest. Jesse sank into that place where neither nightmares nor dreams would reach.

A hand on his arm caused him to lurch forward.

Chapter 7

"I have a venison stew simmering over my cook fire. Are you hungry, Mr. Starr?"

Jesse hadn't realized he'd drifted to sleep until the grandmother's voice disturbed his dreams. He blinked up at her. "I could do with some food."

"Then follow me."

"What about the girl?"

"She will not awaken for many hours. The midwives will watch over her."

Jessie unfurled his long legs. He grimaced against the needles of pain that shot through his numb limbs when he stood. The cold hit him as he stepped from the tipi's warmth, and he looked up at a sky littered with stars against an inky night. Small campfires lit the way to the medicine woman's lodge.

She scolded a barking dog and spoke to several of the men who sat huddled outside their own lodges, rifles cradled in the crooks of their arms.

A few steps farther and she opened the flap of her home and invited him in, extending a hand as further invitation to sit. "Remove your coat." And then she said, "I do not have the white man's coffee. Will chicory do?"

Jesse shrugged out of the heavy buffalo hide coat and set it aside before settling on a floor covered with animal pelts. "Anything hot and strong will do fine, ma'am."

She filled two battered tin cups and handed one to Jesse, then busied herself stirring the stew and ladling two heaping bowls.

They ate in silence, sitting on opposite sides of the bright orange embers. She observed Jesse, taking his measure, trying to control her thudding heart and hoping beyond disappointment that the Great Spirit had heard her prayers and now answered them.

Jesse Starr had blue eyes like his father, except Jesse's were a lighter blue. He had the same cleft chin and smile as his father. She cautioned herself to go slow, to ask all the right questions, to not reveal her identity. Not until she knew for certain.

"You do not speak the same as the white men who occasionally visit our village."

Jesse looked up from the bowl. "How do you mean?"

As if weighing her answer, she offered a smile. "You are not from this region. Where is your home?"

"I haven't had a place to call home for a long time." The look of annoyance on her face caused him to quickly add, "My apologies, ma'am. Living with rough men, often evil men, causes one to forget proper manners. I was raised in England, and I was raised to be a gentleman."

A slight smile touched her lips. "Tell me about yourself, Mr. Starr."

Jesse drank deep from the cup of chicory. "My father came to America from England to hunt buffalo. He was injured and brought to a Kiowa camp, where his wounds were tended by a young woman. They fell in love and had a son. When it was time for my father to return to England, she refused to go with him and instead sent her son with him to have a better life. I'm on a mission to find my mother. At the upper Kiowa reservation, I was told she might live on the reservation in southwestern Oklahoma. Her name is—"

Tears pooled in Leotie's eyes. The Great Spirit had indeed answered her prayers. "His name was Addison Starr Fitzroy. He called her Starr's Woman. She had a son and named him Red Wolf because he was born with a mark on his left hip in the shape of a wolf's head."

Jesse swore under his breath. "Bloody hell."

There was a hot, odd stinging in his eyes. He shut them for a moment, and the feeling abated. His voice came out in a whisper. "Are you my—?"

She lifted on her knees and held out her arms, she cried, "Yes…yes, my son, I am your mother."

Like two dry riverbeds thirsting for water, mother and son talked long into the night, each with as many questions as the other.

"Even on his deathbed, Father tried to speak your name. He made me promise to find you."

Leotie refilled their cups with the strong chicory coffee. "Addison was still a young man. How did he die?"

"Father was a great lover of horses. He had a stable filled with the finest of breeds. He was looking over one of his newest stallions when something spooked the animal. It reared and struck him in the head, and then proceeded to stomp him. Several groomsmen were able to drag Father to safety. At least that is what I was told. I was away at school, at the time." Jesse fell silent for several long moments. "Lawrence and I were with him when he died."

"And his wife?"

"You knew of her?"

"Addison said it was a loveless marriage, an arrangement because of money." Leotie placed a hand against her mouth to suppress a giggle. "He said she was as cold as a dead fish."

Jesse, too, laughed. "Fitting description."

Leotie nodded. "I also knew of Addison's firstborn son."

She didn't miss the flare of anger and how the blue of Jesse's eyes darkened when he spoke. "Lawrence."

"You do not like your brother?"

"Half-brother. There was no love lost between us. From the earliest I can recall, Lawrence and Henrietta made my life miserable. Behind father's back, of course."

Leotie reached out and touched the crook in Jesse's nose, then lightly traced the scar above his eye. "Your father was an honest man. He never lied about his other wife and son. And even though we were married in the tradition of the Kiowa and our love was true, in my heart, I knew there was no place for me in his homeland. When he received word that his government needed him, I knew that for you to have a life better than a buffalo hide tipi with a dirt floor and many days without enough food, I had to love you enough to send you away. Addison agreed."

She touched her heart. "I was barely eighteen moons, and a widow, when your father was brought to our camp. He was unlike my first husband. Kind, well-spoken. At night he would read to me from one of his many books. "I think I fell in love with him the first moment he said my name in that wonderful accent of his. When you were born, I was certain our lives would go on forever. It tore a hole in my soul to send you away."

Jesse drew a long breath as he gazed at his mother. "Why didn't you go to England with Father?"

It was almost as if she couldn't look at him for a moment. She spoke in a voice that did not belie her feelings. "Addison loved me, of that I have no doubt, and you were the joy of his life. But where would I live? In the house with Henrietta? The way he spoke of her, I knew that would never happen. No, if I couldn't live as Addison's legal wife, then I would not live as his whore tucked away in some little house in the woods."

She shifted to a more comfortable position. "From that time until now, I have honored my vow never to share my bed or my heart with another man. This is why I became a medicine woman."

Jesse looked at the firepit's glowing embers—or rather, in its general direction. "I'm sorry."

"For what, my son?"

"For all of it."

"You are a good man. Like your father."

He harrumphed. "Maybe once. Not anymore for a long time."

"I see the hurt, the bitterness, the anger. It is written in your eyes, the crook of your nose, the scar above your eye, even the tone of your voice. Tell me, my son. Tell me what has caused this hatred to grow and fester in you."

"No, Mother."

"Then I made a mistake sending you to England. Did I not?"

Bloody hell. She was ripping his heart to shreds.

He yanked his woolen shirt loose from his pants and exposed his back, scarred and puckered with rough ridges from the many times he had been flogged. He turned away from Leotie.

She expelled a little cry. "Who did this to you?"

"Do you really want to know?"

Leotie folded her hands in her lap and merely nodded. "I am a mature woman who has seen much tragedy. In the Kiowa way we believe that, good or bad, our stories are written before we are born. There is nothing you can say that will cause me to disrespect your story."

Chapter 8

An involuntary shudder ran down Jesse's spine. He'd lived and survived the lashings. He didn't want to live it again. He struggled to control the temper rising in him. He lifted his head and stared into the glittering brown eyes of the woman who had given him life.

Maybe the telling wouldn't be as bad as the living of it.

"Henrietta let it be known that she didn't want that dirty little heathen bastard near her son. Father hired a nanny. Her name was Bessie. She was kind and loving, and protective."

Leotie said, "Did your half-brother hurt you?"

"Lawrence was too much of a coward. No, Henrietta contrived ways. When out of Bessie or Father's sight, she would pinch me, yank my ears, thump me on the head. When I was about five, somehow my bedroom mysteriously caught fire. To this day, I believe it was Henrietta I saw slipping from my room that night."

"Did you tell your father?"

"I did. Of course she called me a liar and wanted Father to send me back to live with the savages. He would have none of it, of course. After that, a bed was moved into my room for Bessie. She slept in my room until my tenth birthday. I determined then I was too old to have a female watching over me like a baby. Out of the blue, Bessie resigned with the excuse her grandmother was ill. We later learned she didn't have a grandmother.

"Although we shared the same genes as our father, it seemed that Lawrence was more like his mother. He was frail and always whining. He didn't like sports, or horses, or even the outdoors. Yet he didn't excel at academics, either. He didn't like reading or music or art, although he did eventually conquer playing the pianoforte.

"To father's consternation, Lawrence enjoyed dressing in frills and outrageous wigs. Even though he was foppish, he had a mean streak, almost sadistic. The young housemaids were afraid of him, and the older maids tried to keep their daughters away from him.

"When Lawrence was thirteen, Father and I heard the most horrific screaming coming from the barn. We found Lawrence laughing as he lashed a prized Arabian mare until her flanks were bloody."

Leotie wiped her eyes.

"Shall I stop?"

"As painful as it is to hear, no, my son, continue."

"Father arranged for Lawrence's admission to Eton College. It wasn't long before he was permanently expelled. The headmaster's letter said Lawrence was deranged and should be placed in an asylum."

Jesse drew a long sigh. "I could go on and on. For my own safety, Father sent me to Eton. I was there for three years. Father came to visit often. And I have to say it was the best three years of my life. I was safe, and I enjoyed my studies.

"Shortly after my sixteenth birthday, I was summoned home. The story was that one of the stallions had kicked father in the head." Jesse clenched his teeth with anger. "To this day, I believe Lawrence murdered our father. I believe he used a cudgel to bash in father's skull."

Leotie clutched her throat. Her eyes widened in dismay. "What makes you think such a thing?"

Still speaking through gritted teeth, Jesse said, "The blow to his head robbed father of his ability to speak. Each time Lawrence entered the bedroom, Father would grip my hand, and his eyes grew wide with panic. As sure as I am sitting here, he feared his own son."

With dismay still written in her expression, Leotie rocked back and forth. "Such savagery. But why?"

Jesse scratched the corner of his mouth. "Both Henrietta and Lawrence were wastrels. As such, father kept a tight rein on their allowances. As the eldest son, Lawrence would inherit everything, including the title of Viscount. The day after the funeral, Mr. Armistead, Father's barrister, arrived at the estate to read the will. We were all shocked when Mr. Armistead conveyed that Lawrence had been disinherited; Henrietta received the townhouse in London with a yearly stipend, and I was the new Viscount of Arlington Estate. The one caveat to the will was that should I die before producing any heirs, all properties and monies would then pass to my stepmother."

Recalling the memories had become too great for Jesse. He was certain his head would explode with outrage. He yearned for a hearty swig of brandy. He'd even settle for a bottle of rotgut.

"At my young age, I determined that the estate manager was capable of overseeing the farm until I graduated from Eton. The night I was returning to school, my carriage was attacked, our faithful driver shot, and I was bashed over the head by someone wearing a black hood. Before the world went dark, I remember my mouth being forced open and a foul-tasting liquid forced down my throat.

"I don't know how many days I was unconscious, but when I awoke, I was on a slave schooner bound for China. It has taken me these many ten years of sailing around the world, of fighting and having to kill or be killed, to get on a ship bound for the Americas. Once we docked in San Francisco Bay, I jumped ship, determined to find you and to begin a new life."

Jesse then went on to explain how he had happened upon Frank Donnelly, the circumstances with Rebecca, and how her father had disowned her.

Leotie's lips parted in what Jesse thought was disgust. "The white-eyes dare to call our people savages. I have heard enough for one night. We will talk more after the sun rises. For now, sleep, my son."

Jesse slid to a comfortable position and, rolling to his side, pulled the heavy coat over his body, fury clouding his eyes.

"My son?"

"Yes, Mother?"

"What do you plan to do about the girl?"

He lay very still, silently struggling, finding no solace. "I need to think on that."

"Will you tell her you are the son of a rich man?"

"She has already guessed that I'm British. For now, all she needs to know is that I'm a penniless drifter and that you are my mother."

"Your secret is safe, my son."

Chapter 9

As Rebecca's eyes fluttered open, panic struck her heart at the unfamiliar surroundings. She lifted the doeskin blanket and wondered why she was naked.

"It is good to see you awake."

She looked into the smiling face. "I remember— you are Grandmother? It seems like I slept a long time."

"Yes, for two days." Leotie nodded. "Your birthing time is near." She handed Rebecca a cup of warm liquid. "This is wild cherry bark tea. It will hasten your contractions. You must drink it as we walk." She and one of the midwives helped lift Rebecca to her feet.

As Rebecca walked around the confines of the tent, she asked, "Where is Mr. Starr?"

Leotie said, "He is with the men in the sweat lodge."

"Did he find his mother?"

Leotie's smile widened as she nodded. "He is my son. To me he is Red Wolf."

"Oh, yes, he told me about the birthmark on his thigh. I'm happy for both of you."

Rebecca's eyes offered a sad smile. She hadn't realized how thirsty she was and drank the flavorful liquid without hesitation. "I miss my mother. She... Never mind. It isn't important."

In truth, Rebecca craved the warmth of her mother's arms around her. She'd never thought about having a baby. This was an important time in every girl's life. She heaved a sigh. Maybe one day in the distant future she would return home and her mother would welcome her with open arms.

A grimace passed over her face as she rubbed her protruding belly. "Will he come visit me today...Mr. Starr?"

"Men are forbidden to enter the birthing tent. He will see you afterward."

Leotie continued to talk as she escorted Rebecca around within the confines of the tent. "The baby has moved downward, but you are small, which makes it difficult for the baby to make its way into the world."

"Shouldn't I be lying down instead of doing all this walking?"

Leotie laughed. "Being upright and walking encourages the little one to make its entrance into the world." She added, "How much do you know about birthing?"

Rebecca worried her bottom lip to keep from crying out. "Nothing. I've never even seen a kitten born." She gasped. "Is it supposed to hurt this badly?"

Leotie slipped her arm tighter around Rebecca's waist. "The pain will get worse."

The look of horror on Rebecca's face caused the woman to hasten on. "When it is time, you will squat over the pot," she pointed to a large, round clay bowl nestled in a hole in the center of the tent's floor. "The pot will be filled with laurel leaves. The smoke from the leaves will help relax your woman parts so the baby can be born."

Panic bubbled up in Rebecca. "I want to lie down, please."

"The baby cannot make its way downward then. You must squat over the bowl."

Rebecca sucked in a deep breath as the next pain knifed through her abdomen. "I can't. What if I fall? Please, I must lie down."

Leotie smoothed a sweat-soaked strand of hair from Rebecca's forehead, and cooed, "We have birthed many babies. We will not let you fall."

Rebecca felt alternately hot and cold. Beads of sweat formed above her top lip and lined her forehead. She moaned as the contractions gripped her insides.

"Think happy thoughts, Rebecca. I learned about Christmas from the missionaries. Did you celebrate this holiday with your family?"

Rebecca gave another moan. "We always had a tall tree with beautiful decorations."

"Think about the Christmas tree. It will help ease your pain."

The Kiowa woman's voice sounded far away. Rebecca's knees and thighs quivered as she squatted over the pot. She thought about all the wonderful dreams she had planned for her life—finishing school, a European holiday, wearing beautiful gowns, attending grand balls, marrying a handsome prince, living in a palace…silly dreams from a silly girl. She wanted to scream her rage to the world. Instead, she silently took Leotie's hand, all the while trying desperately to think how she was going to survive this catastrophe that had befallen her. Damn Frank Donnelly for profiting from her innocence. Damn her father for disowning her, and damn her mother for being too spineless to take up for her own child.

Damn them all.

"For the love of God, deliver me of this child!" Rebecca writhed in agony, her eyes wild with fear, her body covered with sweat as she strained against her burden. How many hours had she been like this, with no sign of progress?

Leotie held the cup to Rebecca's lips and encouraged her to sip more of the wild cherry bark tea. The midwives sponged her pale face and neck with a cold cloth. The stifling heat inside the tipi didn't help.

Rebecca steeled herself not to panic when she looked at the warm blood trickling down her legs. She knew nothing of childbirth but was sure the copious amount of blood wasn't a good sign.

"Are we going to die?" She sobbed. "Please don't let my baby die."

"Shh, hush those thoughts. It isn't good for you or the baby."

"Oh, please, can't you just get it out? I don't have any more energy to walk or squat."

"It's time. The baby comes, Rebecca." Leotie commanded, "Push. Hard."

Leotie and two midwives held tight to Rebecca as she squatted over the pot. She grunted and groaned and bore downward. She scrunched her face until it hurt almost as badly as the raw searing of her insides.

An odious brown fluid gushed. The sickening, metallic stench of blood was thick in the confines of the hot room.

Rebecca screamed.

"Push again. One more time, Rebecca. Again. Harder!"

Leotie caught the baby as it slid from Rebecca's womb. One of the midwives then drew out a knife and cut the umbilical cord.

The child weakly flailed its tiny arms and legs, giving out a faint mew of protest at leaving the cozy home it had known for the past months.

The midwives set about washing Rebecca's body. The delivery pot and its putrid contents were removed from the tipi. Bathed and refreshed, Rebecca was helped to a bed of fresh pelts, where she lay back, exhausted.

Leotie knelt beside her. "It is a girl. A beautiful baby girl."

Rebecca slowly sat up, and Leotie placed the infant in the new mother's outstretched arms. Rebecca stared down in amazement at the newborn, her tiny fists clenched and waving about as if she were trying to find the boundaries of this new world.

"Oh, my," she breathed. "A girl." Awe was written all over Rebecca's face. "Oh, my, she is beautiful, isn't she?"

Her face crumpled into tears as she looked at Leotie. "Thank you." Then she wiped her eyes with the back of her hand. "I have so much to think about—what to do next."

"First, you must rest," Leotie exclaimed. "Until your milk comes down, I have arranged for a wet nurse." She waggled a finger at Rebecca. "You must eat to make milk. You need milk to give nourishment to your little one."

A cough sounded outside the tipi. Leotie lifted the flap. "You may move her to my house, where I will look after her as if she were my own child."

Jesse knelt and lifted the new mother and infant into his arms. The night air refreshed Rebecca.

Suddenly she was tired. Drained of all energy. Her head lolled against his chest.

Neither she nor Jesse spoke until he arrived at his mother's tipi and he had made certain Rebecca and the infant were comfortable.

"I am eternally grateful to you and your mother, Mr. Starr." Rebecca smiled down at her sleeping child. "What is today's date, and time? I will want to record her birth in my journal."

Jesse gently trailed a finger across the peach-colored fuzz on the baby's head. "December 25th, 1881, Oklahoma Territory near Oklahoma City, and by my best calculation, she was born at midnight. Have you decided on a name?"

For a moment tears clouded Rebecca's eyes. The deep ache in her heart spoke only of remorse and regret at her misdeeds. "I had thought to name her after my mother. Given the circumstances, I no longer think my mother deserves that honor."

Rebecca yawned. Her eyelids closed. She jerked them open. "What does Leotie mean in English?"

"Rose of the Prairie."

"It's Christmas, and I have received the most perfect gift." Rebecca kissed the sleeping infant on the head. She smiled up at Jesse. "Mr. Starr, may I present to you Noelle Rose Donnelly."

"A beautiful name, Mrs. Donnelly." His blue eyes were remarkably tender as he smiled down at her.

Neither was aware that Leotie had entered the tipi until she gave a little gasp. This time tears filled her eyes as she knelt beside Rebecca. "I am humbled and honored by your generosity, Rebecca. I shall treasure my namesake as if she were my own grandchild."

Leotie motioned for the woman standing in the shadows to come forward. "This is Corn Mother. She will wet-nurse little Noelle Rose until your breasts fill with milk." She lifted the baby from Rebecca's arms. "It is time for you to sleep. In the morning, we will celebrate the new birth with a feast."

Rebecca drew a tired breath as she smiled up at her companions. She still felt dazed as she closed her eyes and welcomed the sleep. Her dreams were of a tall Christmas tree, beautifully decorated, with a glowing star adorning the top.

"A star for Christmas," she whispered.

****

Jesse sat close to his mother. To keep from disturbing Rebecca's much-needed slumber, they kept their voices to a whisper.

He thought she wore her exhaustion well. "You are an amazing woman, Mother."

Leotie fortified herself with a scoop of pemmican and a cup of warm ginger tea. She rewarded Jesse with a smile. "What do you plan to do about the girl?"

Several long moments passed while he puzzled over how to answer the question. "I need time to think through a probable solution." He lifted his own cup of tea. "For one so young, she sure managed to get herself in a very large mess."

"When the baby is old enough, take Rebecca to Oklahoma City and put her aboard the train. I cannot imagine her mother turning her own child away."

"A worthy idea to consider, except for one thing."

Leotie popped another scoop of pemmican into her mouth. "What is that one thing, my son?"

"I have no money."

"Ah, yes. That is a problem." Leotie yawned. She scooted beneath the heavy fur blanket. "You will think of a way. G'night, my son."

Jesse rested his hands behind his head and stared up through the small opening at the top of the conical roof. One lone star winked in the cold December sky. He had a sinking feeling that he was the only person who could get Rebecca out of her dire situation. In any case, he needed to think about a solution.

Chapter 10

In the weeks that followed baby Noelle's birth, Rebecca had the unsettled feeling that her whole world had turned topsy-turvy. At times she was overwhelmed, torn between excitement at being a new mother and apprehension of her destiny, wanting desperately to return to Chicago yet still fearful of the rejection she might face from her family.

With another day gone and the snow piled in high drifts, the village was quiet. Dressed in her coat and with the doeskin blanket draped around her, she used the scant light from the fire to write in her journal:

January 25th

If I have counted the days correctly, my sweet Noelle Rose is one month old today. Time moves at its own pace in the wilderness. In some ways, it seems like yesterday that I was enduring excruciating labor pains and cursing Frank for causing me to suffer this agony.

Even though he is dead, I still curse him for so many reasons. In reality, I curse myself for becoming his victim. Yes, his victim. He knew from the very beginning that I was a naive young girl with a wealthy father.

Part of me will forever despise Frank Donnelly. Yet he gave me two great gifts. The first is the gift of reality. Becoming a pregnant widow, stranded all alone on the prairie, has forced me to realize what a spoiled, ungrateful brat I was, and how I took my father's wealth for granted. Little did I realize that one day I would be sitting in a buffalo-hide tipi, sipping ginger tea from a battered tin cup, and walking to the woods to relieve myself, and at times being so hungry that my stomach hurts.

My second and most valuable gift is my precious Noelle Rose. I find complete joy in her smile, the way she grips my finger, and how she hungrily seeks my breasts for nourishment. My greatest fear is that, without enough food, I cannot produce ample milk to keep her healthy. This makes me afraid. I do not want us to die and be buried in this faraway land without my family knowing where to find our final resting place.

I have come to admire the resourcefulness of the Kiowa women. They never complain about the bitter cold that cuts through the tipis, or when the hunting parties fail to return with game, and how the women weave fish-traps, and laugh with triumph when the baskets are filled with bass, and shiners, and lamprey. No matter how meager the catch, everyone shares.

Christmas dinner was unlike any I've ever experienced. I cannot imagine my parents or sisters sitting cross-legged in a circle and passing around a community bowl of berries wrapped in buffalo fat or drinking chicory coffee. There was wild turkey and venison roasted over an open fire, and boiled wild greens.

There were no packages wrapped in fancy paper. In fact, there were no presents. I think about my life in Chicago and all the money frittered away on useless frippery and impractical dresses.

Mr. Starr explained that the Kiowa believe friends

and family are gifts, and that life is the greatest of all rewards. Every time my sweet Noelle Rose smiles, I know she is my greatest gift.

Jesse Starr is an unusual man, so different from Frank. He is quiet, soft-spoken, and though he is half Kiowa, he divulged that his father was an Englishman who came to America to hunt buffalo, but circumstances caused him to go back to England and never return to Leotie. Sad. So sad.

I told him about our beautiful Christmas trees and how much I missed not having one. A week after Christmas, he took Noelle Rose and me to the woods. He had found a perfectly shaped loblolly fir. It was his gift to me. We didn't cut it because the Kiowa believe we shouldn't take from Mother Earth unless it is to sustain our lives. Instead, he carved R & N in the trunk.

Mr. Starr's mother is Leotie, which means Rose of the Prairie. She is the sister to Chief Charging Bear. This makes her a princess, royalty of a different kind, and Mr. Starr is a prince.

Leotie is different from you, Mother. I have learned much from her. Although she is a Kiowa princess, she is not "high-toned" or superficial. She is a practical woman with knowledge beyond any rich white woman's realm. She has adopted Noelle Rose as her granddaughter.

My eyes grow tired from the wood smoke and the dim light. I shall write more another day.

Rebecca closed the leather journal and placed it and the pencil inside her valise. The baby had grown fussy. Rebecca lifted the tiny girl and was set to nurse her when a customary scratching on the tipi signaled a visitor was asking entrance.

She puzzled over this, as no one ever visited. Drawing the front of her dress closed, she gasped when she opened the flap. The pockmarked face greeting her was less than friendly. In her lifetime she had seen a rattlesnake only once. She would never forget the evil in the coiled viper's eyes. The man who stood before her had eyes that reminded her of the venomous snake. She had seen him on occasion but did not know his name.

All of the able-bodied men were out hunting. It struck her odd that this man was not with them.

"If you seek Mr. Starr, he is out hunting with the other men."

The man tried to push around her to enter the tent. Rebecca blocked his way. "I did not give you permission to enter. What do you want?"

"I do not look for the one you call Starr. I am Two Knives. I have come to offer marriage to you."

"Thank you, Two Knives," she finally managed, though her heart pounded wildly. "I-I do not wish to marry you or anyone else."

He reached to touch the infant. Rebecca's motherly instinct caused her to slap his hand. Her voice brooked no nonsense. "Do not touch my baby."

Two Knives' face twisted into a hideous grin. His voice was harsh and demanding. "I have made my marriage offer, woman. Since you have no one to receive the bride price, I am not obligated to pay. Tomorrow, I will come to claim you. Have your belongings ready."

With a look that chilled her to the bone, he stalked away from the tent.

Frightened beyond belief, Rebecca held Noelle

Rose tightly against her breast. The need to escape this place was imminent, but there was nowhere to run. Dear Lord, she had to do *something*. Taking deep breaths to calm herself, she paced back and forth across the small enclosure.

She wished desperately that Jesse or Leotie would soon return. They would know what to do.

****

After long hours in the birthing tent, Leotie walked across the snowy compound to her own abode. She longed to wash her body and then settle down with a cup of strong chicory coffee. She turned at the sound of voices—many voices, and the whinnying of horses. One particular rider stood out among all the others. He sat tall and regal, dark and commanding. Noble. Pride swelled her heart as he lifted his hand in greeting and smiled at her.

"Hullo, Mother." Jesse urged his horse toward her. Behind him trailed a packhorse with a large buck strapped across its back. "Mother Earth has blessed us. There is enough to last until spring." He pointed to more horses packing game.

"I will gather the women to prepare the meat for storage and the hides for tanning."

"No, Mother. I see the blood on your dress and the tiredness in your face. Let one of Charging Bear's wives see to this. You must rest."

She was weary. The girl was young and had delivered months before her time. Sadness enveloped her. Not all babies could be saved. It was the way of the life cycle.

"I'll come to the tipi shortly. I am in need of coffee."

"We are both in need of chicory, my son." Leotie trudged toward her tent.

She entered the confines of her home and opened the flap wide to let in light and let out some of the smokiness.

Yesterday, the children had gathered cattails, and the women had ground the roots into flour. After days of subsisting on boiled acorns and berries, they would feast tonight on fried bread and roasted venison. She longed for honey to sweeten the bread. Like the other women, she yearned for spring to arrive.

"Rebecca?"

"I'm here."

The opened flap let in enough light to make Rebecca's frightened face visible. She sat crouched on the far side of the tipi. She rocked back and forth, the sleeping baby held tight in her arms.

Forgetting about her aching bones and how she craved to stretch out on her sleeping mat, Leotie knelt before Rebecca. "What is it? Noelle Rose, is she…"

Rebecca swiped a tear, leaving a smoky streak down her cheek. Her teeth chattered as she spoke. "The baby is fine."

A fierce trembling took control of her body.

Leotie reached out and grabbed Rebecca's shoulders. "Are you ill? Tell me."

"A man came."

Leotie's scalp itched with anger. "What man…did he hurt you?"

"H-he said his name was Two Knives. He said he was claiming me as his wife, and he will come to get me tomorrow." Sobs wracked Rebecca. "What am I to do, Leotie?"

The Kiowa woman controlled her rising anger. "You are a single woman, and it has been more than time for you to heal from delivering the child. This makes you an eligible woman."

Rebecca's eyes widened in panic. "No. No. I won't do it. He is evil, and ugly. No. I-I will kill myself and Noelle Rose before allowing him to touch either of us."

The baby let out a loud wail as if to protest her mother's tight grip. Leotie reached forward. "Let me hold Noelle Rose. The men have returned from a successful hunting trip. Busy yourself making a fresh pot of chicory. Red Wolf is in need of a cup."

Rebecca nodded as she relinquished the tiny girl into the outstretched arms. Without a word, she walked to the open door to collect snow to melt for fresh water.

In afterthought, Leotie said, "Quiet your fears, little one. Red Wolf and I will speak to my brother."

Chapter 11

Jesse watched Rebecca striding toward the woods. Respecting her privacy to take care of her personal needs, he didn't follow or call after her. Once inside the tent, he lifted Noelle from his mother's arms. "I believe she is the most beautiful baby I have ever seen."

Leotie smiled. "And how many babies have you seen in your lifetime?"

He chuckled. "Besides Noelle, one. Maybe two."

He could not discern the expression on his mother's face. It was apparent she was troubled. "What disturbs you, Mother?"

Leotie cut her glance toward the tent's closed flap. "We must hurry before Rebecca returns. I sent her to get fresh snow to make chicory."

Jesse waited.

"There is a man in our village who is known as Two Knives. He has a thirst for the white man's firewater, and he gets crazy when he drinks too much. He comes from the northern reservation. He is a pock-faced man with the eyes of a demon."

Life had taught Jesse how to survive under the harshest circumstance. Little disturbed him. He vaguely remembered seeing such a man but had thought nothing of him. His mother's silence now did give him cause to be concerned. "What about this bounder troubles you?"

"Rebecca is a rare beauty, with her small stature

and hair the color of the sun. Eyes like hers, with a hint of mischief, can lead a man to believe that when she smiles it means more than friendship." His mother's next words were like a kick in the gut. "She said Two Knives came today and offered marriage, and since she has no guardians to accept a bride price, he will come to claim her tomorrow."

An unfathomable depth of contempt for the man named Two Knives swept over Jesse. "Before Frank Donnelly died, he made me promise to take care of his wife. I gave him my word. This makes me her guardian. What happens if I refuse to give Two Knives permission to marry her?"

A lengthy silence passed between them. Leotie held the gaze of her son. "Two Knives can offer you what he thinks Rebecca is worth. You can refuse his price and name your own. If he cannot pay, then there is no marriage. But if he can pay, he gets to claim Rebecca."

Jesse said nothing; his silence sent a clear message of his disapproval. He ran his hands through his thick black hair. Bloody hell! He hadn't asked for this.

Leotie reached forward and covered his clenched fists with her own papery hands. "This man makes me afraid. You must take Rebecca and the baby and leave tonight."

His stomach roiled. He blamed himself for bringing her here. He should have insisted Rebecca remain at the cabin until he returned with either his mother or a woman who could have acted as a midwife. But castigating himself would not solve the problem of Two Knives.

At that untimely moment, a mourning dove fell

through the top opening of the tipi and lay still. Jesse and his mother stood over the motionless form almost too stunned to move.

Leotie gasped. "It is an omen of death. The Great Spirit is warning you. You must go as far away as you can. Rebecca wants to return to her home in the east. Take her."

Jesse stooped to lift the bird. Its neck dangled. The poor creature obviously had mis-navigated and flown into one of the tipi poles. He would bury it later.

He took stock of the woman who stood before him and did a quick mental calculation of her age. She was only forty-four years old. Her dark, weathered skin gave the impression of a much older woman. Strands of silver peppered her thick black hair. Deep lines at the corner of her eyes testified to a hard life of dependency on the prairie. He regretted that he was the cause of her present grief.

"I am no coward to skulk away in the night. If need be, I will stand toe to toe with this blighter."

Jesse paced the circular structure like a caged tiger. Fighting for his life was nothing new. He was an expert marksman, more than proficient with an épée, and had once used his bare fists to kill a man. He had even survived a keelhauling. No, it wasn't fear that caused his hesitation to do as his mother pleaded. The truth of the matter was that he was near penniless.

Frustrated, he jammed his hands into his pants pockets. "It is nearly a ten-day journey by train to Chicago. I haven't the funds to pay passage for one person, let alone two."

Undaunted, his mother said, "Travel by horseback. I will give you my share of today's game. You are a skilled hunter; you can forage off the land while you travel."

He shook his head as he contradicted his mother. "Rebecca is fragile. I have great doubt that she would survive a seven-hundred-mile trip by horseback, in the winter. Little Noelle most certainly would perish, if not from the cold, then from hunger."

Jesse clicked his tongue sardonically. "The only way this Two Knives fellow will ever lay claim to Rebecca is over my dead body."

A hopeful smile graced Leotie's face. "Then you will claim her as your wife?"

The question took Jesse by surprise. He answered without hesitation. "No, Mother, if I ever marry, which is most unlikely, it will be for love, not out of duty."

He found himself thinking about Rebecca Donnelly. He didn't think he had ever seen a more gently and perfectly sculpted face than the one she had revealed the morning she had opened the cabin door to find him with the dead body of her husband draped over the saddle of a horse. In spite of her advanced pregnancy, he had so wanted to feel the softness of her skin, to ease his fingers through her mass of golden tresses. He wanted to feel the whisper softness of her breath on his cheek, her mouth pressed against his. The image splintered as he imagined her in the arms of Two Knives, and anger raged within him.

He had refused to allow his feelings to grow beyond trying to protect her. She had been cruelly used by a scoundrel. He had nothing to offer her, and he'd be bloody damned if he'd use her to warm his bed and satisfy his physical needs. He did know that he wanted to protect her.

A painful silence fell between mother and son. Leotie's hand shot out and gripped his upper arm. A gleeful smile filled her almond-shaped eyes. She leaned close, her voice a whisper. "I have money. All these years it has lain hidden in my parfleche. White man's money is nothing to me. So I put it away and forgot about it."

Jesse furrowed his brow in skepticism. He too kept his voice low. "Where would you get money, Mother?"

"Your father. When Addison knew he had to leave, he gave me a leather case filled with paper money. He said I was to use it to better my life. Humph! Where would a Kiowa woman go to make a better life for herself?"

She made a *pfft* sound as she stooped to lift a layer of animal pelts from her sleeping place, revealing a flat, elongated, smooth stone. She set the stone aside to expose a shallow hole lined with hide as if to protect the interior from weather elements. She withdrew a package wrapped in a tanned pelt and handed it to Jesse.

Slowly, he unwrapped the skin to expose a leather wallet. Unexpected emotions arose in him at the sight of two rearing lions, each with the tail of a Phoenix— the Arlington crest—and the initials ASF embossed in gold, now tarnished. He sighed deeply. Feelings of longing and anger meshed together. He gently traced his father's initials with a finger. Old resentments toward his half-brother flared, and a pulse throbbed in Jesse's temples. It had been a long time since he had yearned to claim his right as Viscount of Arlington. Suddenly, he wanted to go home—home to England.

He opened the wallet. His eyes widened as he

thumbed through the layer of fifty-dollar bills that totaled three thousand American dollars.

"Is it enough, my son?"

Jesse managed a small smile. "More than enough."

****

A miasma hung in the atmosphere that morning, a sense of foreboding that seemed to follow Rebecca as she strode toward the woods. She was totally worn out by the emotions she had summoned up to deal with Two Knives' threat to claim her as his wife.

The wind stung her cheeks. She drew the coat sleeve across her nose to wipe away the impending drip. Snow soaked the hem of her skirt, sending chills to skitter up her legs. She dreaded digging the hole in the ground, hiking her skirt, and squatting to relieve herself. She longed for the comforts of a real water closet with a pull-chain toilet.

She would beg her family's forgiveness—grovel, if it came to that. As much as she'd come to admire Leotie and some of the other women, it was not her desire to spend the rest of her life in a Kiowa camp. In time, Jesse would leave. He had no obligation to her or to her baby. She reasoned that, if she promised not to be a burden, maybe she could convince him to take her with him.

Perhaps he would take her to the nearest town. She would wire her grandmother for money to buy passage home. Her heart sagged. What if her grandmother despised her as much as her father and mother did?

Melancholy gripped her so tightly her insides quivered. She looked up at the slate gray sky. It mirrored her woeful misery. "I want to go home. Do you hear me, God? Please, I want to go home."

She stood stock still, staring upward, hopeful. A snowflake fell wet on her left eye, and she blinked.

As if a sixth sense warned her, she turned to face Two Knives' dark, piercing gaze. She had been so lost in her misery she had not heard his approach.

Without warning, his hand darted out and snatched one of her wrists. She was too surprised to protest as he yanked her closer to him so he could grab her other wrist. His eyes narrowed dangerously, even as his mouth curled into a sneering grin.

"Look at me," he commanded.

Had her wrists not been so firmly pinched between his fingers, she would have slapped his face. She pulled away from him violently. He pulled her back just as violently and held her tightly against his chest, his large hand severing the feeling in her wrists.

His mouth slobbered over hers. His fetid breath and the sour taste of his mouth caused her to retch.

Rebecca screamed, "No!"

She wrenched away from him, pushing at him wildly, catching him off balance. She managed to free one wrist. With all her might, she raked her nails down the front of his face, drawing blood. He hated her for that—she saw it in his eyes, and in the flexing of the muscle in his jaw, and in his reddening cheeks.

He drew back his hand and slapped her. The force of the blow jerked her head to one side, and blood spurted from her cut lip. His eyes raked her in a way that made her skin crawl, made her want to vomit.

His hideous gaze was crazed with mania and lust. "You will learn that as my woman you will never raise your hand to me again."

Rebecca's knees crumpled, and she sagged to the

ground. Tears stung her eyes. Knowing she had no hope of fighting him, she prayed for death.

In a catlike move, he straddled her, and without warning his hand slid beneath her long woolen skirt. For a moment he seemed surprised, then perplexed, as his fingers met with the resistance of her cotton pantaloons.

She tried to buck against his weight, and she screamed again and again until he placed a filthy, calloused hand over her mouth.

She was near suffocating; her head began to swim, and her vision blurred. Her fears had come true. She was going to die in this wilderness, and her parents would never know where to find her bones; they would never know about their beautiful granddaughter. Before the world spiraled into darkness, her last thought was of her sweet baby Noelle Rose.

Chapter 12

Snow spewed in the wake of Jesse's pounding feet as he raced across the white expanse to the woods. Rebecca's panicked cries chilled him more than the wintry wind. Her legs flailing up and down as she fought against the blackguard's weight made Jesse's blood run both hot and cold at the same time. He would rip Two Knives' cod sack out and force it down his miserable throat for daring to molest an innocent woman.

With little more than a guttural growl for a warning, Jesse lunged across the short span of space that now separated them. He reached forward with an iron grip and jerked the unsuspecting bastard off Rebecca and flung him aside.

The heavier of the two, Two Knives bounded to his feet with more agility than Jesse expected. In a flash, the warrior whipped a knife from the sheath at his side. Both men crouched and circled one another. This wasn't the first time Jesse had done this dance. It was almost as if he read his enemy's next move. Two Knives jabbed forward. Jesse spun around and, with a bone-crushing blow, kicked the knife out of the Indian's hand.

Black fury raged in Jesse as he pinned Two Knives to the ground. The Indian managed to pull himself away. They struggled toward the knife, rolling and tumbling, pummeling and pounding each other brutally, viciously, murder in their hearts.

Two Knives bashed and battered Jesse unmercifully, blackening his eye, bloodying his nose, before Jesse head-butted powerfully, knocking the man backward.

Two Knives lunged for the blade, curling his fingers around the hilt, but Jesse caught hold of his wrist and beat it to the ground ruthlessly, again and again, until the Indian was forced to let it go. The knife slid over the snow, just out of reach. Wildly tearing free of each other, both men sprang to their feet, their faces now marred by cuts and bruises and covered with blood. Their hard, virile bodies strained with effort, they stood toe to toe, each slugging the other, grunting and groaning, wincing with pain. A loud sharp crack testified to a broken rib. Two Knives grimaced, positioning one arm to shield the vulnerable spot. Jesse's smile was diabolical as he homed in, his fist hammering the man's face and belly unmercifully, then landing a hard uppercut on the chin, sending Two Knives sprawling.

Jesse launched himself upon his fallen opponent, and Two Knives' legs came up, kicking him squarely in the groin, hurling him back, making him stumble and double over. Suddenly, each was on the ground again and at the other's throat, choking, strangling. Gurgling, trying to gulp air, Two Knives' mashed his splayed hand hard against Jesse's face, flattening his nose in a desperate attempt to force him off, while Jesse beat Two Knives' head violently against the ground until, in an underhanded trick, stretching out his arm, Two Knives' grabbed a handful of snow and threw it straight into Jesse's eyes, blinding him. Rolling over, Two Knives snatched up his lost knife and staggered to his feet.

Leotie raced across the snow. She hurled herself at the man. "No, I won't let you! I won't let you!" She screamed, her hands clawing like a wild thing at Two Knives' face until he seized her around the waist and jammed the knife against her throat.

Her eyes widened with helpless terror and met Jesse's own horrified, stricken glance in a desperate, silent, emotional outpouring of all the words there was not time to speak before a terrible roaring explosion deafened their ears.

Slowly, Charging Bear lowered the rifle. He stared at the grotesque corpse sprawled in a heap upon the ground. His dark eyes flashed like the blade of the double-edged knife that glinted against the snow.

"Brother! My brother," Leotie cried, springing to her feet and rushing to his side. "Thank you for saving my son."

Charging Bear emitted a sound of disgust. "A rabid animal deserves to die like a rabid animal."

A little silence fell at that. Charging Bear ordered a group of men to get rid of the body but to leave the eyes open. "The Great Father above will not want his black soul."

Rebecca wobbled as she pushed to her feet. Her throat hurt from where Two Knives had tried to squeeze the life from her. Her head throbbed, and she felt ages older than her seventeen years. There was nothing to say. She had survived.

Jesse gritted his teeth as Leotie and Rebecca helped him to his feet. With his arms draped over their shoulders, the two women managed to get him back to the tipi.

****

A strained silence fell between them as Rebecca and Leotie struggled under Jesse's weight. The walk back to Leotie's tipi was slow and tedious. Rebecca tried not to respond to Jesse's painful moans or to his nearness.

In a rush of tears, she realized how much she cared for him, even loved him…would give the world if he loved her back. But Jesse Starr had early on made it abundantly clear that he had paid his debt to her deceased husband when he brought her to the Kiowa village. She was safe, had a roof over her head, and scarce as it might be at times, food in her belly. He had also succinctly stated that he had no need for a woman in his life, and that he would move on as soon as the spring thaw began.

After giving her a curious glance, Jesse struggled to speak through his swollen lips. "Why are you crying, Mrs. Donnelly?"

She shrugged her shoulders and expelled a sorrowful sigh. "It's been a trying day. I'll cry if I want to. And for the thousandth time, I want to go home."

He cocked his head aside to view her through a black-and-blue swollen eye. "We'll talk about your going home later. I'm the one who is in pain. Dry your tears."

Unable to speak, she nodded gently against the warmth of his chest. It felt good to have his arm around her, even if he offered her no commitments.

Barely conscious by the time the two women managed to get Jesse inside the tipi, the terrible grimace on his face spoke of the great pain he suffered as they lowered him to his sleeping mat.

Leotie ordered, "Lift his shoulders while I remove his shirt."

Rebecca positioned herself at his head and did as his mother commanded. Her arms strained to hold up his dead weight. Both women sucked in deep breaths at the sight of his battered body.

"How badly is he hurt?" She blinked up at Leotie.

His mother gently pressed along his rib cage and across his abdomen. "I do not feel any broken bones." Her eyes expressed the worry that matched the frown lines in her furrowed brow. "Sometimes things get broken inside the body, and it causes bleeding that cannot be stopped."

Rebecca was certain she knew death was then inevitable. "If so, then he will…" She couldn't bring herself to say the word *die*.

Leotie merely nodded her understanding. "Let us pray the Great Spirit is not ready to receive my son."

From her medicine basket she withdrew a salve of mashed yarrow root and buffalo tallow. As she applied it to Jesse's wounds, Rebecca used cool water to cleanse the blood from his face. "This cut above his eye needs stitching, Leotie."

The older woman pursed her lips. "I will require a clean strand of hair from a horse's tail. But alas, my bone needles are too large."

Rebecca's eyes brightened. "I have needles in my sewing case. Big ones, and several small ones for making tiny stitches."

Leotie gave the girl's arm a grateful pat. "Get your needles. I will return shortly with the hair."

While Leotie was outside, Rebecca collected the silver needle case from her blue velveteen etui. The sixteenth birthday gift from her grandmother Minerva brought a stab of nostalgia. It seemed like a lifetime since she had blown out the candles on a three-tiered cake adorned with a spray of dainty pink roses made of sugary confection.

Upon her return, Leotie poured a small cup of water and set it on a fire stone to heat. She dropped the long brown strand of horsetail hair in the water. Once she was satisfied the thread was clean, she treated it with yarrow salve.

Rebecca handed her the slimmest needle. After a couple of missed stabs, Leotie said, "The light is too dim. I cannot see the tiny eye." She stretched her hand forward.

Rebecca hesitated. "I will thread the needle, but I cannot stitch this cut."

Leotie harrumphed. "I have watched you sew perfect stitches in Noelle's new doeskin booties. With your skillful hand, Red Wolf will not bear an ugly scar to mar his handsome face."

Rebecca shook her head. "I can't. I don't want to hurt him."

"Calm yourself, child. I have given him a sip of my special tea. He will sleep deeply and feel no pain." She nodded as if to reassure Rebecca that she spoke the truth.

Rebecca heaved a huge sigh. "I will do my best."

"That is all any of us can do, my child."

Rebecca willed her hands to not shake as she threaded the needle. She leaned forward and used her other hand to pinch the skin above his eyebrow together. She had to apply pressure to push the needle through the flesh. Her stomach roiled as blood from the gash seeped to stain her fingers.

She drew another breath and skillfully placed the needle under and then over the thread to lock the stitch. Over and under, again and again she stitched, careful not to pucker the flesh. She counted each over and under suture until she had completely closed the gap with twenty-four tiny stitches.

Leotie smoothed a thin layer of salve to keep the area safe from infection. "You have done well, my child. Let us have a cup of chamomile tea. It will help us sleep."

"What about Jesse?"

Leotie brushed a strand of hair from her son's face. "If he rouses during the night, I will tend to him. Take to your bed. This day has not been one that you will want to remember."

Rebecca accepted the cup of brew. It didn't take long before the delicate floral flavor began to work its magic. She yawned as she lay next to the sleeping baby. She didn't want to close her eyes for fear of seeing Two Knives' evil eyes.

"Leotie?"

"Yes?"

"When Two Knives had his hands around my throat, I was sure I was going to die. It's strange that I wasn't afraid for myself, only for my baby and what would happen to her." Rebecca propped on an elbow. "If I should die before I can get back to Chicago, please promise you will see to it that Jesse takes Noelle to my grandmother. Her name is Minerva Stanton. She is my mother's mother. She isn't at all like my mother. I'm certain Grandmother Stanton would gladly see to Noelle's care. I will write her address in my journal because I want Grandmother to have it. Maybe, after reading it, she will convince Mother and Father that I wasn't such an ungrateful sinner after all."

At Leotie's lack of response, Rebecca was afraid she had somehow insulted the woman. "I-I'm sorry. I didn't mean to imply that you wouldn't love Noelle Rose and raise her up right. It's just that, well—"

The Kiowa woman interrupted her voice gentle and kind. "I take no offense, Rebecca. I had the same love for my son when he was a tiny boy. That is why I sent him to live with his father in England. My bones are weary. We will talk no more." She pulled the fur blanket over her head to signal no more talking.

Chapter 13

As the days passed, Rebecca spent her time between caring for Jesse and helping the women with their daily chores. In all of it, she grew to admire the tenacity of the Kiowa women and how they went about the rigors of their mundane lives without complaint. There were times when she chuckled inwardly as she imagined her mother and sisters gutting fish, helping to skin a rabbit, and melting snow for water.

In many ways, she envied the women because they had nothing to compare their lives to. Unlike herself, they knew only one way, and that was the life they had been born into.

One rare day, a group of excited children raced back to the camp to show their treasures to the women. While searching for twigs and pine cones to use as fire starter, the children had happened upon a turkey nest filled with six eggs.

Rebecca joined in the excitement. She clapped her hands together like a jubilant child. "Leotie, let's celebrate by baking a cake."

The Kiowa women looked puzzled as they mumbled among themselves. Leotie said, "Are you speaking of fried bread?"

"Oh, no. Cake is sweet and luscious. It makes your taste buds happy."

One woman boldly stepped forward. "I do not

know who this taste bud is, and I have no desire to share my egg with this person." She crossed her arms over her bony frame and glowered at Rebecca.

Rebecca swallowed back the giggle that desperately wanted to burst from her throat. She didn't wish to make an enemy of this woman by offending her. "Leotie, please explain that 'taste buds' is not a person." She struggled with a simple explanation. She stuck out her tongue and pointed to the inside of her mouth. "It is when you put a special food inside your mouth and it makes your stomach happy and you smile."

Leotie gave her a skeptical look, but explained to the group of women, and then she added, "Are we so stuck in our ways that we refuse to learn new things?"

A wizened woman pushed forward. Her voice raspy with age, Grandmother Blue Duck said, "I am old and have seen many changes in my life—some bad, some good. If this cake will make my tongue happy, then give my egg to the girl with hair like sunshine."

Leotie agreed. "I, too, will give my egg."

A boy about age six tugged at his mother's skirt and said, "I want my taste buds to be happy."

The woman patted her son on the head. "It has been a hard winter. We need a bit of happiness. There are not enough eggs for the entire camp. I would like to try this cake."

Leotie smiled. "Tell us what you need, Rebecca."

Rebecca ticked off the ingredients. "Cattail flour, salt, eggs, mint leaves, milk, and melted lard."

The bony woman with the frown said, "We have no cow."

Someone spoke up. "My mare has a new foal. Will

mare's milk do?"

Nervousness built inside Rebecca. She had eaten plenty of cake, and had watched their cook bake cakes, but she had never actually made one. She prayed this undertaking wouldn't be a disaster. With a slight grimace, she said, "Yes, mare's milk will do."

She demonstrated how to separate the yolks from the egg whites and showed the children how to vigorously beat the whites, giving each of them a turn, while hoping the froth would become stiff with only crushed mint leaves to use as sweetener.

When the batter was prepared and divided into separate tortoise shells, then covered with thin sheets of river birch, they were lowered into a hole in the ground that the women used as an oven. The beaten egg whites were placed in the snow to keep chilled.

Women and children alike formed a circle around the oven area. No one made a sound. Rebecca's apprehension increased. Self-doubt crept over her. She leaned near and whispered to Leotie, "Why don't they go about their usual business?"

"This is a new adventure for them…for me. You have given us a reason to forget about what hardship we may face tomorrow."

"Oh, I wish you hadn't said that. These women gave up a precious gift. I'm assuming that you don't get eggs very often. I don't wish to disappoint them."

Leotie gave Rebecca's hand an encouraging squeeze. Nothing more was said. It seemed an eternity before a delectable aroma sweetened the air. Noses sniffed. Men gathered at the circle. Children clapped their hands, and women chattered like happy magpies.

Rebecca respected Leotie's position as a matriarch

of the village. "Tell them the cakes will need to cool completely before we put the icing on." Rebecca shivered. "In this weather, it shouldn't take long."

And they waited.

As soon as the tortoise shells were removed, Rebecca turned each one upside down on a wooden table lined with birch leaves. She tapped the shells with a wooden spoon and held her breath as she lifted each one and watched the misshapen golden-brown layers plop out. Her delighted squeal escaped before she could draw it back.

Sounds of amazement filtered through the observers. Some came forward to sniff and then smiled their pleasure.

Rebecca asked the little girl who stood at her elbow to bring the icing. She counted all the people and hoped there was enough cake to go around. She used the same wooden spoon to ladle a glop of icing onto the layers. She dipped her finger into the empty bowl and stuck it into her mouth, then encouraged the children to do the same. She was more than pleased at the happy sounds and amazed smiles.

Rebecca showed Leotie how to cut the layers into small squares. It was a mere morsel, but it was enough. Rebecca held the small square forward. "Grandmother Blue Duck was the first to encourage the making of this cake. I am honored to give her the first piece."

The old woman accepted the tidbit covered with sticky white icing. She looked at the golden morsel as if it were a treasure. And then she placed it inside her mouth.

Total silence fell. It was as if even the wind held its breath. Waiting.

Grandmother Blue Duck smacked her lips. She ran her tongue around the outer edges of her mouth to lick at a speck of frosting. She licked the sweetness from her fingers. Her mouth widened into a toothless grin. "Girl with the Hair of Sunshine, you have made my taste buds happy."

Not the smallest crumb was left. Women hugged Rebecca, the men merely grunted to hide their pleasure, and the children planned another hunt to find more turkey eggs.

Rebecca escaped to Leotie's tipi and knelt beside Jesse. Her body betrayed her with a quick excited pulse at the sight of his still-bruised face. "I saved you a piece."

She thought he looked much better now that his lips were no longer swollen and he was able to open both eyes. The stitches above his eyebrow needed a few more days before she would remove them.

He grimaced as he scooted to a sitting position. "What about you?"

"Yes, and a tiny piece for Noelle Rose."

He savored the bite. "It's been a very long time since I've had cake. I believe it's the best I've ever eaten."

His compliment brought a blush to Rebecca's cheeks.

****

As his body healed, Jesse's restlessness increased. He needed to move. Wanted to move. Needed to get his strength back. In the dark, he rolled to his side to face where Rebecca lay sleeping. His thoughts meandered. He had looked into her eyes and behind the smile he had seen the depths of her sadness. She still believed she had brought shame to her family. She had brought an unexpected joy to his mother's people. It was "his mother's people" that jarred him. They were just that— *her* people. It didn't matter that he was half-Kiowa or that he could ride and shoot and hunt as well as any of the warriors; they were not his people. He was not one of them.

In truth, he didn't belong. Not to the Kiowa, not to the whites, and not to the British. He was a man without a true identity. He tried to quiet the thoughts that begged to be heard. It was time to leave. The old resentment toward his half-brother rose hot and furious. Lawrence had stolen his life.

He reasoned that in many ways he and Rebecca were alike. At sixteen her innocence had been stolen and she was coerced into leaving her family, then left penniless and without a home.

At sixteen he had been shanghaied when his half-brother had given the order to have Jesse's carriage attacked. All had been taken from him—his home, his money, his title, and ten years of his life.

Rebecca rolled over, her face a vision in the dim light. It astounded him how much he ached for her. He imagined her unbuttoning his shirt and running her hands over his chest. In his mind, she didn't stop there. The dress would come first, and then the pins holding her hair in place. His fists clenched around the fur pelts as he envisioned her slipping into bed with him.

He expelled a deep sigh. He would run his fingers through that mass of golden silk hair, tugging lightly to pull her mouth to his, and then...the spell was broken when the baby cried out.

After a moment, he wondered if Rebecca felt the

same desire for him.

Did she…?

No, he would not allow himself to wonder if she thought of him in any way other than a man who was as dishonorable as her dead husband. If she did, it was probably without the slightest of tender feelings. He wasn't worth her affection. He was a drifter with nothing to offer.

What about him?

And so Jesse lay back, his arms folded behind his head. Oh, bloody hell, his stomach ached at the thought of life without Rebecca. It made him physically sick to his stomach.

Turmoil twisted like a tornado in his mind. He discarded idea after idea about when he would leave, how he would say goodbye, and which direction he would allow the wind to blow him.

The stitches above his eye itched. Tomorrow he would ask Rebecca to remove them. Tomorrow he would go to the sweat lodge to rid his body of impurities. Tomorrow he would tell Rebecca of his decision to leave. Tomorrow he would ask his mother an important question.

So much depended on tomorrow!

Chapter 14

Rebecca stood at the far fringe of the village, gazing out over the blanket of white. In every direction lay a vast expanse of nothing. She brushed a lock of golden hair off her face and closed her eyes, trying to visualize the tall buildings and busy streets of Chicago, with the varied aromas of home. For a moment, she imagined the children's distant laughter as those of her sisters. How she longed to see Beth and Melinda. She wondered if they thought about her or even missed her.

How far was it to Chicago? She tried to remember how many days she and Frank had traveled by train, changing at different rail stations so often that she'd lost track. A frown flitted across her face as she considered that, in reality; she had no idea which direction would take her back to civilization.

She steeled herself, knowing she had greater hardships yet to face and she could only pray she had enough mettle to face whatever the future held.

Spring was in the air. The woods echoed with the noisy chitter of red-breasted robins. Here and there sprigs of green pushed through the snow, and buds lined the trees' winter-bare branches.

Even baby Noelle was blooming. She was sitting up, making delightful baby sounds, and grabbing everything within arm's reach. Soon she would crawl, then walk, and talk, and ask questions. Rebecca dreaded the future.

Swept away in her musings, she hadn't heeded the soft crunch of steps behind her until he spoke. "Rebecca, it's dangerous this far from the camp."

She shrugged her shoulders, and did not immediately answer.

"It's time for the bears to leave their dens. They are hungry and mean, and standing out here alone, you make a mighty tempting morsel. The wolves are also on the prowl. And…"

His voice prattled on and on like an annoying mosquito that buzzed and buzzed until she wanted to smack the life out of it.

"Please stop." She said, cutting him off, sounding exasperated. "I came out here for a bit of peace and quiet. And…and you're just making matters worse."

"Turn around, Mrs. Donnelly."

She ignored his command and instead reminded, "Rebecca…remember?"

"Aye, Rebecca, turn around, if you please."

Arms folded across her breasts, she stoically stood her ground.

"Go away." He was leaving. She was certain that was why he'd interrupted her solitude. "If you're going to leave, just go. No excuses, no goodbyes."

"Bloody hell, woman, I came out here to ask for your help."

She cautioned herself. Why ever would Jesse Starr need her help? She turned. The raw scar above his eyebrow stood out like a badge of courage. His hair was as black as any villain's, but there were glints of dark auburn when it caught the light.

Sharp blue eyes…a hard mouth, and a face with the

look of a pirate or a highwayman and the kind of expression that boasted of no scruples. Just like Frank. The kind of man whom even *she* in her ignorance understood it was best to avoid and never allow her feelings to go awry.

A flush crept up her cheeks to warm her face. She hated the way she wanted to cover her face with her hands.

And why did his eyes have to rake over her in quite that fashion? Why was there such a twist to his lips as if he despised what he saw?

And why did she mind so much?

She lifted her head and stared boldly into his glittering blue eyes. "I can't imagine why you would need my help with anything."

She counted the minutes, waiting for his answer. "Well?"

"I'm leaving."

She pressed her lips together and hardened her gaze. "Why are you telling me this?"

He almost snorted his reply, his impatience obvious. "I need you to help me convince my mother to come with us."

His words echoed inside her brain. Did he just say "us"?

The thought of leaving the Kiowa village, this wilderness, exhilarated her and frightened her. "*Us*...as in the baby and me, too?"

He offered a cockeyed smile. "Well?"

She inclined her head in assent.

Without touching, Rebecca and Jesse walked to Leotie's tipi. He held the flap aside for Rebecca to enter. His mother placed a finger against her lips to motion silence. She pointed to the sleeping baby.

Rebecca knelt and busied herself pouring cups of chicory coffee for each of them. She took her usual place and gazed at Jesse with a combination of fascination and expectation.

"Red Wolf, my son, you look as if you have swallowed a porcupine quill. What troubles you?"

"There is no need to beat around the bush," Jesse responded. "If I am to escort Mrs. Donnelly—Rebecca—to Chicago, she will need a companion to help with the baby."

Before Leotie managed to protest, Jesse said, "I also crave to see my home in England and to visit my father's grave. It was his dying wish that you see his homeland, Mother."

Leotie looked at him, startled. "Except for long rides and the move from the northern reservation to here, I have never left my village. I do not think the white-eyes would take kindly to a Kiowa woman in their midst." She held her hands out, her fingers splayed. "I thank you for the offer, but my answer is no."

Jesse exchanged looks with Rebecca. She interposed, "I know what it's like to leave the only home you have ever known. It is truly frightening." She said with feeling, "Once Jesse—Red Wolf—leaves, he may never return to this place. You may never see him again. Is it such a small sacrifice to spend the rest of your life getting to know the son that was once lost to you?"

In a moment of very tense silence, Leotie stared at her son. "Addison told me much of his homeland. I never stopped loving your father, my son. On nights when loneliness and longing gnawed at me with its vicious fangs, I would close my eyes and try to imagine the rooms in his big house, and the gardens filled with purple flowers, and a room called a kitchen with a thing called a stove for cooking food."

Leotie fussed with the cup in her hands. She turned it round and round. Rebecca understood the fretful expression on her face. And then the lines smoothed out and the tone of her voice changed as she said, "You speak wise words for one so young, Rebecca. It is true; I do not wish to lose Red Wolf again. The thought of leaving all that is familiar frightens me to the core of my soul." She gave a swift nod. "So be it. I will go with you."

The unspoken love between mother and son gratified Rebecca. She yearned to have her own mother express the same kind of affection. While wondering about what had taken place to cause Jesse to have a change of heart about taking her home, it hit her— where did a penniless drifter suddenly acquire money? It was none of her business, she surmised. Her father's favorite saying was to never look a gift horse in the mouth.

"Jesse, how do you plan for us to travel such a long distance?" She prayed it wasn't by horseback. The day's ride from the cabin to the Kiowa village had been almost more than she could bear. "How will I manage holding Noelle in my arms while trying to control a horse?"

It puzzled her when Jesse cut his eyes toward Leotie, and the way she had busied herself with doing nothing.

"By train."

Succinct. It appeared he didn't wish to divulge any details. She pressed on. "When will we leave?"

"In ten days. April is when the fair winds blow. We should have good traveling weather."

"Jesse…" Her voice trailed off.

"What is it, Rebecca?"

She opened her mouth and closed it again. Her lips felt dry. She moistened them with the tip of her tongue.

"Rebecca?"

She knitted her brows together. "It is not my intention to impose on your generosity." She heaved a sigh. "Your mother needs new clothing." And then she hastened on. "I mean no disrespect, Leotie."

Rebecca thought Jesse stiffened a little as he shifted his gaze from her face to his mother's. "Aye, you are astute for one so young. What about you, Rebecca?"

Unsure if he was joking or if he had issued an insult, her words were as crisp as the outside air. "Nothing for me. But, if you please, Noelle will need clothing, and some tins of milk. I will gladly make a list so you won't forget."

By the way he sat, she knew he was easy in his skin. He laughed and thrust a hand through his black hair. She said, "I didn't mean that quite the way it rolled out of my mouth."

He eyed his mother. "A list will be helpful, especially with sizes and colors."

He was quiet for a moment. When he spoke, his voice was solemn. "Mother, I'll need four good ponies to trade for a wagon. Once we get to Oklahoma City, I'll then sell the team. The money will be yours."

Leotie simply nodded her agreement.

Jesse set his jaw. He spoke in a calm, gentle voice. "Rebecca, would you like for me to send a telegram to your father?"

It was a simple question. Rebecca wrapped her arms tightly around her waist and held on as she tried to anchor her emotions. She sat silently for a few minutes, trying to regain her equilibrium. She averted her eyes but only briefly. When she spoke, her voice was a raw whisper. "The cowardly part of me wants to say…no. I'll just arrive on their doorstep and then deal with the consequences. The other part of me, the child part, wants so much to return home, to know that my parents have forgiven me and will welcome me and my baby with open arms."

Her throat thickened to the point where she could barely breathe, but she nodded. "Send the telegram."

Thoughts raced through her head like willy-nilly children. "What if they don't want me? Where will I go? How will I take care of Noelle? It's difficult for an honest woman to find work, and…and I have no skills."

Leotie reached over to clasp Rebecca's hands. Her expression was truly empathetic. "There is no need to fret over what is beyond your control. If the news is what you desire, then we will bid you farewell. If the news is bad, then we"—she pointed to herself and Jesse—"are your family. All will be as it should."

Rebecca nodded, but she was still troubled. "My head is muddled. I need some fresh air." Rising somewhat unsteadily from the floor, she made for the door. No one tried to stop her.

Chapter 15

Two days later, Jesse rode out of the village leading four horses. The fort was closer than Oklahoma City. Barring no trouble, he figured to arrive in two days. After twelve hours in the saddle, he was relieved to bed down for the night. He hobbled the horses, then banked a small cook fire to boil enough water for coffee and keep the wolves at bay.

Bone weary, wrapped in his buffalo hide coat and a fur-lined blanket, he settled against his saddle and stretched his long legs toward the fire. The air, crisp and fresh, braced him a little. Stars draped the sky in a silvery net. It reminded him of the many lonely nights he'd spent on the ocean, but he didn't miss the sting of wind-driven salt that had stung his eyes and the inside of his nostrils. Unwanted memories caused a shiver to skitter through him. He swallowed half a cup of hot coffee to warm his innards.

His mind kept straying back to the village, back to Rebecca. He envisioned her leaning over the cook fire stirring a stew, or writing in her journal, and how she tried to find privacy in the dark recesses of the tipi to nurse baby Noelle. He found himself lingering on the last image. His insides ground with desire. Something powerful leapt inside his mind—an odd mingling of joy and despair. The word *love* sprang to mind. Maybe he was in love with Rebecca. He didn't know because he'd never been in one port long enough to do more than bed a woman to satisfy his physical desires. The only love he had truly known was from his father.

He sensed Rebecca was drawn to him. On occasion he had seen the depth of her feelings when she thought he wasn't looking. Being drawn to him didn't mean her emotions ran deep enough to be love. He knew she didn't fully trust him. After the way Frank Donnelly had used her, it remained doubtful that she would ever fully trust another man. He also knew how much she wanted to return to her family. Other than nurturing Noelle, returning to Chicago was Rebecca's first priority. If things didn't work out the way she hoped, he might ask for her hand in marriage. This thought rattled him. Men like him didn't marry. They became old salts who swilled too much grog, thrived on swapping tales about sea adventures, and ended up dying with a knife in their gut, or rotting to death from dallying with infected jolly girls.

He tossed a small branch on the fire and hunkered down inside his heavy coat before he pulled the blanket over his head. He had nothing to offer Rebecca. No money, no home, no future. Expelling a deep sigh, it was best to keep his emotions and desires to himself, at least for the time being.

Caught in a web of fretful dreams, he didn't rest well that night, and morning hadn't come soon enough.

Leading four horses was slow going. By the time he reached the massive double gates of the fort, the sky was laced in pinks and blue and decorated with wispy white clouds to signal dusk was ready to settle upon the land.

A sentry called out, "State your name and

business."

Jesse rested easy in the saddle. "Jesse Starr. I have horses to trade for goods."

He waited until the massive wooden gates creaked and groaned their protest as two soldiers pushed them wide.

"Take 'em to the corral," one soldier said. "Sergeant Mulroney is officer of the day. Tell him your needs."

Jesse nodded to the men as he rode through. He led the horses to where a stout man with a rotund belly stood. "You Sergeant Mulroney?"

"Aye, that I am, laddie. What's yer business?"

"I'm in need of a buggy or a wagon, and a few goods from the sutler's store. I've brought these horses to trade."

"Ye ain't Irish, but ye be speakin' close to the motherland's tongue. Light down, laddie, and take yer ease."

The sergeant inspected the horses. He ran his hand down each one's withers, down their legs. He opened each animal's mouth and checked their teeth. "These be Ind'an ponies?"

"What difference does it make? These four are sturdier and will outlast any of those broke down nags in the corral."

The sergeant cocked an eye toward Jesse. "Stolen?"

Jesse matched the older man's glare. He knew the game—throw a man off balance by asking accusatory questions. A thief will either blink or look down at the ground.

"Nope. A gift from my mother."

Mulroney let out a raspy guffaw. "A gift from yer mother. Good one, laddie." He slapped his belly. "Laddie, me boy, the Army ain't looking to buy or trade, but Mr. Pike over to the store might do you a fair deal." He placed a hand on Jesse's shoulder. "Buy me a beer and I'll put in a good word fer ye."

He called out, "Private Jones, get yer head outta yer arse and take care of these 'orses." Then he said, "Where be ye from, laddie?"

"From all over."

"Aw, yer a bit cheeky, ain't ye? Ain't becomin', so I'll ask again, where ye be from?"

"England."

Mulroney guffawed again. "Bloody 'ell, wot brings ye to America?"

Jesse followed the sergeant across the yard and toward a neat line of wooden buildings. The one at the very end was identified by a weatherbeaten sign with fading letters that read Pike's Sutler Store.

Jesse blanched at the man's questions. He didn't know if the sergeant was being friendly or conducting an interrogation. "Heard the streets were paved with gold. Thought I'd come and make myself a rich man."

"I likes a man wid a sense o' humor."

The wind's biting cold sting caused tears to well in Jesse's eyes. It took little encouragement to cross the yard and sprint up the steps and inside a spacious room. The first thing he noticed was the warmth. The second thing was the scowl on the face of a tall lanky man who wore an apron.

"'Ey, Pike, this yer laddie has 'orses to trade, and he be treatin' me to a mug o' the good stuff. So don't ye go puttin' a big 'ead o' froth on me ale."

The storekeeper cut his eyes toward Jesse.

"I can pay."

The storekeeper nodded. "Sergeant Mulroney's credit is no good, and his limit is one drink. What about you, a mug?"

"Coffee and a sandwich if you have it."

A young corporal bounded into the room. "Sergeant Mulroney, sir, Cap'n requests you get your a…umm…wishes to see you post haste." He snapped a salute and left with the same speed he came in.

"Well, laddie, 'tis a sorry day when a good Irishman cain't wet 'is whistle." The sergeant continued to grumble as he left the store.

The storekeeper extended his hand. "Ezra Pike. My wife, Sarey, and me run the store. I apologize for my testiness. Mulroney doesn't know his limit when it comes to drinking, and he never has any money." He called out, "Sarey, one ham sandwich and a cup of coffee. We have a customer." He turned back to Jesse. "Now, what's this about having horses to trade?"

"I need to escort two women, a young widow with an infant, and her traveling companion, to Oklahoma City. I'm in need of a wagon or a buggy."

Pike let out a low whistle. "Rare occurrence to find white women on the prairie."

An elderly woman with an impish smile set a plate and a steaming cup of coffee in front of him. "When you finish, I'll bring you a slice of apple pie."

He tried to protest, "Thank you, ma'am, but I didn't—"

She patted him on the arm. A smile crinkled the corner of her clover-green eyes. "Comes with the meal." She hastened through an open door to what he assumed was the kitchen.

Jesse didn't miss the slight nod she offered to her husband. He turned a questioning look toward the storekeeper.

"My Sarey has a knack for knowing things about people. She said you are trustworthy. She's never wrong. Now, you were gonna tell me about the women."

An odd feeling crept over Jesse. He didn't quite know what to make of Mrs. Pike's unusual talent. He savored a mouthful of sandwich and followed with a swig of coffee. "The young woman's husband brought her out here from the east. His horse threw him. When I happened across the man, he was lying at the bottom of Devil's Canyon, near dead. I promised I'd see his wife and her companion got to the train station in Oklahoma City so they could return to the east. The one woman is elderly, and the widow is young, with a suckling infant. This is why I'm in need of a wagon.

"The ponies I brought are good stock. Gentle broke, and gelded. I figure they're worth about fifty dollars each." Jesse pulled a paper from his shirt pocket. "I also have a list of goods the women need for the trip."

Mrs. Pike seemed to appear from nowhere. She set a plate of pie in front of him and refilled his cup. She took the list from Jesse and read it out loud. "Three wool dresses: blue, black, and brown. Heavy stockings: two pair. Three yards of cotton for diapers; two outfits suitable for baby girl; ten cans of milk, one baby feeding bottle, and a used valise."

She tapped her fingers together. "My Ezra ordered me a new fandangle pedal sewing machine. I make diapers. So much easier than your young lady having to measure and cut and hand-stitch the material. Readymade is the same price as the yardage." She cocked her head and gave him a questioning smile.

Jesse blinked. "Yes, ma'am, I'm sure Mrs. Donnelly will appreciate the readymade nappies. For the record, I have no designs on her."

"Well, if you say so." She again smiled. "I sense there is something else you'd like, Mr. Starr. A wedding ring, perhaps?"

Jesse choked on the piece of pie he swallowed.

Sarey Pike thumped him on the back. "It's quite all right." A mischievous twinkle in her eye, she said, "Your secret is safe with me."

Before he could speak, she had disappeared.

Pike laughed. "I've been married to that woman for more'n thirty years, and it still unsettles me the way she pops in and out, almost like a ghost only she's as real as you and me."

Lost for words, Jesse merely nodded. "I suppose you'd like to check the horses to see if we have a deal?" And then he remembered, "I hope you have a wagon."

Pike lifted a heavy jacket off the coat tree. "Mind the store, Sarey. Back in a bit."

She poked her head around the kitchen door. "Mr. Starr, I believe the young widow might like to have a new traveling suit, too. Which do you prefer—green or mauve?"

Jesse tripped over his reply. "Ma'am?"

"Color. Green or mauve?"

He shrugged his shoulders. "She has brown eyes and blonde hair, and a creamy complexion."

Giving him a knowing look, Mrs. Pike smiled.

"Then green it is." She made a fluttering motion with her hands as if she were shooing the men out of the store.

"How does she do that?" Jesse wanted to know.

"Danged if I can tell you. Something she was born with, I reckon. Anyhow, my Sarey doesn't have a mean bone in her body. Jest don't get on her wrong side." His teeth chattered against the cold.

The ponies stood tied to the corral railing. Two roans, a pinto, and a sorrel. Pike ran his hands over each animal. Like the sergeant, he checked their teeth and inside the ears. He lifted feet and checked hooves. "Three-year-olds, and sound as a dollar. Fifty each is a fair price."

He motioned Jesse to follow. "Whisky drummer come through here last spring. Fancied himself a gambler." Pike harrumphed. "Shoulda stuck to selling whisky."

"What happened?"

"Got caught with five aces. A fistfight occurred. The drummer got knocked off his feet. When he fell forward, there was a blast. Queerest thing. He had a derringer hidden inside his vest pocket. Dang thing fired. Bullet pierced his heart. Killed him deader'n a doorknob. Beats all I ever did see. Anyhow, nobody ever come to claim his buggy. It's yours if it suits you."

The men rounded the back of a barn. Under a lean-to sat the buggy. Pike snatched off a large oilcloth that protected the one-horse, two-wheeled, covered carriage from the elements.

Relief washed over Jesse. This conveyance was more than he could have hoped for. "It will comfort the women to know they'll be sheltered from the weather."

He offered his hand. "I'll take it, Mr. Pike."

"Then let's get ourselves back to the store. The wind is cuttin' right through me." The storekeeper gathered the collar of his coat up around his neck.

Jesse didn't need any encouragement to follow.

Mrs. Pike greeted them. Two cups sat on the table that Jesse had just occupied. "Hot coffee with a splash of whisky to warm you up." She patted a brown leather satchel. "The whisky drummer had this. It's been sitting in the closet collecting dust. I've packed all your purchases inside, nice and neat."

She placed a finger to her cheek, and tipped her head as if thinking. "Ezra, we can't sell what we never owned. I don't think that poor dead whisky drummer would mind if we gifted Mr. Starr with his bag."

"If that's what you think, Sarey, then it's good 'nough for me." Pike hung his jacket on the coat tree.

Jesse sat. He wrapped his cold hands around the warm mug. Pike joined him. Mrs. Pike seated herself, too. She laid an envelope in front of Jesse, along with an itemized receipt of all the goods he had purchased. "Your change, Mr. Starr."

Jesse thumbed through the money in the envelope. He offered a questioning look at Sarey and her husband. "I believe there's been a mistake."

"Ezra, dear, you explain it."

The storekeeper was matter-of-fact in his explanation. "The buggy didn't cost me anything. I figure storing it and keeping it for a year is worth fifty dollars." He placed his finger on the receipt. "You spent thirty dollars in goods. Now, I can get at least two hundred or more for the horses. So that leaves me owing you one hundred twenty dollars. Are we

114

square?"

It was rare to come across honest people. The Pikes' sincerity humbled Jesse. "Thank you doesn't seem like enough. Somehow I feel like I'm cheating you."

Sarey reached for the envelope. She lifted out a twenty-dollar bill and shoved it in her apron pocket, leaving Jesse confounded. She placed a small square box covered in blue velvet in front of him. She commanded, "Open it."

His curiosity compelled him to obey. His eyes widened. Inside laid a sapphire-and-pearl rose-gold band. "It's elegant, but as I said before, I have no plans to marry."

Jesse had always thought of himself as incapable of that finer emotion called love. But if there ever was a woman to fall in love with, it was Rebecca. She was smart, compassionate, and beautiful. She made him want to take care of someone other than himself. She made him want to settle down, own a home, and father his own children.

Yes, she was a woman he could love.

But…love led to loss. No one knew that better than Rebecca. Look what his mother had sacrificed for love, and he had loved his father only to watch him die.

Losing people you loved didn't hold a candle to losing a poker game. He had frequently wagered and lost. Love and marriage was too much of a gamble. He ran his fist along his jaw, lost in thought.

Sarey's hand on his shoulder startled him. An unexplainable force compelled him to look into her eyes. It felt as if she were looking into the depths of his soul.

She said, "There's no hurry. You will know when it's time, and so will she. Take the ring. Tuck it away. Let it be your hidden treasure."

He did as she said and placed the blue velvet box inside a hidden pocket of his coat, where he also placed the envelope of money. "It's been a long day. Would there be an objection if I slept in the hayloft? That way I can leave before sunrise."

Ezra Pike scribbled out a note and handed it to Jesse. "Give this to the guard on duty. He won't give you any guff. Come by the store before you leave. Man can't travel on an empty stomach."

Sarey brought a thick quilt and handed it to Jesse. "Pleasant dreams, Mr. Starr."

Jesse tipped his hat. "Goodnight to you both."

He had one more chore to take care of before turning in. He opened the door and stepped inside the telegrapher's office. A corporal looked up. "Evening."

Jesse nodded. "Is this telegraph reserved for the fort's use, or can anyone use it?"

The corporal shrugged. "Reckon I can send a telegram for you. You plan to stick around for an answer? Might take a day or two."

"Nope. The answer is to be sent to the telegraph office in Oklahoma City."

The corporal said, "Can you write, or do I need to write it out for you?"

"I can write."

"Good enough." He shoved a yellow piece of paper and a pencil forward.

Jesse thought about how to word the message. After several false starts and equally as many yellow paper wads, he finished the message and shoved it

116

forward. "How much?"

The corporal skimmed over the message and let loose a low whistle. "Reckon two bits will do. Hope you get the answer you desire."

Jesse merely nodded his response. He hoped Rebecca's father didn't disappoint her. Time seemed suspended. He didn't quite remember walking to the barn or climbing the ladder to the hayloft. He settled in a bed of straw, snug under the patchwork quilt. Sarey Pike was a puzzle. In his many travels he'd encountered a few men who considered themselves prophets, but he had never met anyone with the ability to know what was going to happen before it happened. Maybe it was his imagination.

He awoke before daylight, not remembering he'd fallen asleep. He hitched his horse to the buggy and placed the saddle on the seat. He led the gray to where Sarey stood on the porch, waiting.

He tipped his hat. "G'morning, Mrs. Pike." He handed her the quilt and thanked her for her courtesy. In turn, she handed him a small cloth sack and a mason jar wrapped in a blue checkered napkin. "The jar is hot. I thought you might like coffee to go with your boiled eggs and the slice of buttered cornbread."

He stepped into the buggy and gathered the reins. "Very kind of you, ma'am. Thank you for...everything."

She lifted her hand in a farewell wave. Jesse slapped the leathers against the horse's rump. As the wagon rolled forward, she called out, "The journey your mother embarks on is one of much happiness."

The hairs on the back of Jesse's neck stood up. He hoped Sarey Pike's prediction was correct. His mother was an intelligent woman whose life had been filled with prejudice because she was Kiowa. She had known hardships that many women would never experience.

He slapped the leathers again to urge the horse into a lope. Miles from the fort, he slackened the pace to allow the animal to rest. Jesse wrapped his hand around the glass jar and unscrewed the lid. The coffee was strong and rich and still warm. Satisfying his thirst, he reached into the bag and enjoyed breakfast.

He pondered Sarey's predictions. For certain, the woman was an enigma. He shook away his morbid feelings. The dead past had nothing to do with the living, or with the new future.

He smiled as he reached to touch the little blue box secreted away in his coat pocket.

Chapter 16

Rebecca walked with the other women and a gaggle of noisy children toward the woods to search for berries, nuts, and arrowroot, and to check the traps. The winter had been harsh, leaving the food stores nearly depleted. Unlike a few of the other young mothers, who carried their babies in cradle boards, she had left Noelle Rose in Corn Woman's care.

Rebecca sorted through her thoughts, trying to make sense of things, evaluating what she had learned this past year, trying to decide where she was headed.

Her elopement, taking her father's money without permission, the loss of her maidenhead, and birthing a baby—all terrible enough, but they were not the worst of it. It was the loss of her family that grieved her the most. She had also lost faith in her ability to make sound decisions. She had lost her faith in love. In fact, she had lost her faith in just about everything. And she wanted that back.

True, she longed to return home. Now she had her doubts. As difficult as life was on the prairie, it was equally as difficult, if not impossible, for a woman to find honest work in a big city, especially an unskilled mother with a young child.

As much as she prayed her family would welcome her with open arms, she wasn't at all sure she could face a lifetime under someone else's roof, even if they happened to be her parents.

Her thoughts ran rampant. After all, what else was there to do in this desolate place except to think? Think. Think. Her thoughts plagued her until she wanted to run and hide from them.

She sniffled, touched the back of her hand to her cheek. She recalled the first time Frank had stolen a kiss. Her first kiss. She had felt giddy, and naughty. Had she loved Frank? She must have loved him to have lost her head so completely. All he had to do was smile and she would forget her own name. He was so intoxicating her knees would go weak when he stood next to her. He had made her feel worldly and alive. Now she knew she had been so blinded by the physical reactions he stirred in her that she didn't stop to question his intentions.

After they were wed, she discovered he was a charlatan just as her father had said. Frank was rough and cruel in their lovemaking. Rebecca corrected her thought. What he did to her was shameful to the point that she'd dreaded being alone with him; he made her wish she was dead. That thought echoed loudly inside her head, and she shuddered, fearing she had spoken it out loud.

"Rebecca? Rebecca, what is wrong? You look as if you are in great pain." Leotie's voice expressed concern.

"What? Oh. I was thinking…about things."

The worry on Leotie's face forced Rebecca to make her voice light and airy. "I'm not ill. At least not in the physical sort of way. I suppose I'm a little anxious about how my father will respond to the telegram. Please, don't fret."

Leotie smiled. "Even though you were visiting a world far away, you have managed to fill your basket with hickory nuts." She touched Rebecca on the arm. "Come, let us get out of the cold, and warm ourselves with a cup of chicory."

Once inside the tipi, Rebecca thanked Corn Woman for taking care of the baby. While Rebecca nursed Noelle, Leotie busied herself preparing a light meal and the coffee. "He's only been gone a day, and already I miss my son." Leotie expelled a deep sigh.

Rebecca caressed the baby's pink cheek. Her thoughts were wistful. "Do you have any concerns about leaving your people and traveling to a faraway land?"

"I will always hold my people here"—Leotie touched her heart—"and I do have a fear of the unknown, but I hope someday my son will marry and have many children. The thought of being a true grandmother gladdens my heart and eases the apprehension."

Rebecca gently laid the sleeping baby on her bed of pelts and tucked the blanket around her. She rose to her knees to give Leotie a hug. The Kiowa woman's eyes widened in surprise.

A rush of emotions filled Rebecca. She coughed to clear the rasp from her throat. "You are a rare woman, with courage any woman would envy. I shall sorely miss you."

She excused herself and settled beside the sleeping baby to go over her thoughts once more. She closed her eyes and envisioned Jesse, recalling the scent of his masculinity and how she enjoyed his nearness the day she had tended his battered body after his fight with

Two Knives. She had seen the way Jesse often looked at her. But she'd seen that same look in Frank's eyes: lust. And if she ever allowed another man in her life, she wanted more than what animals did to each other. Still, there were times, in the dark quiet hours, when her body would betray her. Yet the pain of those physical yearnings was nothing compared to the tortuous regret she had lived with every day for the past year.

She drew a deep, resolute breath. There was no getting past the fact that she missed Jesse. The one thing she had never seen in his eyes was blame or pity. There was something about Jesse Starr that revitalized her, made her feel as if she could do anything, as long as he was nearby. She felt a deep fondness for him. In fact, she felt a powerful attraction to him and wondered if she was falling in love. She thought she'd loved Frank, but in the end she'd come to despise him. She vowed never to make that mistake again.

She lay staring up at a lone star winking through the hole at the top of the tipi. *If I could wish upon a star, I would wish for—*

"Rebecca, are you asleep?"

"No."

"You and Red Wolf are destined for each other. I think both of you are just too stubborn to open your eyes to see what your hearts are telling you."

Rebecca was utterly mortified that somehow Leotie was able to read her thoughts. She sighed. "You and Jesse's lives are together in England. Mine is in Chicago. That is the only destiny I can see."

She rolled to her side to signal that the subject of her future with Jesse was closed.

A painful ache tugged at her heart. *Jesse, I don't*

want to want you.

Thunder echoed across the night. A low howling intruded into Rebecca's sleep. She sat up and listened, remembering how the wolves had scratched beneath the door to the cabin. The baby whimpered in her sleep, and as any protective mother would do, Rebecca lifted the child into her arms and held her close.

The howling came again, this time sharper and louder. The sound caused fear to ripple through Rebecca's body. In the darkness, her eyes shifted toward the leather flap that served as a door. Certainly not a barrier strong enough to protect against a pack of winter-starved wolves.

Her eyes shifted back to the lump lying curled next to the glowing embers. Surely Leotie had heard the howls. A loud clap of thunder vibrated the ground beneath the tipi. Baby Noelle cried out, and her little arms flailed. Rebecca kissed the child's forehead and offered a soothing shush.

Leotie rolled over and lifted on an elbow. Her voice, heavy with sleep, said, "Don't be frightened, Rebecca. Be thankful for the rain. It's the Great Spirit's way of telling us he is washing away winter. Soon the land will be lush with food, and hunting will be good."

The baby mewled and nuzzled Rebecca's breast. She opened her blouse to make it easier for little Noelle to nurse. The shrill whine sounded near the tipi again.

Rebecca tried to keep the tremor from her voice. "Don't you hear them...the wolves?"

"No, child, it is merely the wind. There is nothing to fear."

"Are you sure?"

"I am certain. If there were wolves in the camp, the

dogs would warn us. Close your eyes. The morning will soon be upon us."

"Leotie, do you think Jesse will arrive tomorrow? It's been three days."

Rebecca heard the older woman's suppressed yawn. "He will be here, unless the rain slows his travel."

Baby Noelle had drifted back to sleep. Rebecca's body remained tense as she laid her beneath the blanket. Her fingers trembled as she buttoned her blouse. Hesitant to go back to sleep, she kept watch on the door and listened to the keening wind. Curled into a tight ball, she craved the security of a safe place.

Morning arrived, bringing with it a bone-numbing chill and a muddy ground soggy with melting snow. Rebecca's feet were cold from the moisture seeping into the leather leggings, and mud clung to the hem of her skirt. She surmised the day ahead was sure to be a difficult one, and the effects of a sleepless night had left her emotions raw.

She was busy washing the diapers she had sewn from one of her petticoats when the camp dogs set up a ruckus. Men appeared from tipis, weapons ready, and raced toward where the horses were pastured.

She placed a hand over her eyes, shading them from the glare, and saw what first appeared as a big black bird rising from the horizon. After several long minutes, the large bird evolved into a black buggy jostling toward the encampment.

Leotie came to stand by Rebecca's side. She, too, shaded her eyes. "I hope it ain't that fool from the Indian Agency. He treats us like we are ignorant children, not smart enough to know we aren't getting the food allotments allowed to us. Thinks he can come out here and take his pick of the women and bed them, and we're supposed to clamp our jaws shut or suffer having what little food stores we get cut off."

Rebecca was startled, to say the least. "Can't you report him to someone?"

"Humph. Who would listen?"

The conversation was forgotten when the buggy, escorted by a troop of whooping warriors, rolled to a halt a few feet from where Rebecca and Leotie stood.

Jesse climbed down from the buggy. The brim of his hat shadowed his features so that Rebecca could not see his eyes, but she was intensely aware of him, all the same. She could, in fact, sense his regard touching the deepest parts of her being.

He swept off his hat and bowed as if he were a prince. "Ladies, your carriage awaits."

Rebecca's heart swelled in her chest, threatening to shatter from elation. She giggled at his gallant display of chivalry. She clutched her hands together. "It's more than we could hope for."

He approached Rebecca and laid his hand on her shoulder. "I believe the rain has moved out. We should have fair winds all the way to Oklahoma City."

She lightly touched her fingers to his. She was certain lightning had struck her. It took a moment to find her voice. "When can we leave?"

His voice was quiet. "My horse needs a good feed, and time to rest. Is two days soon enough?"

Rebecca cast a questioning glance toward Leotie. The Kiowa woman merely smiled her answer.

Jesse walked to the rear of the buggy and opened the luggage box. The curious expressions on the women's faces when he held the valise up made him want to laugh out loud. Rebecca clapped her hands together. She prattled, "I can't wait to see Leotie's new traveling outfits, and did you get the cloth for the diapers, and the feeding bottle, and—"

This time, he did laugh. He remembered, as a young lad, how exciting it was to open gifts on special holidays. "Do all women get this agog over pieces of fabric?"

It struck him that she had not requested anything for herself, and yet she was exuding delight for his mother. Whatever mystical insights Sarey Pike possessed, he knew it would give him pleasure to watch Rebecca when she learned the green traveling outfit was for her.

Rebecca wrinkled her nose and stuck her tongue out. She looped arms with Leotie and followed Jesse inside the tipi.

Chapter 17

After tying his own horse to the back of the buggy, Jesse secured a cache of food—venison jerky, pemmican, dried apples, and nuts, along with the two valises inside the luggage box. He walked to his mother's side of the carriage, where Leotie held the reins while Rebecca cradled Noelle Rose. Her cherished quilt tucked around and over their laps, Rebecca sat snug against the Kiowa woman.

Concern filled Jesse's eyes. "You're sure you can handle the reins, Mother?"

She offered him a reassuring smile. "I've ridden half-wild mustangs my entire life. Rebecca's gelding is gentle and calm. I am certain all will be well."

Rebecca's horse was old and placid. Still, a bear or wolf might cause the most reliable animal to panic and try to run away. He patted his mother's arm. "If the weather holds, we should make a good fifty miles today."

Rebecca leaned forward. "How many days?"

Jesse looked upward. "'Tis a fair sky. Clear and with no clouds. As the sailors say, 'We'll have smooth sailin'.' If the weather holds and we don't run into any trouble, about four days."

He walked around to Rebecca's side of the buggy and handed her a revolver. "I don't expect any trouble, but keep it tucked under the quilt…just in case."

She swallowed in an obvious effort to control a surge of fright. "But I don't know how to shoot."

With an inward smile, he said, "All you need to know is to pull back the hammer, point at the enemy, and pull the trigger."

The pink in her cheeks faded. Nonetheless, she tucked the pistol between herself and Leotie. When he turned away, she said, "You did send the telegram, didn't you?"

He nodded and patted his chest where the message lay in his coat pocket. "Once we get to Oklahoma City, I'll go to the telegraph office to pick up the reply." He then walked toward the pinto gelding given to him by Charging Bear. Once astride, he urged the horse forward. As he passed the buggy, he said, "I'll try to stay in sight. If I'm scouting for a place to settle for the night, just keep heading north."

Leotie slapped the reins. "Hy-yup, horse."

As the wagon moved forward, she waved at the group of people who had stood waiting to say their goodbyes. The women yodeled, dogs barked, and children shouted. Several men, old and young, rode alongside the buggy, whooping and calling out for the Great Spirit to protect the travelers from harm. After a mile or so, the escort ended, and the men raised their spears in a gesture of farewell.

****

The Great Spirit had favored Jesse and the women with fair weather. The buggy provided much comfort from the wind, making travel that much easier. As the days each rolled into another, Rebecca wondered if they were lost, or if Jesse was leading them in the right direction. Nothing seemed familiar. She tried to recall how the landscape had looked when she had trailed behind Frank, riding toward a dilapidated shack instead of the promised house with a white picket fence. Leotie's voice intruded on her thoughts.

"Rebecca, look." Leotie pulled the buggy to a halt as Jesse galloped toward them. He hauled up on the reins, wearing a weary grin. "Oklahoma City is over the top of that knoll."

"Should we change into our new dresses?" Leotie relaxed the reins in her hands.

Rebecca gave the Kiowa woman a narrow look. "My mercy, no. It's been forever since I've had a good soaking bath." She wrinkled her nose. "Even I can't stand to smell myself. You can understand why I'd rather have a bath before donning new clothes."

Leotie shifted on the seat. Deep concern covered her face. "I do understand, but I cannot be seen in what I am wearing. First, I have committed a crime by leaving the reservation without permission, and second, I am Kiowa. I do not wish to bring trouble or shame to either of you."

Rebecca nodded her understanding. She looked at Jesse for a solution. "What shall we do?"

Noelle Rose grew fussy. Rebecca cooed to quiet the squalling infant. "I'd cry too, if I were you." She lifted the baby to her shoulder and patted her on the back. "I imagine your little body is sore from being jostled around for four days. Besides you're sopping wet." She sniffed and wrinkled her nose. "Oh, dear. She has soiled herself."

Jesse cleared his throat. He gave Rebecca a sympathetic smile. She looked at him and wished with all her soul that she might love him. He was a fine and honest man. She looked away. Her jaw clenched and unclenched. No, she wasn't going to change her mind about falling in love again. She was the first to break the short, vibrant silence. "I'm not the only one who needs an all-over bath."

He heaved a sigh. ""Follow me to the edge of town and wait. I'll ride in. If there's an alley"—he met Rebecca's gaze—"I will ride back here to get you."

"What if there isn't an alley?"

"We'll cross that bridge when we come to it," he responded.

They were close enough to hear the plinky sounds of an out-of-tune piano when Jesse signaled to halt. He rode to his mother's side of the buggy. "This close to town you might encounter some drifters. Keep the revolver handy, and if need be, don't be afraid to use it."

Leotie nodded her understanding as she patted the weapon hidden between herself and Rebecca. "How long will we have to wait?"

Jesse flashed a reassuring grin. "Not long."

He tipped his hat and gigged the pinto into a trot.

Rebecca unbuttoned her blouse, hoping to entice the fretful baby to nurse. Her voice was troubled. "Leotie, I barely have any milk. What is happening?"

The Kiowa woman relaxed the reins she held. Her tone was reasonable. "To make milk, the mother must eat. If you do not feed your body, you cannot feed your child."

Tears welled in Rebecca's eyes. "I ate what food we had."

"It is true, the winter was harsh, and the hunting was poor." She touched Rebecca's hand.

"Do not fret. I have heard that in the white man's town no one goes hungry. A few good meals and you will make milk again."

Rebecca expressed her doubts. "What if it doesn't happen? Noelle Rose is my life; I cannot let her starve."

Leotie smoothed the baby's head. "Have you forgotten about the thing that Red Wolf brought from the fort, the thing called a feeding bottle?"

Rebecca expelled an audible sigh. "Of course, and the cans of milk. I am such a ninny to have forgotten."

****

Oklahoma City bustled with activity. Three loud blasts from a train whistle sounded. It appeared to Jesse that no one gave him a second glance as he cantered the pinto down the busy street. For a man used to the quiet solitude of the sea and then of the prairie, he found the drone of voices annoying.

He glanced from side to side, reading the names of the various businesses, and supposed the tall brick red buildings would impress most people. He wasn't most people. He'd seen the richest and the poorest, the cleanest and the dirtiest towns and villages all over the world. For a mere moment, he allowed himself to recall the regal beauty of his childhood home in northern Yorkshire. He blinked away the image. Now wasn't the time to drift into melancholy.

A young lad called out, "Hey, mister, I'll watch your horse for a nickel."

Jesse wheeled the pinto to where a freckle-faced boy stood. "Now why do I need you to watch my horse?"

The boy shrugged. "You don't want him stole, do ya?"

The seriousness on the youngster's face caused Jesse to tamp down a smile. He sat tall in the saddle, his voice all business. "You are telling me that this fair city is rife with thieves?"

The boy scrunched up his face. "You talk funny, mister."

This time Jesse laughed. "Aye, I suppose I do. Can you point me to a fine hotel?"

"Yep, for a nickel."

Jesse reached inside his heavy coat pocket. He held up the coin. "Directions first, then the nickel."

The lad seemed to give Jesse's ultimatum thought. He pointed. "Down yonder. Got a big sign with the name on it—Main Street Hotel."

"My thanks. Does the hotel have an alley?"

The lad shrugged. "Mebbe. Mebbe not."

Jesse kept his tone serious. "Let me guess…it'll cost another nickel?"

Once again, Jesse lifted a coin from his pocket and held it up.

"Yep, got an alley that leads to 'nother road that leads to the livery, then out of town."

Jesse flipped the nickel into the outstretched hands. "You're a good lad. I'm thanking you for the information." He turned the pinto and eased him forward.

The boy called out, "If'n yer horse gets stole, don't say I didn't warn ya."

Jesse lifted his hand in acknowledgement and rode toward the hotel. Just as the boy had said, there was an alley. He entered the narrow lane, looking for a set of stairs that would lead to the hotel's back entrance. As good fortune would have it, the stairs were at the very rear of the building. Much to his chagrin, the alley wasn't wide enough for a buggy. Like the boy said, the alley opened into a dirt road. Satisfied with his find, he followed the road which led to the livery stable.

The sign above the stable indicated the proprietor was Hiram Doolittle, and beneath the man's name, in bold black letters, were the words We Buy, Sell, And Trade. Jesse counted this as his lucky day. Anxious to share his findings with Leotie and Rebecca, he touched his heel to the pinto's flank.

Chapter 18

Without a mirror and a means to complete a proper toilette, Rebecca did the best she could to plait her hair into a neat braid. "Oh, if only I could make myself more presentable."

"What shall I do? I can't be seen like this." Leotie fretted over the doeskin dress that had seen its better days.

Rebecca was certain Leotie had blushed in concern over her appearance. She hesitated, searching for an answer. She couldn't help feeling a certain despair for the woman she had come to cherish. The sound of hooves rapidly approaching distracted Rebecca.

"What a stunning sight." The words slipped out before Rebecca could call them back as she watched Jesse, tall in the saddle, astride the spirited pinto that galloped toward them. In spite of herself and all her efforts to ignore him, she was aware of him in every sense. His eyes seemed to see past all the barriers she had erected since the day he'd arrived at the cabin. He had removed his heavy coat and tied it behind the saddle. She focused on his broad shoulders and the way the suspenders tapered down to his narrow waistline. He was rugged, and masculine, and beautiful. He had a mystical quality about him, an allure that drew her to him. Not in a physical way but more like in her soul. Quite against her will she watched him until he hauled up on the reins.

His eyes lighted with merriment, and his mouth tilted up in a cocky grin. "Our worries are over. There is a set of stairs leading up to the hotel's rear entrance."

"Your mother is concerned that someone will see her." Rebecca shifted on the buggy seat.

"No need to fret, Mother. There is a back road that leads to the hotel. I didn't see or pass another person on my ride out of town. Once we're at the back entrance, you will climb the stairs and stay there until I open the back door and let you in. We won't tarry. You have my word."

Concern riddled Leotie's face. "For the first time in a long time, I feel like running away," she murmured with a nod.

"Run away?" Jesse teased. "That isn't like you, Mother. You are a spirit woman, remember?"

To alleviate some of the Kiowa woman's anxiety, Rebecca handed baby Noelle to Leotie and took the reins from her. "It seems years since I've enjoyed a cup of real tea." She smiled up at Jesse. "Do you suppose we might have room service deliver a tray of sandwiches, a pot of tea, and a few petit fours?"

She lifted the reins in her hands. "You will love petit fours, Leotie. They are small sweet bites of pure heaven. Oh, and I hope there is a tub in the room. Perhaps we can order lots of hot water," she prattled on, "with real soap, and lilac water." Rebecca laughed, almost giddy. "Lead the way, Jesse." She flapped the reins and clucked the horse forward.

Her heart clamored in her chest. Eagerness built. She was going home.

They rode in silence. She did her best to guide the

horse around dips and holes in the dirt road to keep from jostling the baby. Jesse slowed his mount, allowing Rebecca to pull the buggy alongside. "Go in easy-like. Hold the horse to a walk."

Rebecca nodded. She nearly swooned over the line of red brick buildings. The town had changed in the past year, or perhaps she hadn't really taken notice when she and Frank had departed the train and made the long walk from the depot to a seedy hotel. How she had trusted him. She swallowed hard and wondered why she had the sudden desire to cover her face with both hands and weep inconsolably.

The buggy jerked to a halt. She looked up, blinked, and made the transition from the dark memories to the man holding the horse by the cheek strap. "Are you ill, Rebecca?"

"I…no!" She lifted Noelle from Leotie's arms. The woman looked positively miserable as she stepped down from the buggy.

Jesse dismounted, and tied the pinto behind the buggy next to Rebecca's horse. Rebecca said nothing as she watched him escort his mother up the steep flight of stairs. In seconds, the buggy dipped. He climbed in, took the reins, and guided the horse down the road to the front of the hotel.

"We're here." Jesse stepped down. He held his hand up to assist Rebecca and the baby. "I think it will look better if I register us as man and wife."

Her hand trembled as she placed it in his. She looked into his eyes. He was smiling. Her knees wobbled. "W-what did you say?"

Jesse repeated, "We should register as Mr. and Mrs. Starr."

Rebecca bit the inside of her lower lip. "Of course, that would make sense."

Collecting the valises, he cupped her elbow and led her up the steps and inside the hotel lobby. Rebecca stopped thinking, stopped breathing.

Her voice hitched. "It's beautiful. I'd almost forgotten how luxury looks."

Jesse steered her toward the registration counter. He tapped the bell.

A bald man wearing wire-rimmed spectacles called out, "Be right with you." The smile on his face faded into a frown. His displeasure at Jesse and Rebecca's disheveled appearances was apparent by the scowled greeting. "Ahem. Perhaps you were looking for the Railroad House." He pointed toward the door. "It's located down by the—"

Jesse seethed inside. He withdrew the pen from the inkwell and signed the register. "We will require a room with a bath and plenty of hot water. Fresh linens on the bed, a service of tea and sandwiches piled high with roast beef." He cocked an eyebrow as if offering a challenge to the desk clerk.

The clerk glanced at the register. "Sir, ah, Mr. Starr, this is a quality hotel. Just last year, we installed water closets in every room, with hot and cold running water. So as you can imagine, the price is rather, um, how shall I put this…exorbitant."

Jesse reached over the counter and grabbed a fistful of the man's shirt and pulled him forward. "My patience is wearing thin, little man. We have traveled a long way to get here. My wife and child are exhausted." He fought to control his temper. Even so, he exaggerated his British accent. "It is highly unprofessional to judge one by his appearance…wouldn't you agree?"

The clerk's head bobbed up and down like a cork on water. "Certainly. How long will you be staying?"

Jesse tightened his grip on the shirt. "That depends on the train schedule. Do you happen to know when the next eastbound train leaves?"

"N-no, sir."

"Then how much for the room, and meal?"

The clerk's face turned beet red from lack of oxygen. He rasped, "Fifteen dollars."

Jesse released the man. He removed the money from the leather wallet that had belonged to his father. "Give us a room at the end of the hall. The baby gets fussy sometimes."

The clerk eyed the bills and then up at Jesse. He turned and reached for a key. "Room 310. It's next to the back stairs."

Jesse took the key. A bag in each hand, he said, "Shall we go, love?" He stepped forward, then stopped as if he had changed his mind. "Add a dozen petit fours to my order, Mister—"

"Boggs," the clerk stuttered, "I-I'm sorry. Such delicacies aren't on our menu. Perhaps a slice of chocolate cake would suffice, ah, for an extra dollar."

"One slice won't do. Tell him, Jesse." Rebecca was not smiling when she spoke.

She stifled a gasp when Jesse set the carpet bag on the floor and placed his hand on the gun butt that rode low in the holster on his hip. "Perhaps I can persuade you to change your mind, especially since you are a rude sort of chap."

The clerk adjusted the glasses that had slipped

down his nose. "Yes, yes! On second thought, several slices of cake, on the house."

Jesse nodded. "I thought so."

He collected Rebecca's valise. He winked when he said, "Shall we go, Mrs. Starr?"

At the top of the stairs, he turned. The desk clerk was adjusting his shirt. He jumped when Jesse's deep baritone boomed, "I'd advise that you not tarry with our meal. An empty stomach makes a bloke irritable."

The little man hustled from around the desk and disappeared through a pair of dark green felt curtains.

Jesse gripped Rebecca's elbow lest she trip on the narrow steep stairs.

"Thank you, Jesse."

"For what?"

Her voice was thick with emotion. "For not allowing that pipsqueak of a man to bully you, and for…for the luxury of this hotel, and my train ticket, and for taking care of me and Noelle Rose when you could have just ridden on and left us."

He looked away, not wanting her to know she had discerned his feelings. He looked into her chocolate brown eyes, and for a moment it seemed she knew everything he felt. But of course she didn't have the slightest notion of what he held in his heart right now. The bloody hell of the whole thing was that he couldn't tell her. Through a life of painful experiences, he had learned to guard his feelings, most especially where love was concerned.

He guided her to the door numbered 310 and inserted the key. He spoke against the knot in his throat. "Your quarters, milady."

She slanted a smile toward him, which didn't help

his composure. "Leotie will be happy to come in from the cold. I'll stand here while you let her in. We should all enter this magnificent room together."

He nodded his agreement. At the top of the stairs and down the hall, it took a mere two steps from their room to the exit door. He grasped the knob and turned. Fearing he might harm his mother, he was careful not to swing the door open with force.

Leotie scooted inside. She shivered, whether from the cold or from unease, Jesse didn't know. "Don't worry, Mother. You are safe."

Rebecca stood against room 310's open door. "It's elegant, Leotie. Come see."

Once inside, Jesse locked the door. "When the food arrives, I'll leave you to your privacy."

Rebecca seemed surprised that he planned to go. "I thought you might dine with us."

A knock sounded at the door. Rebecca laid the baby on the bed. She motioned Leotie to stand behind a heavy curtain. She nodded to Jesse.

He said, "Who is it?"

"Boggs, the desk clerk. I've brought your food."

Jesse opened the door wide. The bald clerk and a stringy-looking lad brought in two trays and set them on a small table next to the bed. "Just as ordered, Mr. Starr. I hope you find everything to your satisfaction."

Jesse cocked an eyebrow but kept his vigilance until Boggs and his helper closed the door behind them. Rebecca swept back the large linen napkin that covered a plate stacked with sandwiches laden with thin-sliced roast beef, a small bowl of horseradish, and what was surely half of a chocolate cake. The second tray held a tea service set. She called softly to let Leotie know it was safe to leave her hiding place.

Jesse grabbed one of the sandwiches and spread it with horseradish. "I need to see if I can negotiate a deal with the owner of the livery stable. I also need to purchase our train fare."

He handed the room key to Rebecca. His voice was quiet but gruff when he spoke again. "Lock the door after me. Don't open it for any reason, or for anyone. When I return, I'll knock three times, and then, Mother, I will call your name."

Rebecca sidled close to Leotie. She glanced uneasily at the door. "Are we in some kind of danger?"

He answered, "Shifty-eyed men can't be trusted. You're young and beautiful, Rebecca. The minute Boggs sees me leave the hotel, he may—let's just say I didn't like the way he looked at you."

"But I'm a mother. He saw me with Noelle."

"Heed my word. Keep the door locked. Don't open it until you hear me call my mother's name."

"We will do as you say, my son." In a more serious tone, Leotie added, "I still have the revolver."

"It may be nightfall before I return." He lightened his tone and offered a smile. "Save me a slice of cake."

He reached for the doorknob.

"Jesse?" Rebecca beckoned him. She hesitated before speaking. "You will check at the telegraph office to see if there is a message from my father?"

For her sake, Jesse hoped the man had answered that all was forgiven and with a request for her to return home. "You can count on it."

Chapter 19

Rebecca did as Jesse had instructed. She laid the key on the table after she had locked the door. She placed her hands on her hips and twirled in a circle, taking in the blue floral wallpaper, textured ceiling, tasseled blue drapes, and a rose-patterned floor rug. A brown upholstered settee and a small round table graced the room. The bed was large enough to sleep two people. There was a chifferobe and a floor-length cheval mirror. She had spent most of a year sleeping on the ground, taking spit-baths out of tortoise shells, and hovering by a small fire for a bit of warmth, and her only utensils had been her fingers. The realization that she had taken for granted the comforts her father had provided for her, and the memory of how she had often degraded other girls who had much less both caused her great shame.

"Why do you weep, Rebecca?"

She wiped the tears from her cheeks. "I was a very immature, spoiled, ungrateful child who thought she was a grown woman and knew more than her father." She spread her hands wide. "All of this reminds me of how much I threw away for a man I hardly knew."

Leotie was wide-eyed. "I have never seen the inside of a white man's house. Are they all as rich as this one?"

Rebecca remembered every detail of the

ramshackle cabin Frank had said was their home. "No. Not all."

Both women stood quiet. It was Rebecca who broke the silence. "What was behind the curtain?"

Leotie took Rebecca's hand. "Come. There is a very large horse trough behind the curtain."

Rebecca clasped a hand over her mouth. She didn't want to embarrass Leotie by giggling. She sat on the edge of the clawfoot tub and reached for the knobs. "This is a bathtub. You sit in it and wash your body." She leaned in and placed the stopper in the drain hole, then turned the knobs.

Leotie's eyes widened. She stepped forward and placed her hand to catch the running water. "Is it magic?"

Rebecca was unsure how to explain the workings of faucets with hot and cold running water. "It's an invention that someone thought up to make life easier." She walked around touching each item. "This room is called a water closet." She demonstrated how the pedestal vanity worked, and much to her delight there was a chain-pull toilet. "Leotie, this is the most wonderful contraption. All you have to do is hike up your skirts, pull down your bloomers, sit on the seat, and let nature take its course. Then when you're finished"—she reached up and pulled the chain—"all your stinky business is flushed down a drain. No more freezing your buttocks in the winter or fearing a rattlesnake will bite you while you squat behind a bush. It's wonderful, isn't it?"

Leotie wore a skeptical expression as she walked over to the sink. She gasped and stepped back. "There is someone in the room."

Alarmed, Rebecca glanced around. "Where?"

Leotie pointed. "There."

Rebecca stood behind the Kiowa woman. Filled with relief, she said, "This is a mirror. You are looking at yourself."

Leotie touched her face, her hair. She opened her mouth and looked at her tongue, her teeth. She frowned. "Am I ugly?"

Rebecca wrapped her arms around the Kiowa woman. "You are a most beautiful woman. Now come. I am starving. Let's eat, and then we will bathe."

In the main room, Leotie grabbed a sandwich and proceeded to sit cross-legged on the floor. Rebecca sat in one of the chairs next to the window. She patted the seat of the second chair. "This is a chair. There is no need to sit in the floor."

Leotie sighed. "I think there is much for you to teach me. When I go to Red Wolf's home in England, I do not wish to shame him with my ignorance."

Rebecca reached for the teapot and filled two cups. "It will be my pleasure. Perhaps you should begin by calling him Jesse."

A loud knock startled Rebecca, and she sloshed tea on the table. The women looked at each other. The knock came again. "Mrs. Starr, I've brought more towels."

Rebecca eased to the door. "Are you Mr. Boggs?"

"No, ma'am. I'm the relief clerk."

"Please leave the towels in front of the door. I'll get them in a few minutes."

The doorknob turned. There was a shuffling of feet.

"Unlock the door, Mrs. Starr. It will only take a

second for me to hand them to you."

Leotie pointed the revolver at the door.

"Whoever you are, my husband is not here. It would be improper of me to allow you in without him present."

The doorknob jiggled. Rebecca was certain she heard whispers. Every nerve in her body trembled.

She forced her voice to not quaver. "I have a pistol. It is pointed at the door. The hammer is cocked, and I will pull the trigger."

"There is no need to get testy, Mrs. Starr. I'm simply doing my job. I'm leaving now."

Both she and Leotie placed their ear against the door and listened. Rebecca whispered, "It sounds like they're leaving."

"Don't open the door, Rebecca. Remember what Red Wolf said."

Rebecca sagged into the chair. She lifted the cup with unsteady hands. "I think I need a piece of chocolate cake to settle my nerves."

Leotie laid the pistol on the table. "There must be a way to block the door if he decides to return."

"There is." Rebecca carried a wooden chair across the room, and hooked the back of it under the doorknob.

She didn't speak, and from the concern on Leotie's face, Rebecca guessed they were both hoping Jesse would hurry to complete his business.

The morning passed without further incident. Rebecca reveled in Leotie's delight over her first all-over bath, the shampooing of her long black hair, and most especially trying on the new outfits Jesse had purchased.

To add to Rebecca's elation was the surprising discovery of the traveling suits that lay neatly folded at the bottom of the carpetbag with a note that simply said "For Rebecca." The clothing fit as if they were tailored for her measurements. She and Leotie shared schoolgirlish chitters as they admired themselves in the mirror.

Rebecca's most delight came from when she placed a finger full of chocolate cake in Noelle's mouth. She laughed at the wide-eyed expression on the baby's face, and how she opened her mouth like a little bird waiting for another bite, followed by a smiling gurgle.

After feeding Noelle from the bottle, Rebecca folded the quilt into a thick pallet for the sleepy infant. She gazed down at her daughter. Noelle was the only gift she cherished from her deceased husband.

Rebecca yawned. Sleep beckoned, thanks to the food, the tea, and the bath, coupled with the long days of traveling that had taken their toll. She pulled back the bed's coverlet. "I could use a nap. Leotie, have you ever slept in a bed?"

Leotie seemed to rouse from a sleepy daze. "I have not."

"I caution you, the mattress may bounce a little when you lie down." Rebecca patted the bed.

Leotie sat on the edge. Her eyes widened when the mattress sank under her weight. "Will it throw me off?"

Each of the Kiowa woman's new discoveries was a joy for Rebecca to watch unfold, yet it was also difficult to contain her amusement. "It's like a horse. Once you get on, you have to figure out how to keep from falling off."

Leotie sighed. She used her knees to climb to the center of the mattress. She lay like a wooden log, her arms tucked at her sides.

Rebecca joined her. "Could you scoot over to give me a little more room?"

The coiled bedsprings squeaked, and the mattress bounced up and down. Leotie clutched the edge. "I am uncertain if I like this bed. I will sleep on the floor."

Rebecca rolled to her side to face the woman. She propped on her elbow. "There is so much you must learn. First, on the train, there won't be room for you to sleep on the floor, and the floors are dirty. I've never been on a ship, but I must imagine the cabins are cramped. Sleeping on the floor..." Rebecca paused, searching for gentle words. "It just isn't what one would do."

Leotie frowned. "It was a mistake to think I could fit into the white man's world. I will leave in the morning and return to my people."

Rebecca rolled off the bed. She fisted her hands against her hips, and scolded, "Jesse is your son. That makes *him* your people. Are you such a coward that you would run away rather than try to educate yourself so that you may spend the rest of your years sharing his life, his happiness? And what if some day he takes a wife? Wouldn't you want to be a true grandmother to his children, rather than delivering babies that belong to other women?"

She softened her voice. "It will break Jesse's heart if you run away. If this is your decision, then so be it. A woman must live with her regrets." She smiled lamely. "I should know."

Emotional hurt glistened in Leotie's eyes. She

propped against the headboard. "You speak harsh words, Rebecca, but they are sage words from one so young. The truth in what you say makes me ashamed."

"Oh, Leotie, you are like a mother to me, and a grandmother to Noelle Rose. Please don't be ashamed. I have lived in your world, and I was afraid, and not nearly as brave as you. Just give it a lot of thought before making your decision."

Rebecca climbed beneath the covers. She rolled to her side completely exhausted, both emotionally and physically.

Chapter 20

Jesse bellied up to the bar in the Half Moon saloon. Feeling a little smug over the deal he'd struck with the livery stable owner, he treated himself to a beer and a shot of bourbon. The additional money would more than pay for train fare to Chicago and food along the way. He glanced up from the drinks he had yet to touch and stared in amazement into the greasy mirror. It took a moment to recognize the face staring back at him as his own. He needed a shave and a haircut. A bath wouldn't hurt, nor would a new suit of clothes.

"Howdy, darlin'. Buy a lady a drink?"

He glanced down at the hand covering his and saw long fingernails painted red. His eyes traveled up to her face, with its garishly rouged cheeks and lip paint to match the fingernails. She had eyes that spoke of deceit and misery, and wrinkles that cake makeup couldn't hide. A mass of tangled hair piled on top of her head reminded him of a rodent's nest, her low-cut red silk dress had seen its better days, and she reeked of body odor and cheap perfume.

Another face drifted across hers in his mind's eye, a face so different. Innocent yet wise. Eyes filled with honesty, and sadness. A mouth that needed kissing. Hair, soft and silken. Cheeks that looked as if they'd been kissed by the sun. A smile that brightened even the gloomiest day. Rebecca.

The woman snapped her fingers in front of his face. "Hey, handsome. My name's Charmaine." She smiled and nodded her head toward the stairs. "You look like a man who needs a bit of…entertainment."

He slugged down the whisky, then slid the mug of untouched beer toward her. "Not today." He tipped the brim of his hat and strode out of the saloon.

His mind reeled as he strolled down the boardwalk. He understood Rebecca's need to return home. For her sake, and the baby's, he hoped the telegram held positive news. A feeling in his gut spoke otherwise. He hoped he was wrong.

Jesse tightened his jawline and clenched his fist in a sudden rush of anger. For him, there would be no open arms, no affable welcome. Years of backbreaking work, suffering lashings, weathering hurricanes, and sleeping with one eye open to keep from having his gullet slit for a piece of hard tack, had made him a cautious man.

While spending time in the brig for insulting a captain from one of the many vessels he'd served on, Jesse had entertained himself by watching the ship's cat taunt and tease a large rat until the rodent became disoriented and exhausted from the chase, and then the cat pounced. It was a quick kill. He would be the cat, and his half-brother would be the rat.

"Hey, mister, somebody steal yer horse? Shoulda let me watch it."

Jesse glanced in the direction of the voice. The same lad he had encountered earlier stood propped against a post in front of the telegraph office. Jesse forced his jaw and shoulders to relax. He unclenched his fist. "So, my young friend, we meet again. Do you have a name?"

A smirk twisted the boy's lips. "Name's puddin' tane. Ask me a'gin and I'll tell ya the same."

"Ned Coffin, take your sassing mouth and go help your mother. I don't need you smart-talking or panhandling my customers." When the kid didn't move, the telegrapher said, "Move along, or I'll notify the sheriff."

The boy hawked a wad and spat on the ground. Nonetheless, he jammed his hands inside the pockets of his wool pants and sauntered down the walkway.

The telegrapher sighed. "Sorry 'bout that, mister."

Jesse watched the lad swagger away almost as if he were mocking them. "Why isn't he in school?"

"Habitual truant. Ned is thirteen and working hard to get himself a bad reputation. His pa was a ne'er-do-well. Got drunk and was run over by a freight wagon. Boy has no respect for his poor ma nor anybody else. Good woman, she is. Doesn't deserve to have a son who's turning out jest like his pa."

Jesse didn't make a verbal reply, but his stance must have been an obvious giveaway that he had business inside.

The telegrapher said, "What can I do for you, sir?"

Jesse followed him inside. He stood behind the tall counter. "Looking for a reply to a telegram sent to a Mr. P. Throckmorton, Chicago, Illinois, for a Mrs. Rebecca Throckmorton Donnelly."

The telegrapher looked through a stack of yellow envelopes sitting in a wooden tray. He shook his head. "Don't see one. When was it sent?"

Jesse did a mental count back to the day at the fort. "About nine or ten days ago, from the telegraph office at Fort Sill."

The man pulled opened a desk drawer and removed a bulging folder. He expelled a small humph. "Lots of folks never claim their telegrams. All the same, gotta keep 'em for a couple of years." He began sorting through the envelopes until he reached the last one.

He gave Jesse a doleful look. "Sorry as I can be. Mebbe the lines were down. If you write it out, I'll resend it. No charge."

Jesse complied. He shoved the message forward. "Do you have any idea how many days it will take for the train to reach Chicago?"

"I'd say about ten days or so. Ask Marvin. He's the ticketmaster." He frowned up at Jesse. "Marvin's an ornery cuss. Don't let 'im rile you. Just his nature."

Jesse had met plenty of men with similar temperaments. "How long for the telegram to arrive?"

The telegrapher scrunched his face, scratched his chin. "If this feller Throckmorton answers right away—tomorrow, 'round noon."

Jesse nodded as he touched the brim of his hat. He walked through a door that joined the telegraph office and the railroad office. Several people sat on long benches, some eating sandwiches, others engaged in conversation. Before approaching the ticket booth, he scanned the departure schedules.

The ticket master greeted him with a scowl. "Help you?"

"Is there a charge for an infant to travel on the train?" Jesse wanted to know.

"No, sir. Just the mother."

"Do you have a sleeper car available?"

The ticket master offered Jesse a thorough perusal.

"Sleeper cars are expensive, mister."

Jesse growled. He leaned a little closer to the wire window. "That's not what I asked. My question was do you have a sleeper car available?"

The man's Adam's apple bobbed up and down. "Yessir. One. Twenty dollars. Sleeps two. No meals included."

Jesse forked over the money. "Three tickets for Chicago, Illinois; one sleeper car."

"Train leaves in the morning, seven sharp." He handed Jesse the tickets.

Jesse strode from the window without a word. He stepped next door to the telegrapher's office, and said, "Train departs early. No need to request an answer to that telegram."

"I could request the answer be routed to the Bedford station. Train will stop there for an hour."

Jesse nodded firmly. "Mighty nice of you. Mrs. Donnelly is anxious for a reply."

"By the way, my name's Lester. I s'pose Marvin told you 'bout no food being sold on the train." Lester hitched up his britches. "My wife owns Edith's Cafe. She's a good cook. Tell her I sent you over. She'll make you up a basket and have it ready for you in the morning."

"You're a good bloke, Lester."

Jesse shook hands with the telegrapher. He mentally ticked off the items on his list. His next stop, the mercantile.

A jovial man with a large belly and apple-red cheeks greeted Jesse. "Howdy, stranger. Name's Abbott. Feel free to browse around. If you don't find what you're looking for, I'm here for the asking."

"I'm in need of shirts suitable for dress and some for work. A traveling coat, new hat, long underwear, socks, and boots." Jesse gave the storekeeper his size, and while he set about filling Jesse's order, Jesse meandered around the store. He spied a button-down cape. It was deep plum, trimmed with a black felt collar. He smiled. His mother needed a warm wrap.

"Mr. Abbott, add this cape to my order."

"You got it."

Jesse thought about an appropriate gift for Rebecca. All she had to keep her warm was her quilt. "Mr. Abbot, if you have another cape in a different color, I'll take it, too."

"Dark blue. You got it."

In his wanderings, Jesse spotted a shelf of books. He picked up a volume of poetry by Wadsworth. As a boy, he'd had a passion for reading. Life afterward had left little time or money for such pleasant indulgence.

"You have a love for the arts, mister...ah?" The storekeeper inquired.

"Starr. I did, once."

"Ah, yes. Life does tend to change courses on us. Well, shall I add the book to your bill?"

Jesse shelved the book. "Give me a minute."

A little bell tinkled. A door slammed, and the storekeeper called out a greeting to his customer.

Jesse opened and closed several books. Almost ready to give up his search, his eyes lit on *The Count of Monte Cristo.* He'd read the book as a boy while attending Eton. Now as a man, he could fully relate to Pierre Picaud's plight. Like Picaud, he, too, sought revenge and vindication against the ones who had wronged him.

It had been a long time since he had indulged himself. Thinking his mother might enjoy reading, he had reached for the book of poetry when he spotted a red leather book bound with a strap and fastened by a gold clasp. A tiny gold key dangled from the strap. The perfect gift for Rebecca. Knowing how much she enjoyed writing in her diary, and that she had filled all the pages, he added the journal to his collection and walked to the counter.

"Do you have a valise, Mr. Abbott?"

The storekeeper pursed his lips and rubbed his chin. His eyes brightened into a smile. "Near forgot 'bout the one I took in a trade a year or so ago. It's got a little wear on it."

Jesse returned the smile. "If it will hold all my purchases, I'll take it."

The hand-tooled leather case with silver-buckled straps was more than Jesse expected. A gentleman's satchel, for sure. A sense of satisfaction filled him as he waited for the storekeeper to tally his bill. "My thanks to you, Mr. Abbott."

"A good day to you, Mr. Starr. Come back to see us, anytime."

Jesse ran a hand over his scraggly beard. "Mind if I leave my purchases here while I visit the barber?"

Mr. Abbott beamed a grin. "You got it." He patted the brown leather case. "I'll keep it safe and sound."

Dusk replaced the sun. Gray clouds that threatened a brisk tomorrow hung heavy in the sky. Jesse hastened his steps toward the hotel. Shaved and bathed, he felt like a new man when he entered the lobby. No one attended the registration desk. Dressed in a fresh suit of clothes and a new fleece-lined coat, he had divested the contents from the pockets of his buffalo coat and hung it over a hitching rail; free for the taking. He reached up to feel a small lump to assure himself that the little velvet box was securely hidden. He smiled slowly, then frowned at his thoughts. Rebecca had made it clear that she was not part of any man's future.

Taking the stairs by twos, he stood at the door and knocked three times. "Rebecca, Mother, it's Jesse."

Chapter 21

Rebecca moved the chair aside and turned the key to unlock the door. She stared at him in disbelief. Her breath caught in her throat. The straggly black hair and dark beard had been replaced by a handsome face with magnificent dark brows that curved neatly, a slightly crooked, thin nose, and a firm but almost sensuous mouth. The lean line of his jaw showed more strength than she remembered when he'd first stood in front of her at the old shack. Then her eyes met his, and, if a flicker of doubt remained, it was immediately dispelled as she looked beyond thick, black lashes into eyes bluer than a morning sky.

"Jesse?" The question burst from her.

A faint smile twisted the corner of his mouth. He held the basket of food forward. "I'm hungry enough to eat a bear."

Leotie stepped forward to relieve him of the food. Jesse laughed as she stood, mouth agape, before she said, "You are not my Red Wolf."

Jesse set the leather case on the bed. "I will always be your Red Wolf, Mother." He rested his hand on the handle. With a quirk of his brow, he said, "I come bearing gifts. Shall we dine first?"

Rebecca wanted to giggle and clap her hands like an excited child. Instead, she simply smiled. "Between the delicious aroma of fried chicken and opening presents..." She cut her eyes toward Leotie, who nodded. This time Rebecca didn't contain her laughter. "We choose gifts."

Jesse deftly unbuckled the straps to the leather case. "This time of the year, the winds from the ocean are quite frigid." He smiled as he draped the cape around Leotie's shoulders. "I can't have my mother catching her death."

Tears coated the small woman's lashes. She stood in front of the mirror. "I have never imagined owning something so beautiful." She touched the black velvet collar and ran her hands down the deep plum-colored wool.

Rebecca sucked in a breath. "The color is perfect."

Jesse said, "Then I hope you like this one." He handed her a woolen cloak of the deepest blue, also trimmed in black velvet. His gaze touched a quickness within her, and Rebecca quickly averted her eyes. Frank had never set her to trembling for any reason, much less with a look or mere words. What was there about this man that aroused her so?

Like the Kiowa woman, Rebecca looked into the mirror and admired the gift. "I don't know what to say, Jesse. It's more than beautiful. It's...special. I shall wear it with pride." She slipped it from her shoulders and placed it on the end of the bed. Feeling a bit overwhelmed at his generosity, she said, "Shall we eat?"

"Not quite yet. There's more."

"Jesse, this is too much." Rebecca and Leotie laughed as they spoke in unison.

He handed Rebecca the diary with its gold key. Running her hand over the soft red leather, she blinked back tears. "Thank you doesn't seem like enough."

He simply smiled. "And for you, Mother, a book of poetry by Elizabeth Barrett Browning."

Leotie held the book to her breast. Emotions played across her face, and for a moment she struggled to speak. "Your father used to quote Browning." She stood on tiptoe and placed a kiss on Jesse's cheek. Her voice a mere whisper, she said, "Such a treasure."

Baby Noelle whimpered, and Jesse lifted her from the bed to cradle her in his arms while the two women busied themselves removing food from the basket. Conversation was minimal until Jesse said, "The train leaves in the morning at seven sharp."

He related about his day—the sale of the horses and buggy, the surly young lad he'd met, and that he had procured a sleeper car for the women. He added, "Don't worry. I'll be close by if you need me."

Rebecca spooned a small bite of mashed potatoes into Noelle's mouth. "Did you go to the telegraph office?"

Jesse set his fork aside. He hesitated before answering. "There was no reply. The telegrapher thought a line might have been down, and your father mightn't have received the wire. I sent another, and requested the reply be sent to Bedford Station. We'll have an hour's stop there."

Rebecca's shoulders slumped significantly. A great weariness seemed to settle over her. Afraid she might dissolve into tears at any moment, she lifted the baby from Jesse's arms. "If you will excuse me, I'll get us ready for bed."

Her departure to the water closet acted as a signal that it was time to extinguish the oil lanterns and call it a night.

Rebecca lay in the darkness. The faint scent of Jesse's bay rum aftershave flooded her with memories of her father, who also wore bay rum. Jumbled thoughts raced through her mind. Was it possible the lines were down, as the telegrapher had stated, or had her father received the wire and chosen not to answer it? Why wouldn't he reply? Did he despise her that much? Surely he wouldn't turn her away, not with a baby in her arms. He wasn't that heartless...or was he? And what about her mother—would she welcome them home? Rebecca slammed the door on her negative thoughts. Her father and mother would forgive her. They would dote on their beautiful granddaughter. Still, doubt plagued her.

Rebecca swallowed a heavy sigh lest she disturb Jesse and Leotie. A ray of moonlight settled on her face. She lowered her lashes and peered through mere slits. Although her dead husband had been a disappointing lover, he had introduced her to the possibility of enjoying the sweetest of nectars. She desired to caress the long, sleek hardness of Jesse's thighs, the rippling muscles of his back, the flat, hard belly, and feel the strength of him pressed against her. She stiffened when her eyes met Jesse's. Almost certain he knew she was watching him, she squeezed her eyes shut, determined to sleep.

****

Moonlight filled the room, and Jesse's gaze settled on Rebecca's diminutive form. The quilt pulled to her chin, she had insisted that he was too tall to comfortably sleep on the settee. Lying on his side, his back to his mother, he wasn't sure about his own comfort. It had been years since he'd slept on a real mattress. Aboard ship a deck hand was lucky to claim a swinging hammock as his own; others were left to find relief on the ship's rough plank floors.

Through the dim light came the face of fragile beauty. The half-closed eyes held him entranced. The lips formed voiceless words that enthralled his soul. He thought her lips parted in a low wordless moan. He wanted to touch her, to test the softness of her breasts, caressing, warming, rousing. He wanted to fold her into his embrace and bring her against his hard-muscled chest, and to press a kiss upon her rosebud lips. He wanted to experience the fierce, naked abandon of possessing her, sweeping her with him to breathless, spiraling heights.

The bed springs squeaked, and his mother whispered, "What troubles you, Red Wolf?"

Climbing up from the depths of his daydream, the brilliance of his and Rebecca's union obliterated, he relaxed upon the pillow. "Go back to sleep, Mother. It's nothing important."

Chapter 22

A heavy fog hung over the town, creating ghostly figures of early-hour storekeepers opening their shops. The warmth from Rebecca's bonnet and new woolen cape warded off damp chills. She had bundled baby Noelle in the quilt's thick layers and held her close. Leotie stood at her side while Jesse entered the cafe to collect the basket of food for their trip.

Suddenly, someone barged into Rebecca and almost knocked her down. Nearly frantic, she let out a little yelp. Strong hands reached out to steady her. "Beg pardon, ma'am. Can't hardly see through this pea soup. Didn't hurt ya, did I?"

Before she found her voice, the man had disappeared into the curtain of gray. The baby whimpered, and Rebecca made cooing sounds to soothe the child.

Leotie whispered, "Is Noelle okay?"

"Just startled."

"I'm sorry it was you he bumped into, but happy it wasn't me. What if he'd seen my face? What if he'd contacted the sheriff or the Indian agent? I don't wish to bring trouble to Red Wolf."

It was strange, but Rebecca felt no sense of wrongdoing. It was beyond her why leaving the reservation to follow her son to England was considered a punishable crime. She assured Leotie that neither she nor the baby was harmed. Keeping her voice low, she said, "Then you must stop referring to him as Red Wolf, most especially in public."

Leotie flinched at the comment. "Yes, I must."

In less time than anticipated, Jesse joined them, carrying a large wicker basket covered with a red checkered cloth. The train whistle disturbed the morning's quiet, and Jesse cupped his mother's elbow but spoke to both women. "We should hurry."

As fast as visibility allowed, the trio hastened toward the train depot. It seemed the fog grew denser, and then the locomotive's engine loomed through the gray like a giant black monster. Leotie gasped as she grabbed Jesse's arm. "It doesn't look like a horse at all."

Jesse laughed. "Did someone tell you a train looked like a horse?"

"Do not laugh…Jesse. My people have heard many stories about the great iron horse and how fast it can run."

Another blast from the train's whistle drowned out Jesse's reply. Out of the dark, a man's voice shouted, "Bound for Bedford Station. All 'board. Leaving in ten minutes."

Jesse herded the women toward a dim glow that looked like a winking eye. "Sir, we have seats on Car Five."

Rebecca gave Leotie a reassuring touch as she turned aside to hide her face when the conductor held the lantern high. He pointed. "Last one down. Be quick, and have your tickets ready."

The conductor called out again, "Bound for Bedford Station. Get aboard. Leaving in five minutes."

"The last car. That's good, isn't it, Jesse?" Rebecca blinked away the moisture building on her eyelashes.

"Aye, that it is. Not so many people."

At the last car, a porter assisted Rebecca up the metal steps first and then Leotie.

"I'll take yo luggage, suh. And iff'n yo show me de tickets, I'll seat yo."

Jesse produced the tickets.

"Yez, suh." He held the door wide.

Rebecca hesitated. "You go first, Jesse."

She and Leotie followed him down the long aisle of seats, through another door, and into a narrow hallway, until the porter stopped. "'Dis it. Number ought twelve."

The porter slid the pocket-door back and stepped inside the small cubicle, where he deftly demonstrated how to fold the upper berth down, and folded the two facing seats over to provide a bed large enough for two. He offered a genuine smile. "Der be washrooms at each end of de train." He pointed in each direction. "One for de ladies, and other for de gen'lmen. If'n yo needs anythin', my name is Silas." He tipped his hat and bade Jesse to follow him. He extended his hand to indicate Jesse's seat. "Yo luggage be o'rhead." He showed Jesse how to push the seat back. "Ain't mos' comfor'ble sleepin', tho." He added, "Now, if'n yo and dem ladies wants coffee, tell me now, and I'll bring some whilst it's fresh." He offered a good-natured wink. "And 'fo' it's gone."

Jesse nodded. "I'll be with the ladies." As soon as the porter left, Jesse took the basket of food and returned to share breakfast with his mother and Rebecca.

Very little time had passed before Silas reappeared, balancing a tray that held a blue-speckled coffeepot, three cups, and linen napkins. He settled the salver on a small table. Jesse paid the bill and thanked the man. "Jest sit everthin' outside de do' when yo is finished." At the door, he looked over his shoulder. "Train gonna lurch for'ard in a minute. Might not wanna pour de coffee jest yet." He tipped his hat and slid the door shut.

While he gripped the handle to steady the coffeepot, Jesse cautioned his mother to sit on the seat and hold on to the edge. Rebecca gathered the baby in her arms and settled in the chair facing the Kiowa woman.

A few minutes later, the train did just as Silas had predicted. The metal wheels grated against the iron rails, the coach lurched again, and then in a breath the train eased forward. The fog had lifted enough to see out the window. Several people stood on the depot platform waving.

Leotie sat white-knuckled as she peered out the window. Her voice was filled with both awe and trepidation. "The buildings are moving, but we are not. How is this so?"

Rebecca smiled as she handed the baby to Leotie. "Jesse will explain while I see what we have for breakfast."

After they had eaten, Jesse lifted the tray and set it outside the door as the porter had instructed. He returned to the main car and settled in his seat.

Alone at last, the women stripped down to their chemises and settled in for their long voyage overland.

****

Jesse reclined in the seat. With the rhythmic

movement and the click-clacking of the wheels, he grew drowsy and, scooting his hat forward to cover his eyes, slept.

When he awoke, he did so with a start, unable to determine what had roused him. His mind was unsettled. He glanced around. The seat across the aisle remained unoccupied. There appeared to be no reason for unease.

Disquieted now, he sought diversion to settle his thoughts and stared out the window as the landscape sped by.

"Tickets?"

Jesse looked up at the same conductor who had directed them to their correct coach. He reached into the inside pocket of his coat. "About what time will we arrive at Bedford Station?"

The conductor pursed his lips. "If we don't have to stop for buffalo on the track, or the boiler doesn't blow up, or worse, outlaws"—he pulled a gold watch from his fob pocket—"seventy-two hours."

"How long will we stop?"

"Long enough to take on water. About two hours. There'll be plenty of time for you and the ladies to stretch your legs and get a bite to eat." He returned the punched tickets to Jesse.

Jesse smiled. "So you know about women?"

"I'm the chief of this here train. It's my duty to run it like an accurate timepiece."

"Then tell me, how many days to get to Chicago? We have an infant who will need clean nappies from time to time."

The conductor appeared to do a quick calculation. "Lucky for you, this is a through train. Goes all the way to Union Station. Counting the times we'll stop to take on water, about six days."

Jesse thanked the man. The conductor tipped his hat as Rebecca approached. "Ma'am."

Rebecca nodded a greeting as she stood before Jesse. "Leotie and Noelle are napping. Do you mind if I sit with you for a while?"

"Maybe you'd like some fresh air?"

She smiled and followed him through the doorway and down the narrow hall to the forward end of the car, where he slid a door open. He held her hand as she stepped outside. She lifted her face to catch the breeze.

"The conductor tells me we should arrive at Union Station about Thursday, perhaps Friday, if all goes well."

Her eyes lit. The cold air had reddened her cheeks. "It's a short cab ride to my house." Then she sighed. "Well, I mean, my parents' house."

Without any warning whatsoever, Jesse pulled Rebecca against him, bent his head and kissed her. She squirmed at first, but then responded shamelessly, her lips demanding more.

Finally, he set her away from him, though his hands remained on her arms. "That's all I wanted to know," he said. Then he rasped, "Rebecca?"

Before she could answer, Silas interrupted. "Ahem, sorry as I can be to in'rupt. You folks gonna take lunch in the dinin' parlor, or should I'se bring it to yo car?"

Rebecca gasped. She put her hand to her mouth and pushed past the porter, leaving Jesse standing there.

"Bad timing, Silas." Feeling adrift, Jesse jammed his fists inside his coat pockets to keep from slugging the man. Instead he drew in a quavering sigh, and spoke through gritted teeth. "We have food. A pot of coffee and a glass of milk will do."

"Yezsir. Sho am sorry, again." The porter made a hasty exit.

****

Rebecca opened the door to the ladies' washroom. She placed her hands against her abdomen, and heaved large gulps of air. Every part of her pulsed with a desire that she would never allow to be fulfilled. And at last, at long, long last, she broke down and cried. After several minutes, she leaned forward to peer into the mirror. Her eyes were still puffy, despite all the water she had splashed over her face.

A rap sounded on the door. Rebecca did not wish to talk to anyone, least of all Jesse. The knock came again, and then a woman's voice. "Are you almost finished? My little girl needs to go."

Rebecca unlatched the door and scooted out. At her compartment, she inserted the key and quietly entered. Leotie sat reading aloud from the book of poetry. Afraid something in her voice would betray her feelings, Rebecca sat quietly and listened.

"...In all my old grief, and with my childhood's faith

I love thee with a love I seemed to lose
with my lost saints. I love thee with the breath,
smiles, tears, of all my life; and, if God choose,
I shall but love thee after death."

Leotie closed the book. She wiped a tear from her cheek. "When Addison read the words, I never understood them, until now."

Rebecca drew a deep breath and let it out slowly, trying to collect herself. "You must have loved him very much."

"When I look at my son, the resemblance to his father always surprises me a little bit. It reminds me of how much I've lost by not having either of them in my life." She sounded a little forlorn.

Rebecca bit the inside of her lip. She swallowed hard, resisting the urge to cover her face with both hands and weep inconsolably. Instead she leaned forward in her chair and gave Leotie a hug. "You and Jesse have the rest of your lives for getting to know each other."

Baby Noelle awakened and cooed with exuberance.

Leotie's words were like a stab in the heart. "Jesse would make a good father to Noelle."

Rebecca shook her head and averted her eyes. A sob rose in her throat, but she made no sound. "Someday he will have children of his own to love." She busied herself tending to the baby's needs.

A voice called through the door, "Ladies, I'se brought coffee, and milk for the little'un, jest like Mr. Starr said."

Rebecca opened the door. "Thank you, Silas." In truth, she had no appetite.

Chapter 23

Settled in his seat, Jesse gazed out the window. Lunch and dinner had been strained affairs. Disquieted now, he sought diversion to settle his thoughts. Rebecca's sobs rang in his ear. *What the bloody hell was I thinking of, to kiss her like that?*

Sleep was not within his grasp. He needed fresh air to clear his mind. Outside, he leaned his hip against the cold iron of the railing. The air was crisp, almost biting. Bracing his hands against the bar, he leaned outward, staring into the dark night sky. Fleecy clouds flitted by with the train's movement. A quarter moon, bright and sharp, cast shadows on the ground below, peeking here and there hiding coyly like a flirtatious woman.

His pride nipped at him. What happened had happened. For Rebecca's sake and his, he would not allow it to happen again.

He pulled the collar of his coat up around his neck. It was too cold to remain outside, and he was too restless to sit more long hours. The need for warmth won out.

Silas made his way down the aisle. "Mos' time to turn down de lamps. You be needin' anythin', Mr. Starr?"

"A brandy."

"Sorry, suh, liquor's only 'lowed in de parlor car, and it's closed."

"Quite all right, old man. I'll read for a while."

The porter bade a goodnight and went on his way. Jesse removed the book from his satchel. He stared at the title for a long time before opening to the first chapter. He read, slowly and deliberately. A face began to form in his mind's eye, and an amber gaze mocked him. Lawrence, dragon of his dreams, nightmare of his waking hours.

He stared at the page until the words blurred into a sea of black. *Lawrence Byron Staunton Fitzroy.* The name echoed inside his ears. *I'm coming for you, brother.* Jesse floated in a deep well of dream stuff, a limbo, an endless void. A tremor raced through him. One moment he was asleep, the next wide awake. He could find no reason for it. A small panic began to build when a large black bat loomed over him. Not a bat. The visage grew—Lawrence's, his white teeth flashing in a sneering grin.

Jesse's lips moved in a voiceless plea. The cat-o-nine tails lashed across his back. He gritted his teeth against the searing pain. The taste of blood filled his mouth. Then abruptly he was drifting into dark green, and endless tendrils of seaweed twined around him, pulling him deeper and deeper into the briny depths. He felt no reason to breathe. He tried to banish the vision.

He stretched his eyes wide, and twisted in his seat. This time he was truly awake, and alone. His mind filled with unpleasant remembrances of his father's death, of awakening, bound, gagged, and bleeding, in the stinking hold of a slave ship. Jesse fought to control the overriding anger that threatened to engulf him.

He gradually relaxed. Rebecca. He was profoundly stricken by the sight and scent of her and his desire to make her his. He was not the kind to take advantage of a woman. It was clear they had both charted their courses for home. Rebecca needed the forgiveness of her parents before she could move on with her life.

Like the sails of a ship catching the wind, revenge swelled and billowed, swelled and billowed inside him.

Jesse crossed his arms over his chest, and allowed the train's clickety-clack to lull him.

****

The next evening, and long after the other passengers had settled in for the night, Jesse escorted his mother to the train's rear platform. She gripped the railing. At Jesse's reassurance that she was not in danger of falling, she relaxed.

Looking up at the sky, she said, "The stars are everywhere, and the clouds, too. Is the world such a big place that it stretches on forever?"

"The world is larger than even I can image, Mother, and I have sailed all of the seven seas."

She touched his arm, her voice earnest. "Would life have been different for you if I had followed your father to England?"

Jesse considered her question. His shrug was barely visible in the dim moonlight. "None of us can control destiny, Mother."

"This is so." She stood silent for a moment. "Do you plan to kill your half-brother?"

It was a matter-of-fact question. The Kiowa were once a nation of warriors who counted coup on their enemies. His Kiowa blood spoke to him. "Aye."

"Will your heart then be at peace?"

"Maybe."

A brief silence passed before either spoke. "What

troubles you, Mother?"

Leotie touched his arm. "I dreamed of a door. It was sealed shut. Rebecca stood on the outside. She was surrounded by darkness." She took both his hands into hers. "I fear the path she seeks will bring her great sadness. Whatever your heart holds for her, you must wait until she falls to rescue her."

His mother's psychic insight amazed him. "How will I know, Mother?"

"Trust the Great Spirit to guide you."

"I have never known the kind of love that binds the hearts of two people for life. Frank Donnelly stole Rebecca's innocence and used her selfishly. What her body desires, her heart denies."

Leotie reached up and touched Jesse's cheek. "Sometimes a warrior is cruel when trying to break a wild horse. The animal learns that to trust is to suffer, so the horse either lashes out and tries to hurt the warrior or it runs away to rejoin the herd, and when it is again caught, it remembers. Patience, my son. Rebecca's love for you is strong. She just doesn't know it yet."

He clasped her hand and held it to his heart. "Come, the night air has grown colder."

Jesse escorted his mother back to their compartment. He slid the door open for her to enter. Rebecca sat propped up in the bed, the red leather diary in her lap. Her eyes met Jesse's, and then she looked away.

He cleared the huskiness from his throat. "We will arrive at Bedford Station in the morning. It is a two-hour stop. There might be a general store. Would you like to accompany me to town? The baby might need some things."

She knitted her brows together as if thinking how to answer. Her voice was soft, almost apologetic. "I'll make a list."

He nodded his understanding. "Goodnight."

He was almost out the door when Rebecca called him back. "Jesse…" Whatever she intended to say, she didn't. "Goodnight."

****

Rebecca sat propped against the bed, her blonde hair spilling over her shoulder, the diary resting against her knees.

"You are unsettled."

Rebecca's face clouded. "What if there is no telegram?"

Leotie changed into a nightgown and settled on the bed facing Rebecca. "Do not fret over what you cannot control. Tomorrow will bring what is fated by the Great Father Spirit."

Rebecca wanted to ball up her fist and pound the mattress. This was not what she wanted to hear. She sniffled. "I'm acting like a hysterical fool, aren't I?"

Leotie smiled. "No, you have a baby, and you want your mother and father to love you as you love her; there is nothing wrong with that. But you will make yourself sick if you worry too much."

Concern etching her brow, Rebecca searched Leotie's face. "You don't think…" Tears filled her eyes, tears of dread. "You don't think fate would be so cruel—?"

Leotie met the girl's eyes, squarely. "No. Fate cannot control the actions of others."

As if to signal the conversation was over, Leotie

slid beneath the covers. She propped on her elbow and smiled. "I think I should like to have a diary. When I am very old, or when I have crossed the sky bridge to join my ancestors, perhaps my grandchildren might like to read about my life's journey."

Rebecca carefully tore a page from her journal and jotted several items, including Leotie's request for a diary. She drew up her knees and used them as a prop, then wrote: *Leotie says tomorrow will bring what is fated by the Great Father Spirit. I hope it is a telegram.*

She closed the book and used the little gold key to lock away her thoughts.

Chapter 24

The conductor walked down the aisle. "Bedford Station, folks. Two-hour stop."

Jesse carried the wicker basket as he made his way down the steps. He glanced back toward the sleeper car's window and smiled at Rebecca peering out at him.

To his way of thinking, Bedford Station was hardly more than a cow path with a railroad depot. It boasted a general store, a church, and farther down a sheriff's office. He supposed that said something about the place. The plinking from an out-of-tune piano caught his attention. Every town needed a decent saloon.

He hummed the ditty as he strolled toward the general store. It struck him that he wanted to dance, and not with any of the saloon wenches who plied their trade for a dime or a dollar. He wanted an excuse to hold Rebecca in his arms. He wanted a home, a garden, a stable of fine horses, and children, lots of children, with only one woman as their mother.

He reminded himself that he had no home, no land, no income. It didn't matter that his half-brother had stolen his title, his money, and the greatest part of his life. He had nothing to offer Rebecca—or his mother, for that matter. A dark cloud in the shape of a shark sent Jesse's thoughts in a different direction. He'd often witnessed the unmerciful shark attacks on men who fell from a main royal mast, and men who had survived keelhauling had prayed they would drown before being torn apart by the man-eaters. His half-brother was just as vicious...an inhuman blighter who had murdered their father without just cause. A harpoon was a suitable weapon for killing a shark, especially the two-legged kind.

"Mister, you from train?"

The voice jerked Jesse back to reality. Sunlight glinted off the badge pinned to the man's vest. "Aye?"

"Sheriff Ed Collier. Did you board in Oklahoma City?"

Jesse's gut clenched. He nodded. "What's your interest?"

"Lookin' for a runaway. Sheriff there wired she might've stowed away on the train."

Jesse's throat tightened with a welter of emotions. He refrained from glancing toward the locomotive. He had taken great care to keep his mother out of sight from the other passengers. Silas? Surely, being a man of color, the porter hadn't reported her to the conductor.

He swallowed to calm his voice. "Do you have a description?"

"Yep. Black hair, average height for a woman—"

Jesse steeled himself to hear the words—Kiowa—jumped the reservation. A flood of relief washed over him when the sheriff said, "Walks with a limp, and might call herself Mrs. Jones."

"Sorry, I'm traveling with my family. Because of the baby, we're staying in a sleeper car."

"So you haven't seen her?"

Jesse arched an eyebrow. "I believe that's what I just said." He pulled Rebecca's list from his pocket. "If you will excuse me, I have purchases to make." Then in afterthought he asked, "What makes a runaway woman so important?"

The sheriff spat then pulled his sleeve across his lips. "She gutted her husband."

Relief cascaded over Jesse. He had prepared himself to do whatever necessary to keep his mother from being hauled off the train. He frowned at the sheriff. "Maybe he deserved it." He tipped his hat and entered the general store.

A portly woman with cheeks that reminded him of red apples stood behind a long wooden counter. He handed her the basket and Rebecca's list. "Add a loaf of bread, a pound of sliced ham, a dozen boiled eggs, and the rest of that cake. Any charge to fill the jug from your well?"

"Nope, water's free for the taking."

Jesse stepped outside to fill the water jug. When he returned, she patted the filled basket. "We don't get much call for diaries. Everything else is in there."

He reacted to the cuckoo clock. "Is the time correct?"

"My late husband, God rest his soul, was a clockmaker. His clocks never lost time."

Jesse thanked the woman, took the basket, and made his way to the telegraph office. He spotted Sheriff Collier and two men stooping to look under the train cars; another stepped down from the coach Rebecca and Leotie occupied. A deputy shouted, "Ain't no sign of her, sheriff."

For the second time in one day, relief flooded Jesse.

****

Rebecca pressed her face to the window and

strained to hear. "It's muffled, but it sounded like he said they were searching for a woman with long black hair." Her hand flew to her mouth. She turned around in the small cubicle. "We have to hide you, Leotie, but where?"

"Up there." Leotie pointed to where the luggage was stored.

Standing on tiptoes, Leotie handed the bags down to Rebecca's up-stretched hands. She stood on the seat and then, lifting her foot to the narrow windowsill, levered herself into the shallow space. "Put the luggage back and pull down the curtain."

Rebecca worked quickly, stuffing the valises into place. "Can you breathe?"

"Yes."

"Are you comfortable?"

"Rebecca, if they come, you must calm yourself."

"I'll do my best."

She peered out the window in time to see Jesse enter the telegraph office. If only he would hurry.

A sharp rap seemed to echo against the metal door. Rebecca held her breath.

"Open up."

"Who is it?"

"Deputy. Lookin' fer a fugitive."

"There's only me and my baby. No one else."

"Sorry, ma'am. If you don't open up, I'll get the conductor to unlock the door."

Rebecca's fingers trembled as she unbuttoned the front of her blouse, and pulled it open. "Just a moment, please." She draped a diaper over Noelle and held her as if she were nursing. With her free hand, she unlocked the door and slid it ajar. She let the diaper drop just enough to expose the mound of her breast. "Forgive me. As you can see, I'm a bit indisposed."

The deputy's face reddened to the tip of his ears. He snatched off his hat. Then, clearly flustered, he slapped it back on his head. "'Scuse me, ma'am. I, um, well, sorry to bother you."

"Would you mind sliding the door closed?" Rebecca offered a demure smile. "As you can see, my hands are full."

"Sure. Yes, ma'am. Sorry, again." He let out a yowl as he slammed the door against his finger.

Rebecca suppressed a giggle as she hastily turned the lock. She also drew the window curtains. After placing Noelle on the chair, she whispered, "Shove the bags down one at a time."

"No. What if he returns?"

"You'll suffocate."

"Death is better than what they do to Indians who jump the reservation."

"Oh, I wish Jesse were here."

Rebecca opened the heavy curtains enough to covertly watch the outside activities. Jesse stood in front of the telegraph office. His stance conveyed strength and confidence in himself and the world around him. She had once felt that way, but she had since learned that she had been wrong to trust her own judgment. Her heart fluttered as he strolled down the platform, stopped to speak to the conductor, and then continued toward coach number five.

She opened the door on his command and relieved him of the basket. He was still standing when a muffled voice said, "I'm ready to get down."

Jesse stared at the upper luggage compartment.

"Mother?" He tossed both satchels aside and helped Leotie from narrow space.

Rebecca dithered about the small space. "A deputy insisted he had to search the room. Up there was the only place for her to hide."

Jesse poured Leotie a glass of water. "Aye, I was a bit collywobbled when the sheriff described the woman."

Rebecca exchanged glances with the Kiowa woman. "What did she do?"

Jesse removed his hat and hung it on a hook. "Sheriff said she killed her husband."

Rebecca looked at him wide-eyed and stammered, "That's terrible."

He opened his mouth to reply, but Rebecca spoke first. "I saw you standing outside the telegraph office." She placed her hands behind her back so Jesse couldn't see how tightly she gripped them. She couldn't bring herself to ask the question.

She waited patiently while Jesse tried to delay his answer. He ran a hand through his hair. He shrugged out of his jacket, and loosened the top button of his linen shirt. When she had spotted him standing in front of the telegraph office, she had known by the expression on his face there was no telegram. For whatever damnable reason, she needed to hear his answer. "Jesse?"

He lifted his broad shoulders in a shrug. "I'm sorry."

The small space grew quiet. Silently fuming, and needing to escape, Rebecca glanced toward Leotie. "Please watch Noelle. I need some air."

Rebecca stood on the platform. Her shoulders

shook with the tears she had repressed for so long—tears of anger, frustration, and expectation streamed down her cheeks. She managed to suck in a breath, and that steadied her a little, although her chest hurt from the painful ache in her heart.

****

Jesse blocked the door to keep it from sliding shut. "Bloody hell. I'd like to put my boot up that man's arse."

His mother touched his arm to stop him from stepping over the threshold. She spoke in a gentle voice. "Leave her be. She needs time to sort through the hurt."

Turbulent emotions roiled inside him. "A *father* is supposed to be the one person in the world to love his children unconditionally. He didn't have the bloody decency to even answer the telegram."

Noelle cried out.

Leotie cautioned him to lower his voice. "Calm your rage, my son. I am as angry as you, but there is no need to upset the baby." She sat next to the child and hummed until a smile replaced the tears.

"I will make some food."

"Not hungry, Mother."

"Very well. I will make bottles for the baby."

He heard the echo of his mother's long-ago words: *You could marry her.* The idea of taking Rebecca as his wife sparked every nerve-ending in his body. He imagined the scent of her soft skin, the caress of her lips against his, and the feel of her silken hair.

Bloody hell. If he got down on bended knee she wouldn't have him, whether from pride or in the sheer belief that once she stood on their doorsteps, her family would lovingly open their arms and invite her in.

"Excuse me, Mother. I'm going to my seat."

She offered him a smile.

Removing his hat, he settled in the seat to peer out the window.

"Bang-bang, mister, you're dead."

A frail woman clad in widow's weeds grabbed the youngster by the ear. She offered Jesse a limp smile. "Sorry, he's a handful."

Jesse sighed in vexation. "No harm done."

Listening to the young mother chastise her son set Jesse's mind to wondering. He and Lawrence shared the same father; they were raised with the same advantages, yet they were as different as night and day. What twist of fate had caused his half-brother to be born a monster? A chill coursed through him, a chill that had nothing to do with the weather.

Chapter 25

The next two days ran together as the train continued its course toward Illinois. Rebecca remained distant, tending to the baby's needs, speaking only when necessary, and continuously writing in her diary. She wanted to scream in frustration. She longed to break the unrelenting tedium of the sleeper car's confined quarters. She longed for music, dancing, and laughter. She missed the finely spun cottons, silks, and satins of the exquisitely tailored dresses she used to wear, even though she knew it was a frivolous and useless desire. And worse, her body betrayed her with a quickened excited pulse at every sight of Jesse.

While Leotie practiced writing in her journal, Rebecca fed the baby and settled her for the night. Once assured the child was sleeping soundly, she draped the shawl over her shoulders. "I need a bit of fresh air."

The Kiowa woman smiled her acknowledgment.

Rebecca stepped outside to stand on the platform. The sky was a lovely shade of periwinkle and the moon was just starting to appear. She thought of her prayer, the secret one. And she thought how God must have misunderstood what she was asking for and perhaps she should have been more specific. She prayed for forgiveness for her sins. She also prayed for a second chance at love. She had forgotten to add that she wanted a good man, an honest man, one who would love her back this time. Jesse wasn't that man. Yes, he was handsome, and yes, he was attentive to Noelle and his mother, but he had his own agenda—to return to England to kill a man. And the only thing he had offered her was the opportunity to be ruined all over again.

To kill a man echoed in her brain. She wasn't supposed to know this bit of information. She hadn't meant to eavesdrop on the whispered conversation between Jesse and his mother that night in the tipi. When she had asked him about it, he'd curtly replied it was none of her business.

It occurred to her that beyond the fact that Leotie was his mother, and he was the illegitimate son of an Englishman and that he'd lived a hard life at sea, her knowledge of Jesse wasn't enough to fill a teacup.

The cold night air chased her inside. Instead of returning to the sleeper car, she decided to bid Jesse goodnight. He was asleep when she entered the coach. A small part of her wished he would wake up. But he slept on, looking deceptively gentle and impossibly handsome.

Jesse Starr had become a thorn in her side, her own personal plague. He had moments when he was funny and charming. Mostly he was a constant reminder of the darkest moments in her life, the ones she tried to forget. She hated him for it.

She had already spent enough time and thought in contemplation. The train would arrive at Union Station tomorrow. In a moment of divine restraint, she resisted the urge to lightly kiss his lips. She simply turned to walk away.

"Don't leave," he whispered, but she did anyway.

She didn't go far, just outside the door, where she leaned against the wall. She buried her face in her hands, and tears trickled down her cheeks. She tried to be quiet so no one would hear her.

"Here now, miss. What fo' you be cryin'?"

Rebecca used the backs of her hands to swipe away the tears. "Oh, Silas! I didn't hear you."

"Is der anythin' I'se can get you—coffee, maybe a nice cup of hot cocoa?"

She touched the porter's arm. Her smile wobbled. "A pot of cocoa and two cups, if you please."

"Yessum."

Rebecca had allowed her silly expectations about love to guide her. In the process, she had ruined her life and taken her family down with her. The worst part, she knew, was that Frank never had the slightest twinge of regret.

Making love, though she had not been quite sure what that entailed, had sounded romantic to her naive brain. She hadn't known what to expect, because no one had ever explained it to her. It was a talk mothers had with their daughters before their wedding night. No one told her the intimate act was painful. In the end, all men were alike, Rebecca decided. They took what they wanted and didn't care one whit about hurting you.

Another tear dripped and rolled off the end of her nose. She hurried to the ladies' washroom and splashed cold water over her face. When she emerged, Silas stood in front of their car door, balancing a silver tray, his fist raised ready to knock. "I'll take that." She offered a smile. "What time will we arrive in Chicago tomorrow?"

He relinquished the tray. "'Bout three o'clock."

She thanked him and said goodnight.

Leotie looked up from the book of poetry. "You've been crying?"

"It's nothing. Just me feeling nostalgic." Rebecca set the tray on the table. She poured a cup of steaming cocoa and handed it to Leotie. "Hot chocolate is the nectar of the gods."

No matter how nonchalant she tried to act, her mood was still as black and cloudy as the night sky. "Silas said we would arrive at Union Station tomorrow afternoon."

Leotie was careful to take a small sip of the hot dark brown liquid. A smile lit her eyes. "This is much tastier than chicory. I will ask Silas how to make hot chocolate." She took another sip.

"I can teach you." Rebecca sank into her own chair and lifted the cup to her lips.

Leotie looked at her and raised one eyebrow. "But you are leaving us tomorrow."

Rebecca suddenly felt off balance, as if her life was about to spin out of control. She drew in a deep breath, let it out, and drew in another. "Silly me. I seem to have feathers in my brain."

"Is a father like the chief of our village?"

Rebecca inclined her head. "I suppose. A chief makes the rules, and sets the punishments for those who don't obey. He makes sure there is enough food for everyone in the village. Yes, a chief is like a father."

She savored the sweet, satisfying beverage, and then placed the cup on the saucer. "In your village, what does the chief do when people break the rules?"

The expression on Leotie's face darkened. "The punishments are often harsh, if a person breaks a tribal law. If a person is caught lying, the entire village will laugh and point, and even make the sign of a forked tongue, like that of a rattlesnake.

"The lower chiefs might burn your tipi and all your belongings. If you are caught stealing, you will be taken to the center of the village, tied to a pole, and publicly whipped. But the ultimate punishment is to be banished."

Leotie drew a breath. "What will you do when you return to your father's house?"

Rebecca peered over the rim of her cup. So wrapped up in condemning herself for the sins she had committed, she hadn't planned ahead. "I suppose I really don't know. I'm certain my parents will insist I find something useful to do with myself."

Not wanting to answer more questions, and not wanting to think about her uncertain future, she offered, "If you like, I'd be happy to write the instructions in your journal. When you get settled in England, you will have the recipe."

"Recipe?" Leotie frowned.

The question eased some of Rebecca's tension. She almost wanted to giggle. "Yes, it means a list telling how to prepare a particular food, or in this case, hot cocoa."

Leotie set the cup aside. She reached under the mattress and pulled out the book. "I will enjoy another cup while you write the…recipe."

Her emotions in turmoil, Rebecca carefully printed each letter to make reading easier for the woman who had become like a mother to her.

Chapter 26

Thursday arrived all too soon. The conductor walked up and down the aisle calling, "Union Station. Fifteen minutes. Everyone off that's gettin' off. This train returns to Oklahoma."

Jesse held the sliding door open while Leotie stepped into the hall. Rebecca took a last look at the room that had been her home for the past week. It appeared she hadn't left anything behind.

She handed Jesse both satchels, then gathered the baby in her arms. A myriad of emotions swamped her, leaving her weak as she and Leotie joined the line of disembarking passengers. She was hot and cold, and nauseated. Her entire body hummed with apprehension.

The deafening scream of iron wheels against iron rails protesting the brakes grated on Rebecca's already overwrought nerves. The train lurched. Jesse caught her before she crashed into his mother.

She reacted instantly. "It seems you are always saving me."

He merely smiled.

Her eyes found his, and she wanted to step into his embrace, to soak in the sensual scent of his aftershave. Clad in all black, he looked like the lord of everything and the master of every desire she wanted desperately to suppress.

"Move along, folks," the conductor ordered.

"We're on a schedule."

The spell was broken. She must have moved then, because in the next moment, Silas was helping her down the steps. "Been a pleasure servin' you ladies."

Words of gratitude to the porter were exchanged, and then they were greeted by a blast of cold air laced with droplets of rain as they hastened toward the depot. Rebecca covered the baby's head to protect her.

The train whistle blew, drowning out Jesse's words. He hurried them inside the station depot. "Wait here while I purchase tickets to New York."

Rebecca lamented, "Drat the weather. I had planned to walk home."

Leotie murmured, touching Rebecca's cool hand with a mere brush of her fingers, "We do not wish to say our final farewells in this busy place. A thundering herd of buffalo do not make this much noise."

Rebecca glanced about. After more than a year of living on the prairie, it now seemed people rushed around like angry hornets. She spotted an empty bench. "Come, let's wait over there."

It seemed an eternity had passed. Rebecca scanned the thinning crowd. Jesse was nowhere in sight. She noted the time on the large wall clock. Only a few hours of daylight remained. A small knot of concern formed in her stomach. Surely he wouldn't abandon his mother?

And then his deep baritone voice said, "I have a carriage waiting." He ushered them through a set of double doors, and toward a hansom cab.

The driver opened the door. "Where to, sir?"

Jesse looked at Rebecca. She answered, "Three nineteen Wicker Park."

Once inside the cab, Jesse settled against the cushioned seat. "Mother and I will stay the night in a hotel. There isn't a train to New York until tomorrow morning."

Gray clouds hung heavy in the sky. A rumble of thunder vibrated the carriage. Rebecca's mind soared in an endless circle of what-if's. She was afraid. Then, feeling eyes upon her, she raised her own and forced a smile. "Thank you both for saving my life. I shall always hold you dear to my heart."

"May the Great Spirit's blessings always be with you, and with my godchild."

Refusing to cry, Rebecca bit back the tears. Words lodged in her throat, leaving her to answer Leotie with a nod.

Jesse sat with his arms folded across his chest, his face stoic. She threw him a quick furtive look and shrugged at his questioning gaze. She felt awkward, conscious of him watching her. She kept her eyes toward the window.

The twenty-minute ride ended all too soon. The cabbie held the door wide, and Jesse stepped out. Rebecca leaned forward to embrace the Kiowa woman and then accepted Jesse's hand, allowing him to help her to the sidewalk.

"I'll walk you to the door."

Rebecca placed a hand on his chest. "Please don't. I left here with a man, a bad man. I don't think it wise for the neighbors to see me arriving with a different man. I hope you understand."

"Aye, I respect your wishes."

Without holding her, he leaned forward. His kiss was as fragile as a butterfly's wing, broken in a moment by the merest threat of a breeze. He lifted the blanket and placed a kiss on top of Noelle's head. Poof—and gone.

She squared her shoulders, the carpetbag gripped firmly in her hand, and moved slowly up the long tier of steps that lead to the front door of 319 Wicker Park. She chastened herself. *Don't look back. It's bad luck to look back.*

The reins slapping against the horse sounded like a peal of thunder; the wheels crunching on gravel echoed in her ears. She cast aside the idea of rushing down the steps and calling Jesse's name. Coming home was what she had wished for. What she had demanded. There was no turning back now.

She lifted the gargoyle door knocker and rapped. While she stood in the misting rain, waiting, the butterfly-wet kiss lingered on her lips to remind her of her folly and her guilt.

The door opened. A tall but plump gray-haired woman, dressed in a gray uniform and wearing a starched-stiff white apron, answered the door. "Go 'way. We don't 'low panhandlers."

Rebecca shivered. She wasn't sure if it was from the damp cold or from a bundle of nerves. "Alice, it's me, Rebecca."

The woman peered closer. "Well, bless my bones." She offered a wide grin and repeated, "Well, bless my bones." Still blocking the entrance, she looked over her shoulder, and hesitated. "I-I dunno—"

Noelle whimpered. Rebecca wished she was anywhere but here. "Please. Do you want to be responsible if my baby comes down with a fever?"

The maid's eyes widened. Her lips turned

downward as she held the door wide. Noelle's shrill wails escalated. Rebecca pulled the blanket back to reveal the child's angry red face. "We've had a long journey. Noelle is usually a very pleasant little girl, but if I were wet, and cold, and hungry, I'd pitch a fuss, too."

A growl came from a man who stormed into the massive foyer. A linen napkin hung from the neck of his white shirt. A woman with a crown of golden braids neatly on her head and clad in a royal blue brocade dress followed on his heels.

"Phineas, do I hear a baby crying?"

"Alice, what is this confounded racket?"

"Well, Mr. Throckmorton, Mrs. Throckmorton, you see, I—"

Rebecca stepped from behind the maid. "Mother...Father..."

Her emotions were in turmoil. She was home, she thought yet again, but she was home among strangers. Everything looked as odd to her as she did to the three people gawping at her. Maybe more so.

Throckmorton continued his glare. "Why are you here?"

The question confused her. "Frank is dead. His horse threw him. Didn't you get my telegrams?"

"I chose not to answer them."

"Father, I—" She was further bewildered.

"Rebecca!" Her mother gasped in obvious shock. And then, rather than giving the smile Rebecca had hoped for, her mother frowned. "I hope to high heaven none of the neighbors saw you arrive. It would reflect poorly on your sisters...on all of us."

"I've been gone for over a year. I couldn't stay

away any longer." Rebecca answered. "Whatever it takes, I mean to make amends."

Her father raised his balled fist.

Matilda Throckmorton patted her husband on the arm. "Calm yourself, dear. Let her speak." She cocked an eyebrow toward Rebecca. "Your father asked why you have returned."

Rebecca fought to keep the tremble out of her voice. She lowered the blanket. "This is Noelle Rose. I thought you might like to meet your granddaughter, and…perhaps…forgive me."

Two loud gasps of dismay drew her attention. She was certain her legs were ready to fall out from under her. Her sisters had entered the foyer, witnessing her shame.

Her father's face turned purple. "You are ruined now! Your sisters, too." He opened his arms wide. "This whole family! All because of what you did."

"I was young, and I thought I was in love. All I want is your forgiveness, and to come home." Rebecca didn't know what she hated the most—the fleet of tears in her eyes, or the pleading.

Throckmorton bellowed, "Forgive you—a thief? You brought shame and embarrassment to this family. The neighbors haven't forgotten what you did." He waggled his finger at Noelle, his voice cruel. "Your mother and I have two fine grandsons, and neither one of them are *bastards*."

The flame of hope flickered and died. Rebecca didn't move. Couldn't move. She almost choked on her anger. "Call me what you will, but do not *ever* call my child a bastard. Her father and I were legally wed by a judge."

Rebecca looked at her sisters, seeking support. "Melinda, Beth…?"

Melinda stepped forward. "Father, would it be so bad if—"

Throckmorton sternly commanded, "Remember who butters your bread, daughters." He cut a threatening glare toward his wife.

Matilda Throckmorton stood like a statue. Her face reminded Rebecca of chiseled stone.

Noelle waved her tiny fists in the air, and raised her voice in protest. In a soft voice, Rebecca said, "Alice, would you mind getting a bottle of milk from my carpetbag?"

Her father's lip lifted in a snarl. "You do not give orders in *my* house." He looked at the maid. "If you value your job, Alice, you will go to the kitchen and help the cook."

The maid wrung her hands together. She looked from Rebecca to her boss. "Sir, 'tis an innocent babe."

He drew himself up and exhaled deeply. "Jobs are difficult to find for a woman your age."

Alice gave Rebecca an apologetic look, then bowed her head and shuffled from the room.

Rebecca searched for something to say. She decided to play a wild card. "If I'm not welcomed here, then surely Grandmother Minerva will be more forgiving."

Her mother gasped and pulled a hankie from the cuff of her sleeve. She dabbed at a tear. "It's all your fault. You and that…that…charlatan."

Rebecca forced herself to remain calm. "What? Will one of you tell me what's wrong?"

Her sister Beth said, "When grandmother was told

of your…of your…um…indiscretion, she was so upset that she had a stroke." Beth's voice dipped into an almost inaudible whisper. "She died two days later."

The rage on her father's face caused Rebecca to take a step backward. "A thief, a harlot, *and* a murderer." He walked to the door and jerked it opened. "Leave this house before I summon the chief of police."

"But I'm your daughter, your flesh and blood…"

"We had three daughters. Now we have two. The youngest died a year ago when she chose to commit an unforgiveable sin."

A blast of cold air sent a chill into the room. Rebecca draped the blanket over the baby. "Surely you don't expect me to go out in the rain? Have you no heart?"

Silence was her only answer.

Rebecca slid the handle of the carpetbag so that it rested in the crook of her arm. She defiantly snatched an umbrella from the umbrella rack. She turned to face her accusers. "The Kiowa took me in. They housed me, clothed me, and fed me without judgment or condemnation. Those who call them savages haven't met the lot of you."

She walked outside and heard the door slam behind her. She swallowed in well-justified fright. She had no place to go and no money to spend even if she did. Heart thumping, feet leaden, she uttered a silent prayer, took a deep breath, and walked down the steps.

Rain beat a steady tattoo on the umbrella.

Chapter 27

Jesse slouched in the leather armchair, his long legs stretched forward, a tot of bourbon on the side table, and a book in his hands. An unsettled feeling stole over him.

"My son, what disturbs you?"

He looked up. "Nothing. Why do you ask?"

"Because you have been staring at the same page for many minutes."

He closed the book and set it aside, then stood to look out the hotel window. "Something is not right, Mother."

"Rebecca?"

He grabbed his coat and hat. "I just need to see if she and the baby are safe."

Without another word he was out the door. In the lobby, the doorman held the door open. Jesse commanded, "I need a cab."

"Right away, sir." The man stepped to the sidewalk, blew a whistle, and motioned for a hansom.

Jesse called up to the driver, "Three nineteen Wicker Park." He impatiently thrummed his fingers against his leg. The short ride seemed to take forever. He didn't wait for the driver to open the door. "Shall I wait, sir?"

"Yes."

He bounded up the steps, rapped sharply on the

heavy wooden door, and kept rapping until it opened. "Jesse Starr calling for Mrs. Rebecca Donnelly."

Alice widened her eyes at the man who towered over her.

A man's voice called out, "Who is it, Alice?"

"A Mr. Starr. He's asking 'bout Miss Rebecca. Should I let him in?"

Jesse didn't wait for an invitation. He bulled past the maid.

Phineas Throckmorton demanded, "Send him away. There are no Donnellys here."

Jesse stalked forward, menace in his voice. "Did you send Rebecca away?"

Throckmorton's faced reddened. His jowls quivered. "What kind of barbarian are you, to burst into my home? If you do not leave this instant, I will be forced to get my pistol." He made a shooing motion with his hands. "Alice, show this blackguard out."

Frustration roiled in Jesse's gut. "Bloody hell." He shouted, "Rebecca? Rebecca, are you here?"

Throckmorton's wife and two daughters appeared at the top of the stairs. He commanded they return to their rooms.

Melinda's words were laced with sarcasm. "She's not welcomed here. Father demanded she leave."

Jesse grabbed the short stocky man by the lapels of his smoking jacket, lifting him to eye level. He spoke through gritted teeth. "Remember my name, and remember it well—*Jesse Starr*. I am not a man you want to cross. If any harm has come to Rebecca or the child, you will rue the day."

Throckmorton stood on tiptoes. A flicker of fear flittered past the meanness in his eyes. "I see Rebecca has not lost her penchant for hooking up with gutter trash."

Jesse's anger rose like bile in his throat, almost choking him. He thrust Throckmorton backward, sending him skidding on his backside across the white tile floor. "You are bloody damn lucky I don't break your neck."

Jesse turned on his heel.

Alice held the door wide. She plucked at Jesse's sleeve and whispered, "I don't know where she is, but the old miser called her some terrible names. He even threatened to fire me for trying to speak up for Miss Rebecca."

Hope sparked in Jesse. "Do you know where she went?"

Alice shook her head. "Shame to send her out in this weather, what with the baby and all."

Jesse struggled to hold on to his temper. He thanked the woman and sprinted down the steps, swearing under his breath. As the cabbie opened the hansom's door, Jesse asked him, "I'm searching for a young woman with a baby. Where would you go to get out of the rain if you didn't have any money?"

The cabbie thought for a minute. "The train depot. It's warm, and there are enough people she might not be noticed as a loiterer."

Jesse clapped the man on the arm. "There's an extra dollar for you if you can make that nag step up the pace. I'll ride up top."

A wide smile covered the driver's face. "Hang on to your hat."

The rain had not slackened, and visibility was limited. Jesse stared out into the darkness. Wind whipped around him, and he shivered. He didn't want to imagine the misery Rebecca and the baby must be suffering. He had to find them.

The moon peeked out from behind a string of gray clouds, shedding narrow beams of light against the street. Jesse's hopes rose and fell at the sight of a woman hunched against the weather, her steps deliberate. Then he spotted the walking stick.

"Driver, stop the horse. I wish to speak to this woman."

The cabbie did as requested. Jesse leaned over the side of the coach. "Forgive me, madam, but have you seen a young woman with an infant walking toward the train depot?"

The woman offered him a toothless smile. "Might've, for a dime."

Jesse reached into his coat pocket, and held up a quarter. "Information first."

"Might be she went to the church." The woman shrugged. "Might not."

Impatience and desperation gnawed at Jesse. "Bloody hell, woman, what church?"

"Dunno. Could be the one over at Railroad Street. Could be not."

She cackled when Jesse flipped the coin into her outstretched hands.

The cabbie said, "I know that church. It's in a bad area, and not safe for a woman, especially if she's pretty. Used to never close, but after being robbed and vandalized, and then the priest was beaten, it's no longer open after dark."

Jesse swore under his breath. He blamed himself for not insisting he explain to her father the ordeal

Rebecca had survived.

Grabbing the buggy whip, the driver cracked it over the horse's head. "Step up, Dollar."

Jesse leaned forward, his entire body alert as he carefully regarded each side of the road.

Ten minutes later, the hansom bumped over several railroad tracks littered with trash. The cabbie pointed. "Up ahead. The whitewashed cinderblock building with the tall spire."

He slowed the horse to a plodding walk, making it easier for Jesse to scan the dark surroundings. Had it not been for the dim glow from the buggy's lantern, Jesse might have not spotted the dark, round shadow against the dingy whitewash. Not waiting for the buggy to stop, he jumped to the ground and rushed up the multitude of steps. "Rebecca?"

No answer.

As he neared, the shadow against the massive wooden doors materialized into a large black umbrella. He heaved a sigh and swallowed hard, almost dreading what he might find. Leaning forward to lift the umbrella, a stream of water poured from the brim of his hat.

Rebecca sat cross-legged, hunched in a tight knot, her head down, chin against her breast. He eased the umbrella from her hands. She looked at him, wild-eyed, and screamed, "Mine. Get away!"

Bloody hell! He hardly recognized her—bedraggled, sitting in the dark, trying to shield herself and the baby from the rain, and at a place where sanctuary should have been available.

Rage heated his blood, and he vowed that, if it took until his dying day, Phineas and Matilda Throckmorton and the two cowardly sisters would suffer for turning their backs on Rebecca and her child.

On bended knee, he touched her. "Rebecca, it's me, Jesse. I'm here to take you and Noelle home."

She blinked. "I'm not dreaming? It's really you?"

He smiled and lifted her and the little lump tucked under her sodden blue cloak into his arms. "I'm never letting go of you again." He touched his chin to the top of the soggy bonnet, and whispered, "I've been a fool."

The coachman stood at the base of the steps. He steadied Rebecca until Jesse entered the hansom and then lifted her and the baby into his outstretched arms. The coachman said as he slammed the door shut, "Ol' Dollar has grown lazy from easy pulls. He'll earn his oats tonight."

A fierce trembling beset Rebecca. Her teeth chattered even when she spoke. "Noelle hasn't cried or whimpered in a while. I'm afraid I've suffocated her."

Jesse drew back the cloak. The baby's eyes were closed, her breathing shallow, and her little hands felt like knobs of ice. Even with the protection of Rebecca's cloak, the infant was soaked through and through. With tender care, he held her tiny fists in his and warmed them with his breath.

The baby's purple lips and pallid color concerned Jesse. He removed his wet coat, hoping soon the warm interior would help revive her. "Don't worry. She's sleeping."

There was pain in Rebecca's eyes. Pain and regret. "They wouldn't let me stay. Father called me a harlot. He said I was ruined and that I had ruined their lives. Because of what I did, my grandmother had a stroke and died."

She continued to gaze up at him. Her voice broke. "Father pointed his finger at Noelle and shouted for me to take my…my *bastard* and get out." She dashed her cheeks with the heels of her palms. "Jesse, Noelle Rose is not a bastard. I told them Frank and I were legally married, but father threatened to call the police if I didn't leave."

Jesse silently strengthened his resolve to enact retribution on the Throckmortons—all of them.

"Rebecca, why didn't you seek shelter at the train depot?"

"I tried to find a dark corner, but when I saw the security guard asking to see people's tickets, I left and went to the church. The doors were locked. It used to be a welcoming place."

He folded her into his arms and held her close. "After we dropped you off, I relied on the cab driver to take us to a hotel. If only I had asked him the name before leaving you on the doorstep, so you would know where to find us. I should never have left you." He pulled back. "Look at me, Rebecca. I'm never leaving you again. I love you."

When she spoke, her voice was a raw whisper. "You love me?"

He kissed her forehead, her eyes, her nose, her lips. "Aye, since the first day I saw you standing in the doorway of that ramshackle cabin."

Rebecca gave a little laugh. "You asked how old I was. Did you truly think I was thirteen?"

"Aye."

A little silence passed. He thought she had fallen asleep.

"Am I a bad person, Jesse?"

She reminded him of a wilted flower. "Hush that kind of thinking. You are courageous, a loving mother, and have a kind heart."

"Thank you for saying so."

"Rebecca, I've wanted to ask for a long time, but I needed to let you go to your family. This isn't exactly the place a man should propose to a woman, but Rebecca Ann Throckmorton Donnelly, will you marry me, and allow me to adopt Noelle Rose as my daughter?"

Her eyes widened in surprise. "You're not just doing this because you feel sorry for me?"

Jesse almost laughed out loud. He had unexpectedly surprised himself. He brushed a tendril of wet hair back from her temple with the gentlest motion of his fingers. "There is a lot you don't know about me, and I'm leading you into an uncertain future. I don't need an immediate answer. Know this—I will never harm you, or Noelle, and I will always provide for you and my mother." He hesitated. "In the morning, if your answer is "no," then I will give you half of what money is left, to see you through until you can find employment."

She touched his face. "Say it again—the part about loving me."

He cupped his right hand under her chin, raised her face, and bent to touch his mouth to hers. At first the kiss was not a kiss but a mere mingling of breaths. Then he kissed her without reservation. When their lips parted, Rebecca blinked several times as if she were trying to bring the world back into focus. "I don't need until tomorrow. Noelle and I accept your proposal."

A thrill of jubilation welled in his spirit when she

added, "You are my heart and soul, Jesse Red Wolf Starr."

Rapt in each other, it wasn't until the driver snatched the door open and said, "Hotel, sir. How can I assist you?"

Jesse peered through the gloom of night and toward the hotel's double glass doors and was surprised to see his mother. He removed his coat and wrapped it around the baby. "The woman in the black dress is my mother. Carry the baby to her while I assist Mrs. Donnelly."

He thanked the cabbie and reached to withdraw a coin. The driver said, "No need, sir. You've already paid me and ol' Dollar more'n enough. Godspeed to you." He tipped his hat and climbed to his seat. As soon as his passengers had disembarked, he clucked the horse forward and pulled away from the curb.

Once inside the lobby, Jesse barked orders to the night clerk. "Send up a bowl of soup, a pot of hot tea, a large slice of chocolate cake, and a mug of warm milk." He glared a warning. "Don't dawdle."

To the bellman, he gave instructions to come to the room in thirty minutes to collect all of the wet clothing and have it cleaned, pressed, and returned.

Holding Rebecca in his arms, he let long strides carry him to the elevator. Leotie followed with the baby. "I'll explain everything when we get to the room." He drew a tight breath. "While you see to Rebecca, I'll take care of Noelle."

Grim-faced, Leotie nodded her understanding.

Once inside the room, Leotie ran hot water in the tub. Rebecca protested, "No, please, Noelle first." She wobbled, reaching out to grab Jesse's arm.

205

Leotie's voice and eyes warned that she was in charge. "I will tend to both. Jesse, get out of those wet clothes and wrap yourself in a blanket." She guided Rebecca toward the tub. "The hot water will warm you. Close your eyes and relax while I take care of Noelle."

Leotie removed the layers of wet clothing from the baby. "Poor little one. Cold as a frog, and soiled." She removed the stinky diaper and tossed it in the commode to wash later. "I will bring everything out for the man to make clean. And Jesse, put a few drops of your firewater in Noelle's milk. It will warm her on the inside. I will ask the Great Father Spirit to keep the fever from attacking this innocent one."

Her face was calmer than her voice. "You will tell me all that happened?"

"Aye, Mother, later." Before leaving Rebecca to his mother's ministrations, he looked into the shimmering sheen of misery in her eyes.

Rage burned hotter than the shot of bourbon he planned to down.

Chapter 28

Rebecca barely remembered leaving the hotel. She had stared out the window, relieved when the train left Union Station. The days had leapfrogged over each other until, a week later, they arrived at Grand Central Station. Sleep had eluded her for most of the trip to New York. The ever-hostile expressions on the faces of her sisters and her parents loomed behind her eyes. Their words had slapped her in the face.

It felt like a lifetime ago that she had sneaked from her bedroom to tiptoe down the stairs, ducking behind pillars and furniture to hide until her father had left his office and retired for the night. Even now she remembered the violent beating of her heart, and how her fingers trembled while turning the lock on the safe tucked beneath his desk.

She had tried six ways to Sunday to justify that she wasn't stealing, that she was taking what was rightfully hers, or would have been on her eighteenth birthday. But, oh, what she had been capable of—demeaning herself, dishonoring her mother and her father— deluding herself that Frank Donnelly was her knight in shining armor. What a stupid ignorant girl she had been, to fall victim to his beguilement.

She had been worn out by the emotions she had to summon up to deal with her guilt...her sin. Love for Noelle had been her saving grace. She had to live for her child.

She did her best to shove away the contemptible thoughts and focus on her new but uncertain future. Her eyes blurred with sudden unwanted tears. She loved Jesse. She loved his strength and his resilience and the fact that he was so indomitably male, which made it so easy for her to trust him. And she loved how easily he handled everything, from buying their tickets to choosing the cabin she and Leotie would occupy while sailing to England.

Time seemed suspended in the haze of sun and shade, and the cold wind from the ocean. She leaned over the rail of the luxurious ocean liner, watching the waves as the big ship plowed through deep blue waters. Tucking a wisp of hair off her neck, she felt happy, invigorated, hundreds of miles away from Chicago.

She was wild about Jesse, and had been for a long time. She really did want to marry him. There was just one concern, and she hoped Leotie had the answer.

****

Jesse sat in the men's lounge, nursing a bourbon. He read the last page of *The Count of Monte Cristo* and hoped his own story had a happy ending. His thoughts turned to Rebecca and his mother. What was to become of them if by some freak twist of fate Lawrence managed to kill him?

He closed his eyes so he could savor all the more the sensation of holding Rebecca, of tasting her sweet lips. He desired to savor more than her lips. Much more. His eyes jolted open. Bloody hell. It was expected that a husband pleasure his wife on their wedding night. The thought of undressing Rebecca, exploring every inch of her, tasting her, then making her his caused a growing ache in his groin. He shifted in the large leather chair to ease his discomfort.

His hand trembled as he lifted the glass to his lips and allowed the alcohol to burn its way down his throat. He dare not plant his seed in Rebecca. The thought of his dying and leaving her penniless and with another fatherless child to raise was compounded by his selfish yearning to bed her.

Damn it all to...bloody hell! He was torn between the tempestuous emotions of being honorable, on one hand, and naked desire on the other.

After a quick stroll to his room, he unbuckled the straps to his valise. His fingers wrapped around the small, elongated black box. Relieved that he still had it, he opened the box and smiled. Except for satisfying his urges with a few saloon wenches, he hadn't used the paragon sheath since he'd jumped ship almost a year ago.

****

Rebecca paced up and down the short aisle of the cabin she shared with Noelle and Leotie. She was fraught to know how to approach such an indelicate subject.

Leotie broke the silence. "You are unsettled over uniting with Jesse?"

"Yes...no!" Rebecca flounced on the bed. She hated the betraying blush that heated her cheeks. The question spewed out. "Leotie, how do Kiowa women keep from getting pregnant?"

She twisted her hands in her lap. Her voice soft and apologetic, "I love Jesse, and desire to please him. It's just that Noelle is barely five months old, and doing all the cute things babies are supposed to do. It's selfish of me, I know, but I want to enjoy all those special little moments.

"And then there is the other thing—the man he plans to kill. What if...?" She couldn't bring herself to finish the thought. "I'm only seventeen and already a widow with a child." She sighed. "I want to bear Jesse's children, but not right away. Is that wrong?"

Leotie leaned forward to wrap her hands around Rebecca's. "Let there be no deceit between the two of you. To set your mind at ease, ask Jesse about the man."

Rebecca didn't miss the mischievous spark in Leotie's eyes. "As to your other concern. Many times a young man and a maiden might wander into the forest and after a long while return smiling, and no baby is ever conceived. You see, we Kiowa know how to take the bladder of a deer, a wild pig, or a buffalo, and scrape it until it is silky like dandelion fluff. Then it is sewn into a pouch that fits snug over the man's *watasch*. When the lovemaking is over, the sack is washed clean to use another time."

Rebecca released a long, exasperated sigh. "No wild animals aboard ship." The giddy delight she had awakened with had disappeared.

Leotie sighed, too.

A sharp rap at the door startled both women, followed by relief when Jesse identified himself.

A wicked smile spread from his eyes to the rest of his face and finally seemed to glow from his very essence. He reached to wrap his hands around Rebecca's. "I've arranged with the captain to perform the marriage ceremony."

She averted her smile for a second, thoughts of

murders and babies still swirling around inside her head. She looked into his earnest face and nodded. "When?"

"How about in an hour?"

A moment of very tense silence filled the small space.

He took her hand and dropped to one knee. "I will never give you cause to regret marrying me, Rebecca," he promised, huskily. "I swear."

She forced her voice to sound light and easy so he wouldn't hear the panic bubbling up. "An hour is perfect."

A great tension seemed to leave Jesse at her agreement; his serious expression turned to a smile that Rebecca found endearing.

He lifted Noelle from his mother's arms and brushed a kiss across her downy blonde hair. The baby cooed and grabbed his nose. Jesse's grin widened. "I will call for *all* my ladies at six o'clock."

Rebecca sighed, her folded hands against her stomach, and summoned up a wobbly smile. They had been at sea three days. Some part of her had assumed the wedding would take place after they arrived in London.

She looked out the porthole—or in the general direction of the small round window. She saw her own reflection in the glass. What spell had Jesse cast over her that she would consent to marry again?

Chapter 29

The allotted hour passed all too quickly, and Rebecca felt as if she were marching toward a lynch mob. She wore the green traveling suit Jesse had bought at the fort, and Leotie had fashioned her hair into a neat chignon.

"You can back out," Leotie whispered.

Rebecca didn't mind having a small wedding. At least it was more than she'd had with Frank. The people she needed most were here, Leotie and Noelle. As far as she was concerned, no other witnesses were necessary. Still, she couldn't help feeling that she was about to commit another mistake.

Rebecca whispered back, "I truly do love him."

"Then let us go. You should not arrive late to your own wedding."

Rebecca stood at the threshold of the ship's library, a small room smelling of cedar and with shelves lined with books. The captain, dressed in crisp white slacks and a navy-blue double-breasted jacket lined with gold buttons, stood in front of a mahogany book stand, a prayer book in his hand. Jesse stood to his left, gazing fondly at Rebecca, urging her forward with his eyes.

She swallowed and prayed she wasn't about to make another silly girl's mistake. She wasn't a silly girl, nor was she a fully grown woman. She was a thief, a widow, the mother of an infant. Jesse deserved better.

Outside, rain pattered against the porthole. The weather was certainly in keeping with Rebecca's mood. Somehow she managed to put one foot in front of the other. Somehow she reached Jesse's side, and his arm brushed hers. She closed her eyes and drew in the scent of his cologne. Bay Rum. Her father's cologne. This conjured a hurtful memory. She squeezed her eyes shut and opened them just as quickly. She prayed she wouldn't disgrace herself and Jesse by fainting in front of God and all who were watching.

The captain's solemn voice said, "Dearly beloved, we are gathered here in the sight of God and man to join this man and woman as husband and wife..."

And then it was over. The vows exchanged, Jesse placed the sapphire-and-pearl rose-gold band on the third finger of her left hand. It was as if the ring spoke to her and placed hope in her heart and she knew she was ready. She pressed her lips to his, and if she had any lingering doubts, Jesse kissed them away.

The captain invited them to dine at his table. He ordered a magnum of Champagne and offered a toast for eternal happiness. Finally, when they were through the servings of a savory soup, roast rack of lamb with mint jelly, petite potatoes, and egg custard, the captain excused himself, saying duty called.

****

The bed in Jesse's cabin was wide, with crisp clean sheets. Waves whispered against the ship's movement as Jesse shut the door on the rest of the world, loosening his tie.

Rebecca knew she was ready. Though she had done this once before, she was still a little nervous. Like her second first kiss, this would be her second first time. Did she remember what to do? Had she even known before? Did any of that even matter? It would be different this time, she was certain. She knew Jesse would pleasure her, and that she would do the same for him.

They were in love.

They had waited long enough.

Now that the moment was here, it became impossible to wait a minute longer. The months of longing and abstinence were finally over.

He shrugged out of his coat and let it fall to the floor, followed by his shirt. Rebecca pressed her palms against his chest. "No second thoughts?" he asked, his mouth close to hers.

"No second thoughts. Kiss me, Jesse, now."

The pins escaped her hair beneath his fingers, and the tresses tumbled free of the sedate coil. A blush stained Rebecca's cheeks. His hands smoothed her hair before they moved to cup her face, lifting it so their eyes met. "I love you, Rebecca."

He made hasty work of the buttons on the front of her green traveling suit, and smoothed it over her shoulders and down her arms. Then he dealt with the camisole, and the bloomers which caught at her waist before pooling around her feet.

She mewled against his lips, "And I you." She trembled, standing there in her white cotton hosiery, so ready to give herself to this man and yet frightened because she didn't exactly know what to do.

A small gasp escaped Rebecca as Jesse knelt, his hands boldly touching her knees and quickly pulling off the garters and stockings, tossing them in a small heap upon the floor.

"Don't be scared," he said in a husky voice. "I will never do anything to hurt you."

She placed her hands over her breasts. He gently drew them away. "I want to see you. All of you."

She didn't trust her knees to support her, so she sat on the edge of the bed and watched as her shadowy bridegroom kicked off his boots and slipped out of his trousers. He was naked as the day he was born when he came to her. If he hadn't gently laid her on the bed, she would have fallen, weak as a dandelion in a strong wind.

She tried to quell the rising trepidation, fighting the flooding tide of fear that surged full force. Memories washed over her like a tidal wave. Would she find pleasure or pain in his arms?

Her eyes wavered under his direct stare. She was suddenly like a small girl in a fully-bloomed woman's body. Her lower lip quivered, and as she met his gaze, tears welled in her eyes.

Jesse lifted a finger and wiped away a droplet that traced slowly down her cheek. "You're trembling."

"Please don't hurt me."

Her eyes reminded him of a trapped animal. With infinite care, his arms slipped around her. "It's not nearly as painful as giving birth."

She snuffled. "I'm not talking about that kind of hurt."

He held her away to fully see her, and whispered, "Tell me."

She watched the way his jaw worked, the crease in his brow. He was angry. With her?

She lowered her eyes. "Sometimes...Frank...was cruel."

****

Jesse quelled the growl that rose in his throat. If Frank Donnelly were still alive, his days would be numbered. Jesse knew he must be gentle to keep Rebecca's fear from destroying the moment, but it took extreme exercise of will. Her skin contrasted against his darkness, like a translucent pearl on a bed of warm earth. Once more his embrace enfolded her, bringing her back in close to his lean frame. His lips slowly traced along her throat and shoulder, and his hands caressed her, arousing her, stroking her breasts, moving downward over her belly.

The whisper of a sigh escaped her as she leaned against his shoulder. She lifted her face to meet his; his mouth possessed her trembling lips. He turned her to him. They came together like forging irons, their kisses now fierce and savage, devouring as tongues met with hungry impatience. His hands wandered down her back, pressing her tighter against him. His passion roared within him, and the fire in his loins raged nearly out of control.

His seed was already leaking into the paragon sheath he'd donned before they spoke their vows. He bent a knee upon the bed, pulling her with him. His mouth opened, hot and wet, to sear her breasts.

Rebecca closed her eyes, panting and breathless, pliable beneath his caresses, as he lowered his weight upon her, parting her legs, and entered her, inch by hot inch. He was gentle, slow and restrained, as if it were her first time. But the truth was so much better: it was *their* first time together. He never took his gaze from hers, and when he was totally sheathed within her, he laced his fingers with hers, and pressed his mouth to hers for a deep hungry kiss. His hips began to thrust, slowly at first, and Rebecca moved with him. When he thrust a little bit harder and a little bit faster, she arched against him with a fierce ardor matching his. A wild, soaring ecstasy burst upon them, fusing them together in the all-consuming cauldron of passion.

Jesse felt the thunderous beating of his heart against her naked breasts. Time seemed to verge on eternity before he raised his head. Rebecca lay back upon the pillow, staring at him with wide, searching eyes, amazement etched in the beauteous visage.

Those cocoa eyes held him softly as she whispered, "I never knew lovemaking could be so beautiful."

Jesse smoothed her rumpled hair and traced his mouth along the slim column of her throat, tasting the exotic scent of her. "Did I hurt you?"

Rebecca shook her head. Gently she traced her fingers across the harsh lines of his frown, smoothing them away. Her eyes gleamed as she stared at him. "Never."

He kissed her again. And again. After catching their breaths, they made love many times during the night, each time growing more voracious even as the storm raged outside their porthole. It was after dawn before they were completely sated.

Chapter 30

The dining room was almost empty when the newlyweds entered for breakfast. A wide smile on her face, Leotie waved them forward.

Surprised to see his mother had ventured from her cabin alone, Jesse led Rebecca to the table. He kissed his mother's cheek. "It pleases me to see you venturing out on your own."

"When the bear comes calling, it must be fed."

Jesse laughed aloud. "I suppose that means you were hungry?"

Rebecca lifted the baby and placed a kiss on her forehead. Two red spots graced Rebecca's cheeks. "I'm sorry we kept you waiting."

Leotie offered a sly lift of her eyebrows. "I'm not so old that I have forgotten my days and nights with Addison."

Jesse reached under the table and squeezed Rebecca's knee. The color in her cheeks deepened.

Lighthearted banter and laughter ensued during breakfast. Jesse pushed back his chair, a dashing grin on his face. "I promised Rebecca a stroll on the promenade deck. Will you join us, Mother?"

"While the two of you were still abed, Noelle and I went out for some fresh air." She too rose to her feet. "We will go to the library. I wish to find a book and practice my out loud reading." Leotie held out her arms.

"For now, you need private time together, and the baby is too young to protest when I stumble over the difficult words."

Rebecca kissed the top of Noelle's silky head and gave the Kiowa woman a hug.

****

Outside, the wind churned up the promise of another storm in small, confused whitecaps as clouds hid the sun, and frigid air sent passengers scurrying for warmer quarters. Rebecca and Jesse strolled around the deck until spotting two empty chairs.

Rebecca swallowed back a slight queasiness, thankful that neither she nor Leotie had suffered from the seasickness that had beset several of the passengers. A few deep whiffs of sea air settled her stomach.

"Your frown is like the weather," Rebecca teased.

"How so?"

"It seems a storm is brewing inside of you."

Jesse swiveled to face his wife. His jaw clenched and unclenched. "There is so much I wish to give you. Things that go beyond creature comforts. You deserve more clothes than you have, beautiful gowns, not having to worry about your next meal…a forever home. I can give you none of these things."

He lifted her hands to his lips and kissed the backs of her knuckles. She gazed into his eyes, so blue, so like a bright sky that it almost hurt to look into them. Loosening her hands, she cupped his cheeks. "You, Noelle, and Leotie are all that I need. Whatever happens when we get to London, we will face it together."

Not certain who she was trying to convince, Jesse or herself, Rebecca offered him a reassuring smile. In truth, she was weary of putting on a brave front, carrying on in the face of adversity. Her secret supply of courage and confidence was rapidly dwindling.

Her thoughts shifted. What a difference between the sparkling white travertine floor tiles, marble columns, and expensive Victorian furniture in her father's house and the crumbling cabin with chinked walls that Frank had purchased or the animal-hide tipis with dirt floors. She had known luxury and poverty, abuse, rejection, and love—true love.

She was at odds with herself. She loved Jesse. This she did not doubt. Yet if she were perfectly honest with herself, she would have preferred to remain unmarried. This revelation sent shock waves to the very depth of her soul.

However, a woman, especially one her age, with a child, and without a husband, was in a precarious position, both socially and economically. The upper-class elite houses of pleasure to the lowest of brothels were filled with women without means to support themselves, without a husband, father, brother, or any man to protect and provide for them, women who had few choices in life.

"Rebecca?" Jesse said with a gentle squeeze of her hands. "Where did you go?"

She averted her eyes. "Nowhere. I'm right here."

He tucked his forefinger under her chin and forced her to look at him. He offered her a broken smile. "Are you having doubts—about us?"

She looked at him and wished with all her soul that she didn't love him, because she feared for her heart if she were to lose him. She shivered and pulled the lap blanket up to her waist. "No, never."

"Then...what?"

In spite of the cold, her palms were sweating. "Tell me about the man you seek. Is he the one who put the scars on your back?"

He turned solemn. "No. He's too cowardly." Drawing in a deep breath, he began, "His name is Lawrence, and he is my half-brother."

Jesse related his suspicion that Lawrence had murdered their father. "He may not have wielded the bloody weapon, but certainly he paid someone to do the dirty deed."

With a clenched jaw and gritted teeth, Jesse recounted the attack on his coach by the hooded men who had beaten him senseless. "Days later, when I finally regained consciousness, I was a prisoner on a pirate schooner. The day I was able to climb from the hole to the main deck, the captain ordered my first of many lashings."

Rebecca blinked back the tears. "How old were you?"

"Sixteen. No longer a boy, and not yet a man. Everything stolen from me—home, title, wealth. Those are mere replaceable things." Jesse's eyes flashed with temper and hatred. "My father's life can never be restored."

He stopped long enough to flag a roving waiter and order a hot cocoa for Rebecca and, for himself, a brandy-laced coffee.

"About two years after my capture, the pirates looted a town. I searched until I found where to post a letter to Mr. Armistead, Father's barrister, to let him know I'd been shanghaied, and that Lawrence was most certainly responsible."

The waiter brought the steaming beverages. Jesse indulged in a generous sip.

"A bloody scurvy bugger ratted me out because he thought the captain would reward him. Ten lashes was my punishment." Jesse winced as if he still felt the pain.

Rebecca longed to put her arms around Jesse, though she refrained. "Did he…get the reward?"

Fire snapped in Jesse's blue eyes. "Aye. Captain said there were enough bloody rats on the ship, and it was time to get rid of one. Before any of us could say *bollocks*, Captain whipped out his dagger and sliced the skive across the neck, then ordered him thrown overboard."

Jesse seemed to drift away for a second. "Sometimes I can still hear the screams. Blood draws sharks." Pain flickered in his eyes but was quickly subdued. "Afterward, I was never allowed to leave the ship. I don't know if Mr. Armistead ever received the letter."

Rebecca laid a gentle hand on his arm. "Is Mr. Armistead friend or foe?"

"He was father's most trusted friend. And mine."

"Good. As soon as we reach London, we shall find his office." She set her cup aside. "Whatever happens, Jesse, Leotie and I stand with you." She narrowed her eyes. "Promise that you won't let Lawrence kill you."

He stood and offered his hand.

She came quickly to her feet. She didn't know what else to say. She parted her lips, and he took full advantage.

His breath became hers, and hers his.

Jesse whispered, "If this kiss doesn't stop now, we'll end up making love on the deck."

Rebecca inclined her head toward the door, but she felt herself go crimson hot—not just in the face, but all over.

Chapter 31

They had been at sea for ten days. Jesse rose at dawn to be among the early risers who crowded the rail to get a first glimpse of the harbor at daybreak.

Home, he thought. A knot fisted in his gut. He was coming home—to nothing familiar at all. He gripped the rail tightly as the ship entered the harbor and a scene of bustling activity.

The ship glided closer and closer, to his past and to his future, and the reflected light of the rising sun seemed to blind his vision as the P&O liner crept slowly toward its allotted berth, its foghorn blaring.

For the sake of his wife and his mother, he had tried to remain calm during breakfast, to quell the emotions battling inside him. He would always cherish this idyllic time spent with the women and the daughter he cherished.

At midmorning they gathered to wait until the all-clear to disembark was given. Jesse smiled down at Rebecca, who stood tucked against him. She shielded her eyes against the sun.

Leotie's eyes were bright with all the new sights and sounds. "What are they doing, Jesse?"

"They are vendors, Mother, out to sell their wares, mostly junk, to unsuspecting passengers. There are also petty thieves looking to pick a few pockets."

He felt Rebecca's sigh. Her eyes, too, were bright

with all the new sights and sounds. "I don't know whether to be excited or frightened."

He hoped his smile offered reassurance to the two pairs of questioning eyes looking at him.

The sound of a voice barked through a bullhorn, announcing the ship had docked and passengers should be ready to disembark.

Jesse said, "I'll handle the luggage. Mother, loop your arm through Rebecca's, and hold tight. Both of you stay close and follow me. Don't stop, for any reason."

He held the two bags in front of him to use as leverage to create a path through the throng of travelers. He was home, he thought yet again, but he was home among strangers. Everything looked odd, as odd to him as he was certain it did to Leotie and Rebecca. Maybe more so.

Leotie's voice rose among the droning multitude. "I have never felt so torn between two worlds. I'm as nervous as a warrior about to go into battle."

Jesse successfully led them through the ceremony of going through customs. He asked the agent, "May I inquire if Barrister Armistead's office is still located at Canary Wharf?"

"Aye. A friend, is he?"

"He and my father were teammates at the Berkshire Polo Club."

The agent took a second look at Jesse's documents. His manner changed deferentially. "Well, ye'll be needin' a cab, Mister Starr. 'Tis too far to walk, 'specially wid yer wife totin' a young one."

The agent blew a whistle and motioned to a young man. "Hail a cab." He handed Jesse the stamped documents. "'ow long ye plan to visit?"

Jesse returned the man's smile. "I'm here to stay."

The customs agent nodded. "Luck to ya."

Outside, waiting for the hackney, Jesse said, "I'll book us rooms at the Grand Hotel, where you can freshen up while I call on Armistead."

Rebecca cut an eye toward Leotie, who nodded. Rebecca said, "We will go with you. Whatever happens, we are in this together."

The tension was broken when the cab driver pulled the horse to a halt. The cabbie stepped down and opened the door.

Jesse sighed heavily. "Aye, you deserve to know what the future holds for us."

He handed Rebecca and his mother inside, then gave the address to the driver.

No one spoke. Appearing relaxed and confident, Jesse stretched his long legs forward. Occasionally, the driver shouted, "Make way. Comin' through."

They passed several buildings before turning onto Main Street. It was another ten minutes before the driver pulled up in front of a red brick building with columns on each side of a massive door. The driver appeared instantly to assist his passengers. "Should I wait, gov'ner?"

Jesse dropped the fare into the outstretched hand. "Thank you, no."

The cabbie doffed his hat and climbed aboard the high seat and drove away.

Jesse looked at the numbers on the door and then up at the sign. *26 Canary Wharf.* His courage and determination started to fade. He could just walk away. But he had come half way around the world for this. In fact, it felt like he had crawled from the depths of hell for this chance to reclaim his life and avenge his father.

No, he would not turn back now. He placed his hand on the knob and turned as he opened and held the door wide for Rebecca and his mother to enter. Then he removed his hat and stepped forward.

A woman seated behind a desk greeted them with a smile. "May I help you?"

"I would like to speak with Barrister Armistead."

"Do you have an appointment, Mr.—?"

"I do not. Tell him it is most urgent that Jesse Starr speak to him."

She offered an apologetic shrug. "Sir Oliver's schedule is quite full for several weeks. If you like, I can refer you to one of his associates."

He stood a bit taller, straightened his shoulders and looked the woman in the eye. "I have waited ten years to see Oliver Armistead, and I will not wait a day more."

"Sir, I am sorry for your plight, but you must understand that—"

He chose his words carefully and spoke clearly so there would be no confusion, "Either announce me or I will announce myself."

At that moment, Noelle let out a scream, her high-pitched wails deafening. Rebecca shouted, "I-I'm sorry. She's usually a very quiet baby."

A door slammed against the wall, causing the baby to cry even louder.

A man Jesse barely recognized stormed through doorway and demanded, "What the bloody devil is going on out here?" His glance shifted from the two seated women to the man standing with clenched fist.

He frowned. "Miss Wells, who are these people?"

Leotie handed a bottle to Rebecca. Noelle latched on to the nipple. Her shrieks quieted to snuffles.

"This man insists"—the secretary wrung her hands together—"ah, I told him you were…"

Jesse's scowl deepened. He fixed his gaze on the reedy man who looked more like a scarecrow than a man of the law. "I sent you a letter letting you know I was alive."

Armistead adjusted his glasses, his voice gruff. "I have received no letter. Explain yourself. Who are you?"

"Addison Jesse Starr. Son of Addison Starr Fitzroy, First Viscount of Arlington."

Armistead took a step closer. "The devil take you," he blustered. "Miss Wells cancel all of my appointments for the rest of the day."

"B-but sir…"

Armistead's growl brooked no arguments. "No buts, just do as I say."

He swept his hand toward his office. "Young man, I have my doubts that you are telling the truth. Nonetheless, I should like to hear your, how shall we say, your tale."

Holding the baby, Rebecca stood and, though she blushed from head to foot, said, "It is no tale, sir."

The lawyer peered over his glasses. "And who might you be?"

"I am Mrs. Addison Jesse Starr." She motioned for Leotie to stand. "And this is Leotie Starr, of the Kiowa people in Oklahoma. She is Jesse's mother, and the widow of Jesse's father. And we go where Jesse goes."

"Miss Wells, bring two more chairs." Armistead

threw up his hands in exasperation. "Do come in. The more the merrier."

Although a smile lurked in his eyes, Jesse kept a suitably serious expression. He said as he lifted two straight chairs, "Allow me."

Clearly befuddled, the secretary sputtered, "Sir Oliver, shall I bring tea?"

Armistead cast a sardonic smile. "And scones, too." Rounding the mahogany desk to sit in a leather chair, he leaned forward, eyeing Jesse.

No one spoke. Jesse matched the man's stare.

The barrister pursed his lips and furrowed his brow as if thinking, and then he leaned back. His words were measured. "Start from the beginning and spare no details. I will reserve judgment until I hear you out." He added, "Be forewarned that I shall do my best to poke holes in your"—he arched his eyebrows toward Rebecca—"tale."

Jesse countered with, "Then I ask that you not interrupt until I am finished."

The secretary entered with a salver. Quiet as a church mouse, she served the refreshment.

"That will be all, Miss Wells. You may take the rest of the day off. Lock the door and put out the Closed sign."

She curtsied. "As you wish, Sir Oliver."

Armistead directed his attention to Jesse. "All right, you may begin."

Jesse finished the cup of tea in one gulp. He began his narration with how his father and mother met. He continued through his early years as a boy, the problems with his half-brother, the death of his father, and the details of how he had spent the last ten years of his life, including the search for his mother and the months spent with the Kiowa.

Tension rode him hard. Rage caused him to pace like a caged lion. And when he'd drained his memory of the last pieces of information, including the lashes he had received for posting a letter, he splayed his hands on the desk and leaned forward. "You might find this one last bit of trivia interesting. Father and his lifelong friend were both born on Friday, September 24, 1831. They each received a pony on their sixth birthday."

His temples throbbed, and his chest heaved like a man laboring for breath. Leotie rose and poured Jesse a cup of tea. She touched his arm and whispered, "Only a red wolf has such courage."

****

A numbness crept over Rebecca as she listened to her new husband relate his life story. All that she had suffered paled in comparison to the injustices foisted upon Jesse. Staring at his solemn expression, she schooled her face into quiet reserve to hide the turmoil roiling inside her. She knew Jesse was a complex man with a difficult past, but after hearing the detailed cruelty he'd suffered, she fully understood his need for revenge.

She swore that if worse came to worst, she herself would pick up a pistol and blow Lawrence Fitzroy to kingdom come.

Chapter 32

Sir Oliver Armistead laced his fingers together as he mulled a litany of arguments to deny that this dark-haired man with eyes like blue ice was indeed the son of Addison Starr Fitzroy. He leaned over the side of his chair to pull open a bottom drawer and remove a metal box. He set it on the desk and used a small key to open it. Shuffling through the stack of confidential papers, he withdrew a badly soiled envelope. The ink had bled, making his name almost illegible. Without opening it, he recalled the sparse message: *Lawrence had me shanghaied. Upon my father's grave, I will return. J Starr.*

He cleared the rasp from his throat. His heart told him the man sitting before him was truly the lad he'd last seen ten years ago. The lawyer in him demanded one more piece of proof. "Do you recall the names of those ponies?"

A smile feathered across Jesse's mouth. "Father's was Donatello and yours was Rembrandt."

Armistead held forth the scrap of paper. "When this arrived, it solved the mystery of your disappearance. I was relieved to know you were alive. Forgive me for the cross-examination. I had to be sure."

"Then you believe me?"

Armistead rounded the desk and clasped Jesse by the shoulders. "By Jove, no one could possibly know

231

birthdates and names of ponies except the son of my dearest friend." He blinked to clear the mist clouding his eyes. "We have much to discuss, but that can wait."

He looked at the women. "I shall consider it an honor if you will agree to spend the week at my country estate."

Jesse objected. "I'll secure a hotel room for my family, then ride out to Arlington."

"I must object, my boy. At present, the estate is in ill repair, and there is no staff. Heed my word, it is best to keep your arrival confidential. Do you understand my meaning?"

Jesse looked at the expectant faces staring at him. His jaw clenched. "Understood."

"Excellent." Armistead grabbed his hat and coat. He scribbled a note and placed it on his secretary's desk.

He led them to a back door. "My coachman lives above the stable. As soon as he hitches the horses to my brougham, we shall proceed."

With Jesse's help, the carriage and its matched pair of grays were readied straightaway. The driver efficiently loaded the meager luggage in the time it took the two women to settle themselves in their seats. Sir Oliver rapped on the roof with his knuckles, and the carriage began to move, wheels skimming over the cobbles, the horses' hooves clattering noisily.

****

No one spoke as the carriage moved through the labyrinth of narrow, congested streets of the business sector. Once they reached the outskirts of town, there were miles of fields and grass and trees, and a curious silence between them that Rebecca did not want to breach because she herself was feeling a little overwhelmed.

She was still trying to absorb the fact that her husband was royalty. At least she thought a viscount was royalty, and if so, what did that make her and Leotie?

She was stepping into a world that reminded her of her past. Memory of her parents' harsh words was still not deeply buried. If she had learned anything from her past, it was that love and comfort could be snatched away within the blink of an eye.

She consciously shook off her discomfiting thoughts. All that was important was the safety of her husband and the security of her child.

She glanced at Leotie and saw from the expression on her face how beautiful she found the countryside.

And then the carriage topped a small rise and stopped for an instant, and they caught their first glimpse of Hardwick Hall in the distance.

It was two and a half stories of ivy-covered gray brick, the main section with its broad, shallow, balustrade steps flanked by two ells, the arms of the letter H, the elegant shape of the house.

It stood shimmering in the golden haze of early summer, nestled on the shore of a sparkling blue lake, and cooled by the draping boughs of old gnarled trees.

She imagined herself as mistress of such a grand manor.

Rebecca was brought back to reality as the carriage lurched forward to pass between two stone columns and onto the long sloping track that wound its way through the lush fields and gardens and around the centuries-old trees that dotted the lawns of Hardwick.

As they progressed closer and closer to the house, the driver blew a bugle, and when the carriage finally stopped, a retinue of staff awaited their arrival.

At the top of the steps, in front of the etched-glass double doors of the entry, an extraordinarily tall woman with a pleasant smile waited.

Armistead exited the coach and dashed up the steps to place a kiss on his wife's cheek. He also whispered, "I am relying on you to keep our guests' visit confidential." He winked. "I'll explain later."

He smiled as Jesse assisted Rebecca and the baby up the cascade of stairs. "My dear, please welcome our guest, who arrived from Oklahoma in the American West just this morning: Jesse Starr, with his wife and his mother, Rebecca and Leotie." He gently tweaked the baby. "And this lovely child is Noelle."

He bounded forward to assist Leotie up the last remaining steps. "My wife, Lady Beatrice Armistead."

"Oh, pshaw, Ollie." His wife offered a smiling chastisement. To her guest, she said, "Please, no bowing, or calling me 'Your Lady,' or any of that folderol. In the leisure of our home, we are simply Bea and Ollie."

Leotie nodded. "Pleased to meet you."

Lady Beatrice snapped her fingers. "Albert, the Rose room and the Ivy room." She extended her hand toward the open door. "Welcome to my home."

The reception hall was both overwhelming and comfortable, and yet the house had a homey feel, as well. Lady Beatrice turned to her guests. "My goodness, it's nearly noon. Traveling all the way from America? You must be exhausted." She clapped her hands together. A young maid rushed forward and curtsied. "This is Zoe. She will show you to your rooms. I will arrange for cook to send up a tray of tea and biscuits, so that you might rest. Dinner is at seven."

Before taking her leave, she offered an invitation. "Do either of you ride? Riding gives me pleasure, but I often long for company."

Rebecca and Leotie exchanged smiles. Rebecca answered, "Yes, we do."

"Lovely. Perhaps tomorrow." She flashed a genuine smile. "Enjoy your rest. Until seven." Lady Beatrice turned and snapped her fingers, and a servant immediately appeared.

Armistead said to Jesse, "Join me in my study."

Jesse assured Rebecca and his mother that he would see them later.

There was a dread in Jesse's stomach, a sick feeling as he followed Armistead into the richly paneled room. A manservant entered. "Madam thought you might prefer coffee with your biscuits." He filled two cups and departed, closing the door.

A massive clock chimed twelve times. Armistead opened a cabinet and held up a crystal decanter. "What is your pleasure, cream or brandy?"

"Brandy."

"Good lad." Adding a splash and handing Jesse a cup, Armistead settled in an overstuffed leather chair. Neither man spoke while they partook of the refreshments.

Jesse bit back his impatience. He needed answers to questions...lots of answers. "Tell me about Arlington. Why is it in ill repair?"

Armistead gave a single loud sniff. "After you seemingly dropped off the ends of the earth, your half-brother and his mother decided to remain at Arlington, but he found that running an estate, especially one the size of Arlington, actually required work, and money. A lover of the gaming tables, he lost more than he won. The bloody blighter squandered money set aside to pay the taxes, and the workers.

"He used brutality to squeeze more labor out of underpaid and overworked employees. Worse, he forced unwanted attention on the young maids and terrorized the older ones. One day he awoke to find all the workers had quit. Eventually, his mother abandoned him and went to reside in the townhouse in the Soho district.

"I suppose Lawrence got bored, rambling around in that huge mansion with no one to wait on him hand and foot"—Armistead sniggered—"or to hitch up the carriage."

Armistead raised his eyebrows ever so slightly to emphasize his next words. His tone showed concern, and he spoke in earnest. "At first, he was welcomed in all the social circles. Before long, he was simply tolerated, until his debauchery was no longer acceptable and he was totally ousted. Word is he invites himself to balls and opera parties and makes a bloody arse of himself.

"Make no mistake, Lawrence is still as foppish as ever, but never allow him to fool you into thinking he is a weakling. He is an excellent shot, wicked with the sword, and seems to take fiendish pleasure in mutilating his victims with a dirk.

"Worst, Lawrence has developed a fondness for opium. He frequents the opium dens. I have heard that when he is under the influence, he is like a madman with superhuman strength."

Anger simmered inside Jesse. He gripped the chair's arms until his knuckles hurt. "What kind of law allows such offenses to go unpunished?"

Armistead pursed his lips as if he were considering how to answer the question. "Victims—those who survive—and their families are afraid to press charges. That is, until our then new chief of police had the bollocks to throw Lawrence into gaol for stealing money from the church. I think the good people of London breathed a sigh of relief when he was sentenced to ten years of hard labor."

Jesse almost relaxed back in his chair until he realized the lawyer's eyes were hooded, and the tone of his voice had gone flat. "The magistrate who heard the case and imposed the sentence on Lawrence was discovered the next morning hanging from the public gallows with a sign around his neck—the word 'warning' printed in blood."

Armistead's hand trembled as he lifted the cup to his lips. "That same morning, while the chief of police was investigating the crime, his young wife was assaulted in her own bed, and—well, there's no need to go into the gory details. The chief resigned, and as soon as his wife was able to travel, they left London."

Jesse's breath almost stopped as he envisioned his wife and mother in the grips of a maniac. "Bloody hell! Why is he still walking around free?"

Armistead poured another brace of brandy into his cup and offered the carafe to Jesse, who declined. "Because Lawrence and his gang of pirates, cutthroats, rapists, and other ne'er-do-wells have the current chief of police in their pocket."

He flung his hands wide. "We petitioned the Prime Minister in hopes an investigation would prove corruption and collusion with a criminal, and not only land the chief of police in the gaol but rid us once and for all of Lawrence."

Armistead snorted in disgust. "The petition never reached the Prime Minister. Our courier was found floating face down in the Thames River. We concluded that we had a spy among us, someone loyal to Lawrence. But who? Trust became so fragile that we simply aborted our efforts. And thus, here we are. Still none the wiser, and still quivering like frightened rabbits."

"Dammit," Jesse growled. "So much to consider. Since Lawrence didn't keep the taxes paid on Arlington, who is the present owner?"

Armistead said, "You are."

Jesse sputtered, "But you just said—"

The barrister chuckled. "I know what I just said. Your father had an instinct for business and made many wise investments." He sighed. "Although Addison never discussed it, I will always believe he suspected Lawrence might try to do him harm. What I'm saying is, as your father's best friend, his legal adviser, and his attorney, I was charged with looking after your financial interests. When that scrap of a letter arrived, I was heartened to know you were alive. And until I received some kind of official word and proof of your death, it has been my duty to guard your investments, including paying the taxes on Arlington, and to keep your amassing wealth confidential. You are a very rich man."

Jesse stood. He crossed the room to stare out the

window. He was at war with himself. Should he go after Lawrence first, or bring Arlington back to life?

"Oliver, I'm at loss for words. I'm humbled by your loyalty to my father, and for looking out for my interests. You are truly a man of principle. I'd consider it an honor if you would represent me the way you did my father." He reached out his hand.

Armistead gripped it. "Nothing would please me more, Jesse."

Jesse's voice was low and serious. "My first priority is to settle my family and bring Arlington back to life. Then, whatever may come, Lawrence will suffer the way he made our father suffer." He hesitated, gathering his thoughts. "However, if things should go wrong, I want my family's future secure. Before leaving this room, I'd like to draft my will."

Armistead pulled out several sheets of paper from a desk drawer and dipped a pen in the inkwell. He nodded.

Jesse drew in a deep breath and slowly exhaled. "A stipend of 775 pounds sterling for life to Sir Oliver Armistead for his devotion and trustworthiness. Upon my death, if my mother and my wife and child wish to return to America, all of my holdings are to be dissolved and monetarily divided equally between the honorable Viscountess Rebecca Ann Starr Fitzroy, Lady Leotie Starr Fitzroy, and my daughter, Noelle Rose Starr Fitzroy."

Armistead waited.

"That should do it for now." Jesse stood. "If you will excuse me, Oliver, I'll join my ladies."

"Certainly, Jesse. If you would like to visit Arlington tomorrow, I will arrange for a carriage."

Jesse's smile faded. Though he couldn't have said why, a sudden feeling of doom washed over him.

Chapter 33

The night held no comforts for Jesse. The silvery glow of the moon shining in through the open shutters cast shadows with its brightness, and in its light he rose to prowl the room, with more than occasional glances toward the softly curved form in the bed. He counted himself luckier than most men. In truth, if he hadn't happened upon Frank Donnelly's horse, he would have never met and married Rebecca. For all the abuse he had suffered, it was well worth what he had gained in a wife.

For a long time, he contemplated his sleeping bride. Her golden curls spread like a wide fan over the downy pillow, touching her pale shoulders. Her slender hand rested on the flat of her stomach, and in the gentle glow of moonlight, the sapphire and rose-gold band gleamed with its own luster.

"You are my wife, Rebecca Starr Fitzroy. I swear by all that is holy that any man who dares harm you, my daughter, or my mother will burn in hell." He didn't realize he had spoken aloud.

"Jesse?" Rebecca's voice cracked with sleep, and she rubbed a hand across her brow as if to clear her mind. "I dreamed you had left me." Her velvety brown eyes caught his and held them. "Do dreams come true?"

He shrugged. "Sometimes, but mostly because you want them to and work at it." The bed dipped when he sat beside her. Reaching out a hand, and grinning in a lopsided, roguish way, he smoothed her sleep-tossed curls. "I'll never leave you, Rebecca. Not of my own free will. Never!"

Tears traced down the side of her face. Gently, Jesse pulled her into his arms and kissed her trembling mouth. Her worried whisper came against his lips. "Do you know how much I love you?"

She locked her arms around his neck and nestled in the comfort of his encircling arms. At her soft, inviting smile, he nuzzled her throat while his hand explored softer places. His voice rasped with lust. "Why don't you show me?"

She giggled, nibbling at his ear, and answered his caress by curving her body seductively against his. She kissed him with such passion that he trembled with eagerness, and in a sudden moment, she lay beneath him. He heard his own moaning—such pleasure, such gasping, breaking waves of pleasure, his body out of control and her voice in his ear, whispering in tandem with the pounding pleasure as she kissed him wildly, violently, as if she could not get enough of him. He wanted to absorb every sound of her pleasure into his body.

And then his culmination—that one, long, thrusting, reaching climax to their passionate lovemaking—and he collapsed, rolling to his side and cradling her in his arms.

Instinctively he knew Rebecca was going to bring a lot more to his life than carnal pleasure. Before she came, his life had been a vast wasteland. He rolled over, his hands behind his head, and lay smiling in the darkness. He closed his eyes, drifting on the edges of sleep.

"Jesse?" Her voice sounded urgent. She propped on an elbow, and gazed down at him.

"What?" he demanded quietly.

"Describe your half-brother to me."

"What the bloody—"

"Please. It's important."

He sighed and kissed the tip of her nose. "Lawrence is older by five years. The last time I saw him, he was shorter, coming just above my shoulder, reed thin. His skin and hair were pale. He always looked sickly. He had long fingers and soft hands. His eyes are amber, almost like the eyes of a tiger—cunning and malevolent."

Jesse looked at her pensively, and a bit torn. "Will you tell me what's going on inside of your head?"

"Who looked the most like your father—you or your brother?"

Jesse frowned as he considered her question. "Those who had known my father since birth often remarked that I could easily be mistaken for his younger self. Why do you ask?"

She stared at him. "It hurt me to the depths of my soul to hear all you've suffered because of Lawrence's greed. And now that you have described him, it puzzles me that your father could have sired two sons so totally different in stature, coloring, hair, eyes, character, and morality."

His response was to simply stare at her. She put her hand to her mouth. "I'm sorry. I should have kept such thoughts to myself."

Jesse's gaze narrowed and his jawline tightened. He heaved a great and beleaguered sigh. His mind was on the long ago and the far away. There was something…something he seemed to remember…a memory he couldn't quite call forward.

He assured his wife with a kiss. "It's not anything I haven't thought myself."

He touched her nose and whispered, "Close your eyes, my sweet. You've had a busy day."

"Jesse?"

"Hmm?"

"I don't mean to be contrary…" She hesitated.

"Go on, say it."

"Revenge may be sweet, and there are some people who deserve exactly what they get, but don't let it eat you up on the inside. Men like your half-brother always get their comeuppance. Sooner or later, Lawrence will get his."

She rolled to her side.

Jesse tucked his hands behind his head and stared at the ceiling. Giving deep thought to Rebecca's observations, he allowed his mind to drift backward ten years.

Just before his father gasped his last breath, he had motioned for Jesse to lean close. Jesse had struggled to understand the unintelligible words. He'd been about to ask his father to speak slower when Lawrence had entered the room with his usual simpering swagger. He had climbed up on the massive four-poster bed and, balancing on his knees, hovered over the pale figure that stared up with frightened eyes.

"Dear, dear Papa, whenever are you going to give up the ghost?" Lawrence's laughter reminded Jesse of a braying ass.

He remembered grabbing Lawrence by the arm,

yanking him from the bed, and swinging him so hard that he slammed against the wall and slid into a limp heap. Jesse then lifted his brother to his feet and threw him into the hallway.

He had immediately returned to his father's side. "As long as I'm here, you will never have to fear Lawrence."

Addison managed a smile as he reached up to touch Jesse's face. Jesse watched his father struggle to form words. The effort was too much. Viscount Addison Starr Fitzroy's last utterance had sounded like a whistling teakettle.

Noelle's whimper intruded into Jesse's deep contemplation. He eased to the bassinette and straightened the tangle of blankets to tuck around her tiny form. He stroked her head, murmuring soft words to soothe her.

Lest his bride find his side of the bed empty, he crawled beneath the covers to join her again, but sleep eluded him. He longed for revenge. There was nothing noble about his desire to hurt his brother the way he had been hurt, but it had given him a reason to go on living, and he wasn't ready to relinquish it yet.

He closed his eyes and conjured the image of his father. Those blue eyes, always merry, contrasted with his tanned complexion. Addison was tall, lean, powerfully built with broad shoulders, and exuded casual confidence. His easygoing amiability could be quite misleading to any enemy he might encounter. He was a man to be admired and respected, a man who should have lived to bounce grandchildren on his knees.

Rebecca made a sleepy noise as she rolled over, draping her arm across Jesse's chest. He brushed a strand of hair from her temple, stroked her cheek with the lightest of touches, and ran a thumb over the curve of her lower lip. A surge of emotions swept over him. He looked at her for a long moment until his eyes closed and he sank slowly into soft, luxurious darkness.

****

Brilliant rays of silvery-yellow sunlight streamed through the open window.

Jesse stirred, moaning, mumbling unintelligible words.

Rebecca knelt beside the bed. Her chest ached with worry.

"Not going to…let it hap-happen." He pressed his lips tight. His fists were clenched, and she realized that he was seeing some highly disturbing scene that vividly lived inside his mind.

She gently nudged his shoulder. "Jesse, wake up."

He muttered to himself, looking at her with vivid blue eyes that saw something else.

She sought to calm her rising panic. "Jesse, shall I get your mother? Are you ill?"

The snapping sapphire fire left his eyes and a confused, bewildered look replaced it. He squinted, as if trying to clear the fog. "Re-Rebecca?"

Tears clouded her eyes. She smoothed the heavy wave from his brow. "Yes, it's me. You were dreaming, and mumbling words that didn't make any sense."

He propped himself against the headboard and scrubbed both hands over his face. "I don't remember. What was I saying?"

Rebecca shrugged and shook her head. "It sounded like—'la-ish-ba'ard-nomo-shon." She shrugged her shoulders. "I'm not well versed in foreign languages."

"It's gibberish and nothing else."

She placed her hand in his. "Tell me about your dream."

A knock sounded. Rebecca rushed to open the door a crack. A young maid curtsied. "'Scuse me, mum, but milady sends word that breakfast is 'alf an 'our. Do ye be needin' anythin'?"

Rebecca quickly handed the maid four empty baby bottles. "If you please, these need washing and filled with warm milk." She thanked the maid and assured her they would not be late.

Dressed in her mauve suit, her sleek black hair braided and coiled in a neat tiara, Leotie smiled at the maid and entered the room. Rebecca quickly shut the door and grabbed her mother-in-law's hand. She whispered, "We're a bit slow. Jesse had a terrible nightmare. Would you please see to Noelle while we dress for breakfast?"

Leotie peeked over Rebecca's shoulder at her son clad in white drawers, his back turned. The old puckered scars marred his tanned flesh. She clenched her jaw into a grimace, and answered with a nod.

Jesse faced his mother. He shifted his glance from her to Rebecca and back again. He cocked one eyebrow. "Have neither of you no shame, standing there staring at me in my boxers?"

Leotie laughed. "I have seen you in your bare bottom, my son."

He groaned his response.

Leotie said, "When we go for our morning ride, you must tell me about your dream."

His voice was low and considerate. "It's nothing. I barely remember it."

"Dreams are sacred to the Kiowa people. A dream has its own reality, my son. It is said that all can be found within your night visions."

His mother lifted Noelle from the bassinette. "We will talk more when there are no curious ears listening."

With the baby in her arms, she crossed the room and, before opening the door, said, "Jesse, the young servant said the cook was serving pancakes. What is a pancake, and do we eat it with our fingers?"

He flashed a genuine smile. Rebecca's heart swelled with adoration as he explained that pancakes were much like the Kiowa's fry bread. He tucked the tail of his white linen shirt into the waistband of his pants. "Watch Rebecca and do everything she does."

He shrugged into a black frock coat. "Let's not keep our hosts waiting."

****

Jesse and his ladies joined Lady Beatrice in the Garden Room for breakfast. The Corinthian columns that graced the elegant round room brought a nostalgic shudder to Rebecca, a reminder of the marbled columns in her childhood home.

She said, "This is a lovely room, Bea. It's like an outdoor paradise."

"Thank you, my dear. I especially enjoy it on dreary days like this." Lady Beatrice opened the linen napkin. She directed her attention to Jesse. "Ollie sends his regrets. My poor dear received an urgent message, something about the Scotch Whisky regulations. Oh, well, such is the life of a parliament barrister."

Jesse nodded. He commented that the room with its koi pond and lily pads reminded him of the Zen gardens he'd seen while in Japan.

Lady Bea dabbed her lips with the napkin. She pointed to a pergola with an attached hammock adorned with colorful pillows, and a waterfall made of stacked stones. "Ollie's duties often keep him away for days. This is, as you say, Jesse, my Zen place. The sound of gurgling water is soothing, don't you agree?" She seemed to direct her comment to Leotie.

"I have lived my entire life on the plains of Oklahoma. Never have my eyes seen such as this. The outside is inside. It is mystical."

Breakfast consisted of chitter-chatter until Lady Bea said, "'Tis typical English weather, gray mist which leaves everything feeling damp and limp." She sighed. "That is why Ollie arranged with our stable master to ready a carriage for you. And Rebecca, my dear, if you would rather not expose your precious baby to the elements, our Zoe is one of twelve. She is quite good with children."

A twinge of panic raced through Rebecca. She hesitated. "Noelle has never…I mean…"

Lady Bea tut-tutted. "I quite understand, my dear. Why, I remember when Oliver, Jr. and Olivia—twins, you know—were still in their nappies. I feared that if they were out of my sight for one minute, disaster might strike. But I assure you, Zoe is as trustworthy as they come."

Leotie reached over to lay her hand on Rebecca's, while Jesse reached for another scone and calmly buttered it.

Lady Bea answered Jesse's questions about his father's house. "We hired some of Arlington's staff. In fact, Mrs. Tweedy is in charge of our kitchen." She good-naturedly wagged a finger. "If you intend to hire her away from me, I will double her wages."

Comments were exchanged regarding the house and gardens, and acquiring new staff if Jesse decided to take up permanent residence.

Rebecca realized she had left the conversation while she went woolgathering. Jesse said, "Rebecca?"

"Okay," she said, as much to herself as to the people staring at her. "Thank you for a lovely breakfast, Bea."

Lady Bea smiled and clapped her hands together. "Wonderful. Mrs. Tweedy has prepared a picnic basket for you."

Chapter 34

Jesse clucked the horse into motion. They passed very few houses. It was almost as if the track from Hardwick Hall ran directly to Arlington. He felt as if he were stepping into his past, the memories of his home—the happiness and the grief—deeply buried beneath his skin.

The redolent scent of apples reminded him of accepting Lawrence's dare to climb out on a limb to pluck a particular apple. The limb broke. Lawrence had laughed as he used the heel of his boot to squash the large red pomme. Jesse remembered forcing back tears. He'd cradled his painfully broken arm and walked home.

He'd asked, "Why does Lawrence hate me, Father?"

Addison, sitting in a chair next to the bed, had leaned forward to brush the wave of black hair from Jesse's forehead. "I don't know, son. Sometimes, people are like animals. When they are cross-bred, something gets mixed up in their bloodlines and they seem to lose their kindness."

Jesse's six-year-old mind didn't quite understand what his father had meant. He said, "Maybe you should geld Lawrence like you do the stallions that are mean. You think that would make him like me, Father?"

Addison had laughed. "If only it were that simple."

He'd kissed Jesse on top of the head and bade him close his eyes and dream pleasant dreams.

Time seemed suspended as the sun struggled to break through the haze of gray mist. A sharp breeze made the aspen leaves quake and ripple. Memories swarmed over him, hovering like fog, waiting to swallow him up and sap the very life out of him.

Suddenly, a bolt of lightning flashed, bright and white. The horse whinnied and tried to rear up. Jesse steadied the animal with a calm voice.

Before the flash dimmed, a growing roll of thunder flared rapidly and ended in an ear-splitting crack.

Rebecca grabbed Jesse's arm. "How much farther?"

Rattling gusts of wind shook the buggy. Jesse flapped the leathers to encourage the horse into a gallop. "Any minute now."

Trees swayed to and fro in a nervous frenzy. The gully-washed lane opened to a wide circular drive inlaid with white brick now adorned with leaves and green lichen. In the center of the drive stood a large carved stone fountain, and behind the fountain the massive mansion appeared like a gray ghost.

The rain thrummed a steady drumbeat on the roof of the carriage as Jesse pulled the nervous horse to a halt. Setting the brake, he jumped to the ground and reached up to pull first Rebecca into his strong arms and set her feet to the pavement, and then his mother. The women dashed up the steps with Jesse trailing after.

He gripped the ornate doorknob. "It's locked," he shouted over the deafening downpour. "There is a spare key hidden in the stable. Stay here."

He raced down the steps, leapt into the buggy, and hied-up the horse.

Damp and shivering, Rebecca and Leotie huddled together for warmth. Rebecca put her mouth close to Leotie's ear. "I'm thankful Noelle is safe and warm with Lady Beatrice."

It was several minutes before Jesse appeared with the picnic basket, splashing through the looming darkness. His hands shaking with cold, he handed Rebecca the basket, then inserted the key and turned the knob. The door didn't open. He placed his shoulder against the door and shoved. A strong musty odor greeted them as it opened.

It took a moment for their eyes to adjust to the dark interior. Jesse led the women to the parlor. "Aha," he remarked. "Thankfully, there is kindling."

In moments, he had a fire crackling cheerfully in the hearth, casting wavering shadows across the red silk damask walls. Large cobwebs waved from the three-tiered crystal chandelier.

Leotie sneezed, and sneezed, and sneezed again.

"Mother, are you coming down with a fever?"

She used the hem of her sodden skirt to wipe the itchiness from her eyes. "No, it's from the dust." She cleared the rasp from her throat, her eyes wide with amazement. "This is Addison's home...your home?"

"It is, but I care little for gilt and pomp and finery, and neither did Father." Jesse spread his arms wide. "This was all Henrietta's doing. 'Tis a wonder Father didn't go bankrupt with all her frivolous spending."

Rebecca stepped closer to the fire. She turned to warm her backside. "I thought my parents' house was grand, but theirs pales in comparison to this."

Jesse laughed with little humor. "Let's change the subject." He lifted the picnic basket. "I'm famished."

Rebecca looked away for a moment. "Without candles or a lantern, it's too dark to explore the upper level. How many bedrooms?"

He was thunderstruck at her question. Surely she wasn't…not yet…was she?

She faced him and raised one eyebrow, as if waiting for him to answer her question.

"Ten. Why do you ask?"

She smiled, and again he was thunderstruck. "There are three of us, plus we already have one child." The implication of her smile pleasantly threw him off balance.

"Are you—?"

Mirth lighted her eyes. "I'm merely thinking about the future. And, like you, I'm famished."

Rebecca helped Leotie remove a dust-covered sheet that revealed a gold-colored velvet settee. They spread the cloth on the floor in front of the fireplace. Jesse used his pocket knife to open the bottle of wine.

Lunch was a solemn affair. The house was very quiet, so quiet the next peal of thunder sounded as if it were inside the room. Rebecca gave a startled cry, sloshing wine from her goblet. She managed a feeble smile. "Jesse, tell Leotie about your dream."

He tilted his head to one side, thinking hard. "All I remember is feeling unsettled when I awoke."

Between bits of her sandwich, Rebecca said, "And he mumbled something that sounded like—'la-ish-ba'ard-nomo-shon."

Leotie shrugged her shoulders. "It is not Kiowa or Lakota."

"I've told her—it's gibberish." Jesse stood and walked to the window. "Rain's stopped."

Rebecca and Leotie draped the coverlet over the settee and repacked the wicker basket. Rebecca said, "I am eager to hold Noelle in my arms."

Outside, pink and orange smeared the sky; the dark gray had disappeared. Insects hummed, leaves rustled quietly, and birds called in the treetops.

Jesse brought the carriage around. He assisted Rebecca in first. As he cupped his mother's elbow, she looked up toward the second floor and rubbed her hands up and down her arms as if warding off a chill. "Is that where Addison died?"

Jesse sighed. "It is."

She touched his face. "This house has a soul. It begs for happiness, but—"

He stared into the shadows of her eyes. "But what, Mother?"

She moaned low in her throat. "You must never let your guard down, my son. This is all I know."

****

Lawrence Fitzroy sweltered inside the steam room. Sweating out the aftereffects of smoking the hookah pipes, he wanted to lie down and die. His skin itched incessantly, stomach cramps doubled him over, and the merest taste or scent of food or drink brought on violent bouts of vomiting.

To steady his tremors, he used both hands to ladle more water over the hot stones. He needed more steam to cleanse his pores. Three days was all he needed to get through the withdrawals, three days to clear his brain of the opiate maggots that distorted his mind.

Maybe he was hallucinating. Opium did that.

Maybe he had imagined the security agent from the shipping port had brought news of Jesse Starr's arrival in London. Had he paid the scoundrel, or had he run a rapier through the man's heart? He couldn't remember.

The face of his bastard half-brother was scored into his memory, and nothing could force the image to flee. Clenching his eyes tightly, an almost inhuman, raging howl rose from his throat.

The bathhouse owner shoved the heavy wooden door open. "Blimey, gov'ner, don't ye be a-dyin' in me 'stablishment. 'Tain't good fer me business, ye know."

Certain blood was pouring from his eyes; Lawrence lurched off the wooden bench. His emaciated body fully exposed, he screamed, "Get out, you fool. Lock the door, and don't come back until I call for you."

The squat man stared at the contorted face. "Aye, gov'ner. Scared the bloody bejeebers out'n me, ye did."

It was four days later when a loud pounding on the door caused the snores of the bath attendant, Jonesy, to end in a choking gurgle. He rolled himself upright; a rumbling belch cleared his throat. He let his ire at being so rudely aroused sound in the tone of his bellow.

"Aye, ye bloody bugger!" he roared. "Would ye strip the plank from its hinges? I'm comin'.'"

Standing naked as the day he was born, Lawrence demanded, "Bring my clothes, and make certain they are freshly cleaned."

Jonesy snickered. "Aye, yer 'ighness."

An angry growl warned Jonesy, and he stumbled back behind the door, slamming it with a solid clank.

When the door opened again, Lawrence stopped his agitated prowling and accepted the neatly folded clothing. He sniffed to check their freshness.

"Get out, and this time leave the bloody door open."

Hatred rose in Lawrence's chest, and an odd sense of elation bloomed. Maniacal laughter threatened, and he covered his face with his hands to shut out the vision of Jesse's blue eyes.

Chapter 35

Two days after the storm, Jesse drove Rebecca to Arlington. "I wanted you to see the house alone. Whatever you like or don't like, we'll change."

Rebecca stiffened, somewhat afraid. "You're not leaving, are you?"

He touched her cheek. "Only to the stables to take inventory. Shout if you need me."

She smiled up at him. "I want a home that is warm and welcoming. Not an ostentatious mausoleum."

"Whatever makes you happy, my sweet." He left her then.

The walk up the front steps was a short one, but it could have been a hundred miles, or a thousand. Rebecca's feet, not to mention her heart, were heavy. Only a few weeks ago, she had climbed the steps to her childhood home. It too had been cold and unfeeling, like her parents.

She entered the mansion through the great hall, a massive room lined with gilt chairs and portraits on the walls at either side. She looked at each one and noted there were none of a little boy with black hair and blue eyes, or of a man who had he lived might have resembled Jesse.

From there, she proceeded to the dining room. A table with twelve chairs sat in the center of the room. More pictures of the same people lined the walls.

The kitchen was next. A large room with an indoor water supply, a massive stove in dire need of cleaning, a square pinewood table with eight chairs, and cupboard with doors. The floor, fashioned of lacquered wood, was laden with layers of dust, but nonetheless beautiful. A good mopping and waxing would bring it to life.

She reentered the great hall and went into the parlor, where she, Leotie, and Jesse had picnicked on the morning of the storm. It boasted a floor-to-ceiling fireplace. Her father would have coveted it. The room was overly crowded with furniture, including two settees and several red-cushioned armchairs. She couldn't imagine herself sewing by the fire or Jesse reading the newspaper in a chair next to hers.

She explored the study next—definitely a man's room, with a large mahogany desk, an overstuffed brown leather chair, and a bookcase with empty shelves. Books lay strewn across the room, as if someone had deliberately thrown them from the bookcase. It saddened her to see the abuse of such fine tomes.

The staircase was wide, with a graceful curve of ascending steps. Her hand came away dusty from the banister railing. She made her way upward, slowly, an ominous feeling draped over her, as heavy as the dust on the handrail. The upstairs hallway was divided, with an east wing and a west wing. The east wing consisted of three bedrooms on one side of the hall and three on the other side. The west wing had three smaller bedrooms, and at the end of the hall a set of double doors. Somehow she knew this was Addison's room. She drew in a breath and stepped over the threshold.

The intricately carved four-poster bed sat high off the floor. Another marble fireplace, a twin of the one downstairs, and a large painting of a magnificent dappled gray stallion, and a smaller painting of a little boy sitting in a man's lap. A large slash formed an X through the faces. She struggled to hold her temper and to keep from bursting into tears as she held the pieces together. This had to be Jesse and his father. But who would be cruel enough to destroy such a precious memory?

Anger caused her heart to thump. Two names came to mind—Lawrence or Henrietta.

She continued her tour of the room. The drapes were heavy green velvet, and there were two gigantic wardrobes against one wall. Another door led to a surprising discovery—a clawfoot bathtub, a marble-topped vanity that spanned the entire wall with an equally long mirror, a pull-chain toilet, and a tiled floor.

She was startled, to say the least, when she turned to leave this magnificent suite and found Jesse quietly observing her.

His eyes flashed blue fire. "Do you find this room to your liking?"

She met the sparks in his eyes. "With a lot of cleaning it will do, especially the bed."

He took her by the arms and lifted her onto her tiptoes. He pulled her into his arms and kissed her so hard she feared she might swoon. She surrendered to it, even moaned a little because it aroused such a ferocious need in her.

Then he lifted his head and in complete contrast he put her away from him. "What the bloody hell…" He walked to the ruined painting and gazed at it a long time.

Rebecca touched his arm, her voice almost a whisper. "It's you and your father, isn't it?"

He answered with a nod.

"The cuts are clean. Perhaps Lady Bea knows of a skilled artist who can restore it like new."

He stiffened but managed a somewhat reasonable smile. "Perhaps."

She desired to soothe his underlying anger. "With a few womanly touches here and there, this will make a lovely master bedroom." Trying to keep her voice light, she added, "I promise it will be just the right mixture of masculine and feminine."

His arms tightened around her, and she leaned against him.

"Jesse?"

"Yes?" His voice was low and hollow.

"I promise to make this a happy home."

He smiled. "I know." His arms tightened around her. "Shall we begin tomorrow?"

She linked her arm through his and tugged him toward the doorway. "Let's go tell Leotie and Noelle."

****

Lady Beatrice had volunteered to make contact with friends who could recommend the elite of service staff. Within days, there were maids, kitchen workers, grounds keepers, and stable hands trailing in and out of Arlington—some new and several who had known Jesse since he was a wee lad. Boisterous joviality vibrated through the house as dust covers were stripped from furniture and cleaning rags and polish were applied to every inch of every room. Not to be outdone by his wife, Sir Oliver had procured two invitations to the Kensington royal horse auction, a ten-day-long affair.

Jesse's first order to the workers was to remove every portrait of Henrietta and Lawrence. "If there is any article of clothing, jewelry, or other items that Henrietta or Lawrence left behind, gather it all, as well as any furniture items my ladies wish to discard. Whatever money it brings at the Billingsgate market will be divided equally amongst you."

His comment was met with cocked eyebrows and surprised smiles.

He pointed to a man and a freckle-faced lad of approximately thirteen. "Mr. Poole, you and your son are charged with the responsibility of assisting my wife and mother with this duty."

The man doffed his hat. "'Twill be me and Charlie's pleasure, sire."

Amidst the flurry of activity, Lady Beatrice declared she would simply perish if Mrs. Tweedy returned to Arlington. "Mrs. Caldwell is Mrs. Tweedy's sister, and a very fine cook. I'm quite certain she will serve you well." Then, in a gesture befitting any actress, she dramatically clasped her hands to her breast. "And lastly, my dearest Rebecca, our precious Noelle deserves a special nursemaid who might also serve as governess. Zoe can read and write and do sums. She can embroider and knit, has legible penmanship, and adores Noelle. She is my gift to you to make amends for keeping Mrs. Tweedy."

Rebecca hugged the gregarious woman, assuring her there were no hard feelings. "As soon as the house is ready to receive guests, you will be the very first to see the redecoration, before the invitations are sent for the open house celebration."

Lady Bea clapped her hands together and, with a melodramatic sigh, said, "I do so love parties. Now, my dear, escort me to my carriage. I must be off."

It delighted Rebecca to see the pleasure on Jesse's face when he came to stand beside her. "We'll have a fine stable of thoroughbreds, and I will take great care in selecting mounts for you and Mother."

She reached up and straightened his ascot. "It was good of Sir Oliver to arrange invitations to the royal auction. It sounds...well...royal. Do you think he might acquire tickets for Leotie and me?"

He feigned a frown. "'Tis a rather fancy affair—for men only."

Rebecca placed her hands on her hips. "Oh!" She exaggerated the word.

As he left for the auction, Leotie demurely requested, "The Kiowa are partial to painted ponies. Do not bring me a swaybacked nag. One with a little fire will suit me just fine."

Taking a cue from Leotie, Rebecca made her own request. "I should like a pinto as well, not a tall horse, and one with an even temper."

Jesse laughed. He drew Rebecca close and held her. She bemoaned, "Ten days will seem like a lifetime."

He looked back at the house. "With all the work ahead of you, the time will fly by as if it had sprouted wings."

She playfully slapped his arm. "I suppose."

He stepped into the white brougham and waved. She and Leotie stood together, watching the carriage negotiate the circular drive.

Rebecca ran a little distance and shouted, "No frou-frou sidesaddles."

He poked his head through the open window. "What?"

"Oklahoma women ride astride," Rebecca yelled.

Jesse acknowledged her request with a salute and a loud guffaw.

She sighed. "I am thankful you are with me, Leotie. I don't think I'd enjoy staying in this house alone."

Leotie laughed. "How can you say you are alone when there enough people here to call a tribe?"

They walked arm in arm up the marble steps to the wide sweeping porch. "Our lives were much simpler on the prairie. Do you ever think of going back?"

The Kiowa woman remained quiet for a long moment. "I do not. Yes, our lives were simpler, but the food was scarce, the winters harsh, and death was always scratching at the tipi doors." Her forehead furrowed, pensive. "You can never go back. The place you left is never the way you imagine in your mind. This is our home now. We must make it a joyful place, a place to build memories for Noelle and her brothers and sisters, and for their children. Yes?"

Rebecca hugged her mother-in-law. Leotie's words rang true, a dark reminder of how she had imagined an open-armed welcome from her parents. Instead, she had huddled on the doorsteps of a closed church with only an umbrella to shelter Noelle from the pouring rain. "I hope to someday be as wise as you."

Much to her surprise, the days did seem to have sprouted wings. The trip to Billingsgate market had turned a healthy sum. Mr. Poole and his son Charlie proved their worth. As a reward, Rebecca suggested the boy choose a puppy.

She made him promise to always treat the little dog with kindness. Much to her delight, the boy had thrown his arms around her for a brief hug.

Mr. Poole pulled a handkerchief from his back pocket to blow his nose. "I be thankin' ye kindly, me ledy. Charlie ain't had an easy time of it since the angels took 'is mum from us, and jobs being scarce…" His voice choked with emotion, and he cleared his throat. "We'll serve ye an' Ledy 'otie well, won't we, son?"

Charlie answered with a wide grin that grew even wider when the black-and-white spotted puppy licked him on the face. "'Is name be Spot."

Rebecca patted his arm. Deep inside, she sensed young Charlie and his father were men of their word.

Save for select pieces of furniture, Addison's four-poster bed, and a bed of Leotie's choosing, the mansion was starkly vacant. Rebecca filled her days conversing with furniture makers, wallpaper contractors, seamstresses both for draperies and bedding and for wardrobes for herself, Jesse, Noelle, and Leotie.

She enjoyed selecting elegant but inviting wallpaper patterns for each room and drapery fabrics in bold and subtle blues, warm grays, mauve, and forest green. Quite to her satisfaction was the artist who had seamlessly repaired the painting of Jesse and his father. Impressed with his work, she had commissioned him to paint portraits of Leotie, Noelle, herself, and Jesse.

Leotie had busied herself marking out a large outdoor space for a kitchen garden. Mr. Poole and Charlie had assigned themselves as her designated helpers. When all the rows were planted with carrots, beans, beets, chard, pumpkin, and strawberries, leeks, and a variety of herbs, the three of them tackled the overgrown flower gardens—weeding and pruning to restore the faded beauty of the vibrant red roses, pink geraniums, purple heather, and lilies in colors of the rainbow.

Mr. Poole had even fashioned an enclosed seat swing for Noelle. He and Charlie had taken the garden chairs, sanded away layers of rust, and painted them a bright white, while she and Leotie had labored to sew canvas cushions, pricking their fingers often.

Clear blue water flowed in the garden pond, now filled with colorful koi. Mr. Poole had fashioned a fine mesh cover to keep the birds of prey from stealing the fish.

The sun had set on the thirteenth day, and Rebecca fretted over Jesse's delay. The hypnotic back and forth swaying of Noelle's swing had Rebecca's eyes fluttering shut, but neighs and whinnies and the clattering of many hooves rescued her from the descent into a black abyss of nightmares.

Leotie shouted, "He's home! Jesse is home and bringing a fine string of horses."

Rebecca sat up and widened her eyes to rid them of sleep. A sense of approaching doom rippled up and down her body; she had been somewhere between dark and light and Lawrence and madness.

She grabbed Noelle from the swing, hugging her, and near tears.

Chapter 36

Each month the mansion progressed further from overbearing opulence to comfortable homeyness. After three months of renovations, it had become a place of gaiety and comfort. With Leotie's green thumb, the flower gardens burst with colorful profusions, and the vegetables from the kitchen garden were a particular delight for Mrs. Caldwell.

The stable boasted a sorrel thoroughbred stallion with impressive bloodlines, six brood mares, and a gray dappled gelding that was Jesse's personal mount. He had explained that after the auction he had searched high and low for pintos. The coloration simply didn't exist in England, apparently, but his search was the reason for his delay in returning home.

Forgiving him was easy. Rebecca immediately fell in love with the doe-eyed, flaxen-maned chestnut gelding Jesse had selected for her, and a sassy black mare with a white blaze thrilled Leotie.

The women enjoyed daily rides, while Jesse often spent time in the city learning about the multiple businesses he had inherited from his father.

Rebecca swallowed back the butterflies building in her stomach. She and Leotie had planned the open house down to the last detail, and Jesse had declared the first day of September a time of celebration. Tonight they would host their first gala—an open house to welcome new and old friends.

Rebecca pressed her hands to her stomach. She leaned close to Leotie and said, "Now I understand why my mother was always in a tizzy before party guests arrived."

Leotie clasped her hands together. "I am a Kiowa woman. I am different. What if these people treat me with nastiness like the white-eyes did in Oklahoma?"

Rebecca reached over and took her mother-in-law's hand. "You are a beautiful, intelligent woman. Unkindness toward you will not be tolerated. I pity anyone who dares treat you differently. Such a person will answer to Jesse, unless I get to them first."

Dressed in fawn-colored breeches and matching waistcoat, spit-and-polished black boots, Jesse smiled as he strolled toward his wife and mother.

"He is handsome, isn't he?" Rebecca sighed at the sight of her husband.

"Like his father." Leotie gave Rebecca's hand a little squeeze.

"Carriages are arriving. Time to greet our guests." He offered an arm to each of his ladies to escort them to the great hall.

Smoothing her gown, Rebecca drew in a deep breath, ready to smile and play hostess, which she did with aplomb. After the crush of people had settled, Jesse nodded for the musicians to play.

Sir Oliver danced with Rebecca and then Leotie. As a matter of courtesy, Jesse waltzed with Lady Bea. She tittered, "A lovely party. Simply glorious."

The musicians struck up a rigadoon. Dancing to the lively tune left couples breathless and seeking the punch bowl. Plates were filled and refilled with food.

Events began to drag out interminably, and Rebecca smiled graciously through it all, but her immense relief came when the tall hall clock chimed and, turning, Jesse verified the hour as midnight and announced the guests' carriages awaited. He had given a nod so slight that only she and Mr. Poole recognized it as a signal to advise the valet to alert the drivers the party was over.

Viscount and Viscountess Merryvale declared, "Smashing party. Can't remember when we've had so much fun."

"Ta and ta." Dame Ackerman declared, "I hope your cook won't mind sharing her canapé recipes with my cook."

The Earl of Warwick invited Jesse to join the royal polo club.

It seemed everyone had enjoyed the merrymaking and all were reluctant to leave. An hour passed before the doors were locked and the lights doused.

****

The moon hung low and skimmed the treetops. Where it penetrated the high canopies it lit the cool but oddly tense night with an eerie gray cast. There was an urging in him that made Lawrence edgy. The house seemed to beckon. Its great dark hulk drew him. All the lights were darkened now, and he knew the revelers had departed and those inside were abed.

A familiar bulk loomed beside him, and reaching out his hand Lawrence felt the bole, identifying the apple tree. The one with the rotten limb. He swallowed and nearly choked on the silent chuckle as he recalled how, knowing the limb was rotten, he had cajoled his half-breed brother to pick a particular apple.

He leaned against the wood and stared upward

toward the open doors that marked *their* room. His mind wandered until it touched on a scene of his father's frightened but accusing eyes, blue flints that had damned him. The vision was most distasteful, and Lawrence banished it from his mind. Thus freed, his thoughts trod forward to the night he had watched the men he'd hired attack Jesse's coach. They had beaten him senseless and then forced laudanum down his throat to insure he wouldn't awaken until days out to sea. He'd sold the little wog to Joseph Bunko, a dealer of men. Bunko often sold them into slavery, and the ones he couldn't convert into rapscallions, he fed to the sharks.

A keening wail lodged in Lawrence's throat. All these years, all these bloody years, he'd felt assured that the dark-skinned, dark-haired son of a whore that had stolen his title, prestige, fortune, Arlington—everything—was dead.

He dabbed at his sweat-moistened brow. From head to toe, his body vibrated with tremors. Bloody damn, he'd kill for just one puff on the hookah. No, make that two hundred puffs.

He closed his eyes and rested his head against the tree. She was a beauty, with her fair skin and her hair like spun gold. After he castrated his bastard brother, he'd taste the deliciousness of Jesse's bride, and then he'd slowly disfigure her beautiful face while Jesse watched. And the Indian woman, the bitch his father had shagged…he had special plans for her. In the end, just like his father, they would all die.

He clapped his hands over his mouth to hold in the hysterical giggle.

****

Rebecca came awake with a start and then lay still, wondering what had intruded into her sleep to shatter it so completely. The clock on the mantel delicately chimed the fourth hour as she listened. Jesse's naked body snuggled against her back, and his arm rested on her hip. Then she realized that he, too, lay tense and rigid, his breathing subdued. She shifted on the pillow and in the dim glow from the moon saw that he was propped on an elbow, staring across the dark room toward the door. Then she heard it, the rattle of the doorknob as it twisted and slowly eased back in place. The locked portal gave no entry. She shifted her gaze toward her husband. He lifted a finger to his lips as a caution to remain quiet.

Slipping carefully from the bed, he reached for his breeches and pulled them on. With a quick, noiseless stride he crossed the room, and Rebecca snatched her nightgown over her head. If he was going to confront anyone beyond the door, she was not going to be caught naked.

On tiptoes, she hastened across the room to stand next to Jesse. Grabbing the iron fireplace poker, he gently turned the key in the lock. Then, in one swift movement, he flung the door wide. He stepped into the hall. Rebecca followed.

Only the deep shadows in an empty hall greeted them. Jesse motioned for Rebecca to stay put. His bare feet padded soundlessly along the wide corridor and down the hallway of the second wing where his mother slept.

Empty.

Frowning, he returned to the bedchamber where Rebecca waited next to the open door. He motioned her in and locked the door.

She joined him on the bed. Leaning close, she whispered, "Everyone is asleep. Do you think we have an intruder?"

"Old houses have creaks and groans. I'm sure it's nothing to fret over." He shucked his breeches and climbed under the downy duvet.

"I'm cold." She snuggled close to him.

"And you have on too many clothes, my sweet." His rolled the hem of her gown upward over her hip.

Their bodies were cold, but their kisses flamed the stirring heat of passion. She murmured against his lips. "I'm hungry, and it isn't for cake."

"Then let me satisfy your appetite." Jesse's lips nibbled at the soft flesh of her shoulder and sank warmly against her creamy throat, then paused to taste an earlobe. He abruptly sat up, leaving Rebecca to stare at him in surprise.

"What the bloody hell is that?" He tilted his head to listen better. Into the silence of the room came the faint but angry whinny of a horse. "The horses never make a fuss at night."

He threw back the covers and again snatched on his breeches. "It must be something Mr. Standish can't handle." He grabbed the shirt draped over a chair. "I'll go see." Pulling the shirt over his head, he spoke through the material. "Lock the door behind you. Don't let anyone in unless it's me or Mother."

Chills rippled over Rebecca. She tried to keep the fear from her voice. "Jesse, don't go. I have a bad feeling."

He leaned onto the mattress and placed a quick kiss on her lips. "I won't be gone long. Keep my side of the bed warm."

She followed him to the door, a frown on her face. "Please be careful." She locked the door behind him. Too restless to lie in bed, she shivered in her thin nightgown. Memories of being alone in the cabin and watching the wolves clawing under the door assailed her. A chill had invaded the room. To stave off the shivers, she knelt before the fireplace and placed two oak logs on the hot ash. She gently blew until the ash glowed orange and tiny flames licked upward to caress the logs. Curling up in a white button-tufted chair, she soaked in the fire's beginning warmth and let her mind drift, her eyelids heavy.

Leotie's sharp shriek startled Rebecca. Her mother-in-law cried, "Fire! Jesse, wake up! The stable is on fire!"

Rebecca arose from the chair and raced to the window. Flickering tongues of fire created a macabre sight. Jesse was already racing across the yard to the stable. Her long black braid bouncing back and forth, Leotie, too, sprinted toward the heart-wrenching sound of screaming horses.

Mr. Standish, the new stable manager, joined Jesse and Leotie, as well as Mr. Poole and Charlie. She watched Jesse and Mr. Standish swing the stable doors wide. Jesse waved his arms about as if giving instructions, and then he disappeared inside the burning structure.

"Oh, God!" Rebecca managed a strangled cry. Heedless of her bare feet and thin linen nightgown, she hastened to the door. Shaking fingers fumbled with the key. "Open, damn…damn, open!"

"Milady?"

The voice behind her was low, melodious, menacing. Afraid to turn, she felt the color draining from her face. Terror numbed her.

"Turn around and let me see Arlington's new viscountess."

Her knees trembled, and she feared they might buckle beneath her. Her dread grew, and she closed her eyes for a moment trying to summon the strength to do as he commanded.

Irritation laced his voice. "Patience is not one of my virtues, Rebecca."

This time she was certain all the blood had drained from her body. A scream rose in her throat; she strangled on it. She was literally too frightened to scream.

He sniggered. "Don't look so shocked, my lovely. I know about precious Noelle, and the bitch, Lee-o-tee." He spat. "Only heathens have unpronounceable names."

He stood there, his hands resting lightly on his hips. He was of medium height, with thin shoulders. In the moonlight his face was utterly without expression. His cheeks were bleached of all color, chalk white. The corners of his mouth quivered. He was foppishly attired in brown satin breeches and matching frock coat laced with gold braid, his brownish hair straight and lank. His eyes, gold-flecked, reminded her of a winter-starved wolf stalking its prey.

She didn't remember finding another door when cleaning and redecorating the room. "How did you get in here?"

"Ah, my luv, it seems everyone was too distracted by the gala to notice an uninvited guest wending his way up the stairs." He stepped forward.

Rebecca backed closer to the door, her trembling fingers searching for the key.

"What's the matter, luv? Not afraid, hmm?"

"You're him, aren't you?"

His voice was aloof. He gazed at her with leering eyes. "Who do you think I am?"

She touched the key. Now if only she could make it turn in the lock. "I believe you are truly the…devil."

With a boisterous swagger, and with a swiftness that belied his frailty, he stepped forward, seized her arm, and jerked her savagely, pulling her off balance. Her long nails dug into his hand. His eyes were fierce. The nostrils of his sharp, beaklike nose flared, and there was a sullen curl on his lips. "You little bitch." He drew back his fist and clipped her on the jaw, knocking her down, and as she climbed to her knees, he twined his fingers through her hair, pulling her upright.

He swept over her with expressionless eyes. He exuded an aura of utterly ruthless dominance. His lips curled with a faint smile of satisfaction as he savored his power.

"Frightened?" he inquired.

"Of a cowardly dog? Never!" She clawed at his face and kicked his shin. Without shoes, the only thing she hurt was her own foot.

He backhanded her, hard. Blood spurted from her nose. He dragged her across the room, dumped her on the bed, and stretched her arms over her head and tied her hands to an ornate knob on the headboard.

He moved to her feet. She twisted and turned and lashed out with her feet. She screamed, "Help me! Jesse, Zoe, anyone, please…" Her shrill pleas were silenced when he pressed a pillow over her face.

Chapter 37

Lawrence tossed the pillow to the floor. Rebecca searched deep inside to stay her rapidly fleeting courage. He straddled her. His lean, harsh face tightened with desire. "It will spoil my fun if you die too soon."

She tried to buck against his weight. "How is it possible your father sired an amoral fiend? You and Jesse share nothing in common. Not in looks, intelligence, or goodness."

She gazed up at him cool, composed, not the least bit intimidated by her tirade. During her brief moment of unconsciousness, he had tied her spread-eagle to the bed. The blade in his hand glinted in the moonlight. Rebecca prayed.

Lawrence rocked back on his knees and loosed an exaggerated sigh. "You know what they say about bad seeds—every family has one."

Rebecca knew her best chance of surviving whatever Lawrence had in store for her was to buy time. "You know what I think?"

He seemed to give her question thought. "I really don't give a donkey's fart what you think, but because I'm feeling generous, why don't you tell me."

Rebecca's swallow echoed in her ears. She knew full well what she was about to say might be her last words. "I am the youngest of two sisters. We three have the same color hair. Two of us have eyes the same as our father, and one like our mother. Mother is tall and slender, father is short and pudgy. Two of us inherited our mother's stature, and the other takes after our father."

The dirk's sharp blade sliced through the bodice of her nightgown. The folds of fabric fell open, exposing her creamy flesh. He traced the sharp edge down the valley between her breasts. The thin thread of blood seemed to excite him. "What's your point?"

Rebecca's pulse matched the clock's loud ticking. Time seemed to drag on interminably. Her fear and anger overrode the pain. She gagged against the sweetly odoriferous perspiration beading his forehead and oozing from his pores. "You are the bastard. Not Jesse. I believe your mother was already pregnant and duped Addison Fitzroy into marriage to cover up her sin." It took superhuman effort to maintain her poise. "And that sin was *you*!"

Lawrence's eyes narrowed to mean slits. A snarl contorted his face, and his lips drew back to expose yellowed, rotting teeth. He grabbed the edges of her gown and ripped the thin material to fully expose her nakedness. Again he straddled her. He forced the dirk's blade between her teeth, and reached in to grab her tongue. Wielding the knife, he screamed, "How did you know? Who told you?"

So it was true. She had guessed correctly. Certain he was about to rip her tongue out by the roots, tears leaked from her eyes.

He coughed as if to clear the knot that blocked his voice. "Mommy dearest, that miserable piece of gutter-dung, she lied, but before I cut her tongue out, she confessed all. She'd spread her legs so many times she didn't know who had sired me. She called me a misfit, a joke, a scourge on society. When he brought Jesse home, she'd say, 'Be a good boy. Be like Jesse so your father will love you more.' *My father*." His shoulders shook with silent laughter. "In the end, the joke was on both of us. My dear ol' mum—"

"Why did you kill him, Lawrence?" His face covered with soot and his torn sleeve exposing a long red gash, Jesse sought Rebecca's eyes. A tidal wave of relief washed over her as she reveled in his calm reassurance.

Still gripping her tongue, Lawrence jerked around. Rebecca grimaced in pain.

"You gutless swine," Jesse snarled. "Your fight is with me, not my wife. Let her go and I might let you live."

Lawrence snorted as he let go of her tongue, placed his full hand over Rebecca's face, and shoved her head against the pillow. "Bitch." He slid from the bed, the knife pointed forward.

Jesse reached for the fire poker. He cautioned, "No sudden moves. Step away from my wife." He waved the poker to indicate the direction.

Lawrence acquiesced. "Seems we're at an impasse, brother."

"Answer my question—why did you murder our father?"

"You stupid wog." Lawrence spread his arms wide. "All of this was mine until he returned and foisted his stray mongrel on Mother and me. One day, I found his will. He was giving everything to you." He took a step closer to Jesse, the skirt of his brown frock coat swaying, ruffles fluttering at chest and wrist.

Jesse warned, "Not another step." He kept a keen eye on the dirk Lawrence wielded. "First, I'm not from India, so don't call me that insulting name. Second, I'm Kiowa, grandson of a tribal chief and son of a Kiowa princess and an English viscount. At least I can prove my lineage." Jesse held a large brown journal sealed with a leather strap and a gold lock. "It's Father's journal. A little worse for wear, but the pages are intact."

Lawrence's eyes widened. He stepped forward. Jesse raised the poker. "Don't test me. I'm not the gullible little boy you cajoled into climbing out on a rotten apple tree limb. All I wanted was a big brother, someone to admire. Instead, I got you."

Lawrence stared at Jesse with defiant eyes. "Whose seed did I sprout from? I need to know."

"I only just found the book."

"Where? Tell me! Bloody hell, I searched for years looking for that blasted book."

A wry grin touched Jesse's lips. "You might say it was a gift from Father. It actually fell from the stable attic and conked me on the head. Getting the horses out alive was my main concern." He held the book for Lawrence to see. "I'm certain Father wrote the name of his attacker on one of these pages, but we both know it was you. And when you're sentenced, I will personally request Wakefield Prison as your next home."

Rebecca fought against the bindings that held her prisoner. Her heart skipped a beat and the hairs on her arms stood up when Lawrence let out a blood-curdling shriek and lunged forward, the knife pointed at Jesse's heart. "I'll slit my own throat before I'm sent to that hell hole."

Jesse used the poker to block the attack. As they both fell over the white button-tufted chair and rolled to the floor, he grabbed Lawrence's wrist to keep the blade from plunging into his heart.

Unable to see the fight for life between her husband and a maniac, Rebecca was certain an invisible hand squeezed her heart. It seemed an eternity passed before Jesse stood, blood dripping from his chest. She screamed, "No…no…no!"

Jesse clutched his bleeding shoulder as he stumbled toward the bed. Rebecca's eyes widened in horror. She cried a warning, "Jesse, look out."

Lawrence rose like a monster, the dirk in his chest. "I'm not an easy man to kill." He raised the poker high over his head. He expelled a loud grunt, his face grimaced, and for a moment he seemed suspended in motion before falling face forward, a knife embedded in his back.

Leotie stood in the doorway. "I could not let a monster kill you, my son."

"We'll need the constable, Mother."

"Of course. I'll send Mr. Poole."

Jesse wrapped his arms around his mother. "Thank you for saving my life."

She touched his face. "Today was not your day to die." She bent to pull the knife from Lawrence's back.

Jesse's cautioned, "Leave everything as it is. The constable will need to see the crime scene."

His mother nodded her understanding. She said, "Take care of Rebecca while I send Mr. Poole and then see to Mr. Standish. He was badly burned."

Rebecca's words of gratitude to her mother-in-law

were softly spoken.

When they were alone, Jesse lifted one of his father's rapiers from the wall brackets to free Rebecca from the ropes. He wrapped the duvet around her naked body and carried her into the adjoining suite decorated especially for her, for when she felt the need for privacy. He placed her gently on the bed there.

Finally he brought a ewer of water and a basin to sit at Rebecca's feet. He carefully removed the quilt. Dipping a cloth in the tepid water, he lifted her face and wiped it clean, taking tender care not to duly chafe her bruised cheek and swollen lips. As he washed her hands and arms, his jaw tightened at the red welts around her wrists, the bruises, and the mark of the knifepoint between her breasts that bespoke the cruelty from Lawrence. At least he had sent him to a well-earned end.

Placing her slender feet into the basin, he washed the blood from her ankles, then patted them dry. For a brief moment he let his gaze wander over her in a longing caress. Though she had been roughly used, her beauty stirred his heart. With great care, he slid a fresh nightgown over her head and helped guide her arms into the sleeves. He gathered her in his arms, resting his chin atop her head. His voice broke. "I'm so sorry, my sweet. I shouldn't have left you alone."

She grimaced from the pain. "He said no one noticed him walking up the stairs, but how did he get in the bedroom? The door was locked."

Jesse sighed. "These old houses were built with secret passages in case the family had need to escape from an enemy. I'd forgotten about it."

Rebecca shivered. "I don't want to spend another

night in that room. Your father's death, and now Lawrence's…too many ugly memories."

Jesse agreed. "I'll send Zoe to sit with you while I wait for the constable."

She nodded. "Did we lose any horses in the fire? Were any of our people hurt?"

"Only the stable suffered." He was silent for a moment. "Odd how Lawrence's twisted mind worked. He tied the horses inside their stalls to make it impossible to get them out or for them to escape on their own. Had it not been for the stallion's frantic whinnies and the help from Mr. Standish and Poole, we never could have gotten them out. Charlie cut them loose, and Mother worked her Kiowa magic on them, or all would have been lost."

"Will you read your father's journal?"

"Aye. In time."

Rebecca twisted the hem of the sheet. She blinked back tears. "The constable won't take Leotie to jail, will he?"

"Not when he hears that Sir Oliver is her barrister." Jesse paused. "In fact, the constable might give a huge sigh of relief to be rid of Lawrence."

"He ranted on about cutting out his mother's tongue. Oh, Jesse, I hope it was a lie." She placed her hand to her mouth. "I've never met anyone mentally unbalanced, and I hope I never do again." She thought for a moment. "I have to ask. You don't think your father was…" She couldn't bring herself to say what she wondered, if madness ran in Jesse's veins, too.

He leaned forward and kissed her. "Try to rest. As soon as I deal with the constable, I'll come to bed. We'll read the journal tomorrow—to satisfy both our minds."

Before he subdued it, pain flickered in his eyes. She longed to put her arms around him, though she refrained. She had pain enough of her own. There were so many things she wanted to say. She wanted to say kind, wise words, but those words wouldn't come. They looked at each other in silence, separated by deep emotions tightly contained. After a moment, Jesse scowled and looked away. "Good night, my sweet," he said, and left the room.

Chapter 38

Dressed in a gray flannel robe and wearing a nightcap, the butler greeted Jesse in the grand hall. "Frightful evening, milord. Most tragic…most tragic. Shall I bring you a tea or a hot toddy?" Clarence Jeeves had served as butler for as long as Jesse could remember. He had gone with the other Arlington staff when Lawrence's vile mistreatment and failure to pay wages left them no other choice but to flee.

It was strange being treated like a guest in one's childhood home, and in one where he now served as master. Jesse released a beleaguered sigh.

"Hot toddy." Jesse massaged his throbbing temples.

"Right-o, milord."

Jesse seated himself behind the big old mahogany desk. His father's desk. The slightly burnt leather journal lay before him. Although he was sitting, he was dizzy from the effects of his near-death experience with Lawrence and the cruel way his half-brother had treated Rebecca, overlaid with a new worry: his mother. She had clearly acted in his defense, and her actions were justifiable, but would the courts treat her as cruelly as the Indian agents in the American territories treated the native people? Had he made a mistake by bringing her to England?

Caught up in his dismay and concern, he didn't

hear the butler enter the study. "Pardon, milord." Jeeves set the aromatic toddy in front of him. "I've also brought salve and bandages for your arm." The older man busied himself tending the wound.

"You are a good man, Jeeves. I'm glad you returned to Arlington." Jesse wearily rubbed his eyes.

The old man quirked a smile. "Shall I stay up while you wait for the constable?"

"Go to bed and get your rest. Whatever morning brings with the investigation, I will depend on you to keep the staff calm and going about their duties as usual."

Jeeves gave a little salute. "Right-o." He stopped at the door, his hand on the knob, then turned. "Beggin' your pardon, 'tis not my place to speak so bold, especially of the dead, but if Madam Leotie had not wielded the blade, I would've meself. The devil take 'im. He was rotten to the core. No matter how yer father tried to love 'im, it 'tweren't never good enough. Same with Lawrence's mother. Your father was more than my employer, he was my friend. When you disappeared, we all knew it was Lawrence's doings, and we prayed ye had not met the heavenly saints. There be not one of us who will shed a tear for the blighter. There, I said it, and if you be wanting me letter of resignation—"

Jesse offered a weary smile. "I count myself fortunate to have your loyalty."

The old man nodded. "Right-o." And he silently closed the door.

Jesse peered at the contents of his cup. It had cooled enough that he swallowed the warm honey-laced whisky in one long gulp.

Using a letter opener to break the journal's lock, he gently opened the binding. Jesse immediately recognized his father's handwriting: Addison J. Starr Fitzroy, Viscount of Arlington, Warwickshire.

That gray nagging feeling that had followed him around for the past ten years—and perhaps most of his life—as a constant shadow was darker, more insistent than ever. If that dark and heavy shadow could talk, he feared it would whisper, *Much to my horror, I have passed on the madness to my first born. I pray God has spared my second son of this dreadful mania.*

Jesse hadn't felt this wretched since the first day he awoke, bruised and battered and sick, aboard the slave ship *Scarlett Whydah*. Restless, he rose to settle in a chair by the fire. Tucked inside the pages was a letter. The vellum was old but still spoke of quality. The seal of the Viscount of Arlington informed him that the missive was from his deceased father. He broke the seal and unfolded the sheet, and something fell into his lap—a gold ring set with diamonds and pearls. A woman's ring. He pocketed the band and turned his attention to the page of neatly penned script.

He read the date, September 1879. Performing a mental calculation, he determined the letter was written the year of his sixteenth birthday, and just prior to his father's death.

Dear Jesse,

If you have found this letter, it means you have also discovered my journal, and that I am most likely dead. I have left the Arlington property, in its entirety, to you because Lawrence is no longer my heir. Oliver Armistead has the official copy of my last will and testament.

Rose Manor was purchased for my cherished Leotie. It was my intention to provide this unentailed estate in hopes of bringing her to England. It is only proper that it belong to my younger son. You are so much like your mother that I desire you to own the property I wished for her. Your preferences were always the same: for solitude rather than parties, for horses rather than chess, as well as the wildness and openness of the countryside instead of theatres and operas, and books instead of idle chatter. Your temperaments are the same, too, stemming from the same passionate nature. I have faith that you will achieve great things when you come of age and reach the fullness of your manhood.

Your mother, Leotie, Kiowa Princess and sister of Chief Charging Bear, Oklahoma Territory, America, was everything I am not, everything I needed to feel whole. If I said to you as a child that you should be more like Lawrence, it was my way of wishing you were more like me, or less like her. When I looked at you, I could only see what I had lost and not what I had gained. I fear I will die before I see you set razor to strop and shave the peach fuzz from your cheeks. I am certain a part of me thinks I died the day I kissed my Prairie Rose goodbye and returned to England. If I was never not fair to you or good to you, my son, forgive me, for I am sorry.

Regret is a wretched thing to live with, Jesse. If I have one wish for you, it is to never know the feeling as I do. If I could have a second wish for you, it is that you find your mother and know the goodness and love that she possesses. My third wish is to follow your heart, especially when you find your "forever" love. Be

Kiowa, be passionate, and do not be staidly British.

Included is the ring I intended to place on your mother's finger on the day of our wedding, another regret that erodes my heart every day. I should have stopped being so bloody British and heeded the "when comes forever" beckoning back to Oklahoma and placed it on her finger, Henrietta and Lawrence be damned.

With Love,

Addison Jesse Starr Fitzroy, Viscount of Arlington

Postscriptum: A man does not easily share his private thoughts. You, however, are my son, and the only seed of my loins. The contents of my journal will answer any of your doubts.

Jesse read the letter again to make sure it was real and to be sure he had read it correctly. It must be true and real, judging by the tightness in his chest and that odd, hot stinging in his eyes that he had only felt once, on the day his father died. If he had one wish, it would be that he had found this letter earlier, because he could never bring back his father. He already knew regret. It had kept him company for ten years.

Jesse looked out the window. It was too dark to see what lay beyond the room. He saw his own reflection in the glass—that of a man who ached to regain what had been stolen from him. Beyond that lay a vast land that was his and which would one day belong to his heirs.

He scanned the letter once more, pausing on the line *You, however, are my son, and the only seed of my loins.*

His heart swelled with an unfamiliar emotion. His father had given him a gift more precious than all the wealth in the world.

Jesse held the vellum to his nose and sniffed, hoping to catch a scent of his father's shaving lotion. He closed his eyes and conjured an image of his father—stalwart, tall, full of life, with eyes that bespoke deep sadness and, perhaps, regret.

He'd wanted answers, had bided his time and suspected that when the time was ripe, his father, dead or alive, would find a way to explain all the family secrets. Part of him hesitated. After all, he had promised Rebecca they would find the answers together.

He rationalized that the hour was late, and she had already suffered enough shocks for one night. He silently promised to find a way to placate her. First and foremost, he wanted to understand why his father had married Henrietta in the first place.

With his head down, he read with interest. His eyes grew weary, and his vision blurred. Were it not in his father's script, and his head bent to the crisp clean pages, he would not have been able to comprehend the words. There was much to digest. His tired eyes threatened to close all by themselves. His shoulders slumped forward, and his brain seemed to close down. He jerked awake, blinking to clear away the fatigue, and so he read Addison's words.

I, Addison Jesse Starr Fitzroy, am the youngest son. It was my duty to enlist in the Queen's service. However, my brother, Giles, loved adventure and despised all thoughts of business and following in our father's footsteps. Without father's knowledge, Giles enlisted in the Royal Army and was immediately assigned to the British Raj in India. Alas, my dear brother was felled on the first day of the Great Rebellion. Though but sixteen years of age, I feel responsible for his death.

Mother suffered a cruel and debilitating illness. It was almost a blessing when she closed her eyes and drew her final breath. I will always believe Giles's death hastened her own. We buried Mother today, and my father took up a new residence inside a bottle of whisky. Between his heavy drinking and even heavier losses at the gaming tables, Arlington is near financial collapse, the magnificent thoroughbreds sold to cover unpaid gambling debts and most of the staff dismissed due to lack of funds to pay wages. Because of his debt, father arranged for a forced marriage between me and Henrietta Staunton. The daughter of a tradesman, she is not a woman of beauty, is crude in her manners, and only slightly intelligent, besides being five years my senior. But she is rich, and she traded her dowry for my title. I was but eighteen when the marriage banns were read.

Eager to read more of the details regarding his father's marriage to Henrietta, Jesse quickly scanned the pages until he spotted the continuation of the story.

An inexperienced youth, I was nervous as an unbroke stallion wearing a saddle for the first time. I did not know, until much later, about "popping the cherry." Unbeknownst to me, hers had already been popped! It bothered me that on our wedding night Henrietta was not the shy bride I had expected. She willingly undressed and lay naked with her legs spread, inviting me in. What giddy, wet-behind-the-ears bridegroom would pause? I was ready to dive right in and take all she offered.

As the months passed, she tried to conceal her pregnancy. Tonight, she gave birth to a boy. A man should rejoice and shout from the rooftops that he has sired a son. She named him Lawrence Byron Staunton Fitzroy. She tried to claim the baby was two months premature. Even the physician who delivered the boy declared him full-term. The calendar does not lie. Seven months of marriage does not equate to a ninth-month pregnancy.

At the age of nineteen, instead of being a proud father, I am sickened to have wed a soiled tart who so crassly admits she doesn't know who sired the boy. Her brash announcement that there were at least four, maybe six, others she had shagged sickened me.

I demanded a divorce, but she reminded me it is her money that supports me, my father, and Arlington.

Jeeves knocked before entering. "Beg pardon, milord, Constable Underhill, Vice Constable Gilford, Sir Oliver, and a lady is here."

Jesse rubbed his sleep-deprived eyes. "You are supposed to be abed."

The butler shrugged. "I was, but now I'm here."

"Show them in." Jesse heaved a sigh. He wondered who the lady might be. "Advise Mrs. Caldwell our guest will stay for breakfast, and summon Mr. Poole and Mr. Standish to my study. And Jeeves, bring a large coverlet, one strong enough to cart the body downstairs and out to a wagon."

He didn't wait for the visitors to enter the library. Instead he met them in the hall, where he was surprised to see Sir Oliver's secretary. "My regrets that we meet again under such dire circumstances, Miss Wells." He indicated the stairs. "Follow me. I'm sure you will want to examine the body first."

****

Jesse was surprised to see his mother standing at the top of the landing, fully dressed. Her stature wooden, her face stoic. He sensed she had prepared to be taken away. He rushed up the stairs. He was prepared to do battle before allowing law enforcement to remove her for any reason. "There is no need for you to look at the body, Mother."

She harrumphed. "Why should I fear a *baykok*? He is dead and can do no more harm."

Constable Underhill said, "I thought we were here to examine the body of Lawrence Fitzroy."

Jesse coughed to disguise his amusement. "My mother is a Kiowa princess from the southern Kiowa people of Oklahoma territory. In her language, *baykok* means monster. In a sense, Lawrence was a monster."

"Of course, of course," Underhill sputtered. "Milord, if you will show us the body."

Jesse opened the door and held it wide for the officers and Sir Oliver to enter the bedroom. Leotie followed. A white sheet draped Lawrence's body. Only the upturned dirty soles of his shoes were visible. A large splotch of brownish red stained the newly purchased Parisian rug.

Underhill knelt and lifted the sheet. He looked up and spoke to no one in particular. "Who all were present at the time of the murder?"

Still wearing his bloodied and torn shirt, Jesse felt anger knot his stomach. "There was no murder." He pointed to the large bandage on his shoulder. "He came bloody near to killing me."

Underhill flicked a sardonic smile. "Hmm. It's rather odd that your wound is in the front of your shoulder, but the blade is in the victim's back."

Leotie stepped forward. Jesse was certain her dark eyes sparked anger. She said, "I could not allow a monster to kill my son."

Underhill lowered the sheet and stood. He squinted at Leotie. "So you stabbed the victim in the back?"

Sir Oliver intervened, his voice terse. "Let me remind you, Underhill, that this is not an inquisition, that Viscount Fitzroy voluntarily sent for the law, and further, I am barrister to the Fitzroy family. There will be no interrogations, and no skewed questions. I suggest the body be removed immediately and taken to the morgue, where the coroner will do a formal examination." He looked at Jesse. "Although the hour is late, I will need statements from everyone who witnessed the—incident." He cocked an eyebrow toward the constable.

Constable Underhill did not try to hide his displeasure. "Of course. As you wish." He added, "Under the circumstances, I hesitate to require Lady Rebecca's presence, but it is necessary to obtain her statement."

The gruffness in Jesse's voice spoke his anger. "My wife suffered horrendous physical abuse from Lawrence. I will not allow her to be further tormented."

Wearing a fresh robe, her blonde hair lying in tangles over her shoulder, Rebecca appeared in the doorway. Her swollen, damaged lips made speaking painful, but her voice was firm. "Ask your questions. I have nothing to hide."

Oliver Armistead gawped at the diminutive woman. "My God, Lady Rebecca, shall I summon a doctor?"

Miss Wells clasped her hands over her mouth to

catch her audible gasp.

The finger imprints on Rebecca's neck had turned blue; both eyes were puffed and black and her nose swollen like a bulbous beet. To avoid baring her breasts, she discreetly parted the lapels of the blue robe to expose the long, thin raw slash that started at her throatlatch and continued to her navel. The sleeves of her robe rode up to expose the harsh red and blue chafing on her wrists. She wobbled. In an instant, Jesse and Leotie were at her side. Jesse marveled at his wife's pluck even as she struggled to speak. "If anyone was out to commit murder, it was neither my husband nor my mother-in-law." She pointed at the sheet-covered body. "It was the devil."

Sir Oliver profusely apologized. "I wonder if we might retire to the library. Miss Wells is very adept at note taking. She will not need to ask any of you to repeat what you've already stated." He cut an eye toward his secretary, who answered with a meek nod.

The constable ordered, "You may now remove the body. Vice Constable Gilford will assist."

Cradling his wounded arm, Jesse grimaced with pain. "Mr. Poole, will you carry my wife to the library? And Jeeves—"

"No worries, milord. I've already informed Mrs. Crawley. She is preparing tea and scones as we speak."

Before being engulfed by tears, Rebecca managed to say, "Sir Oliver, Lawrence threatened to cut out my tongue just like he had done to his mother."

"Bloody damn, you say." Constable Underhill threw a glance of surprise her way. "There was rumor that a female corpse from the Upper East Side had been found minus her tongue. She had choked to death on her own blood."

"Your professional tact is positively understated, Constable." Sir Oliver offered the chastisement. "Gilford, while in the city, verify with the chief of police if the deceased is Lady Henrietta Fitzroy. Posthaste. And send a doctor to Viscount Fitzroy's home."

Leotie responded. Her voice emphatic. "I am a medicine woman. There is no need to send a doctor." Jesse and Rebecca affirmed her statement.

Damnation, Jesse thought. It seemed the taking of statements went interminably long. He shook his head as if to clear his mind, trying to focus on Sir Oliver's words.

"Let us take our leave." Sir Oliver patted Jesse's arm. "Nothing to worry about, my boy." He lifted Leotie's hand and kissed it. "Madam, I regret we meet again under these circumstances." His gaze softened as he wrapped Rebecca's small hands in his. "Settle your concerns, my dear. There will be no inquisition. Evidence is quite clear that self-defense against a monstrous intruder was the only recourse. Constable Underhill's report will state, 'Case closed.' "

He cut a commanding glance toward the officer, who frowned as he nodded. Sir Oliver looked at his secretary. "Miss Wells, I trust you will have the statements ready for a full reading by the end of the week?"

"I will, milord."

The sun broke through gray clouds, filling the library with dancing prisms. Leotie turned her face to catch the light. "It is an omen. The Great Spirit Father blesses us with a new beginning."

Chapter 39

Nearly a month passed before they received Sir Oliver's proclamation stating that Lawrence Boyd Staunton Fitzroy's death had been ruled a justifiable homicide, and that no charges had been nor would be imposed against any member of the Fitzroy family.

Rebecca sat in the summerhouse overlooking the lake. She laughed at Noelle's gabbling duck imitations. It felt good to laugh. She looked back at the house, where Leotie tended the kitchen garden, and then her eyes settled on the corral, where Jesse was putting a new thoroughbred stallion through his paces. Her heart swelled with love.

She bent to her journal and wrote, describing the terrible events they had suffered at the hands of a madman. She ended with: *Jesse shared his father's journal entry with Leotie and me. It is a relief to us all that Lawrence's insanity was inherited from someone other than Jesse's father. As Leotie said, the Great Spirit Father smiles on the Fitzroy family.*

A few days after the unpleasant incident, Jesse presented Leotie with his father's journal. After she read it, we visited the family cemetery, and standing next to his father's headstone, Jesse slipped the gold and pearl ring on his mother's finger. It was tears of happiness that we all shed.

Indian summer is upon us. Just as the leaves turn

their brilliant golds and reds, and then wither and die, a new year will begin with the promises of new life.

She dipped the pen into the inkwell and continued. *It is too soon to make the announcement, but I am certain that in the coming summer Jesse will proudly hold his new son or daughter.*

She smiled at the secret she was keeping. A sweet voice warmed Rebecca's heart. "Mommy, ducks go cak-cak-cak."

Joy filled Rebecca. "Yes, they do, my darling girl."

Once again, the pen scratched across the blank pages. *Through his many business associates, Jesse has learned that my father's bank collapsed due to overly zealous and poor investments, and to keep from going to prison, he had to liquidate all of his assets. My sisters' husbands didn't fare quite so well. Both are serving ten years for collusion and embezzlement. I am shocked to learn of such dishonesty from a father who was always so righteously pious. My sisters are now divorced. They live with my parents in a fourth-floor apartment. Father is a night watchman at one of the harbor warehouses, and mother, from what I understand, has permanently taken to her bed.*

On my behalf, Jesse graciously wired a check in the amount of five thousand dollars. Although the money I took from my father's safe was rightfully mine, money that Frank Donnelly squandered, I did take it without permission. My conscience is clear. I have more than paid my debt. I pray the money will bring some measure of comfort to my parents and sisters.

We know the check was cashed, but not a word of appreciation has been received. No matter. Truly, it does not matter. I stopped being a Throckmorton the day I eloped, and I stopped being a daughter and a sister the day my beautiful Noelle was labeled a bastard and I was ordered from the house in the dark of night and in the pouring rain. I shall never forget my father yelling that I was a jezebel and that he had disowned me. Even more painful was the way my mother turned her back and walked up the stairs, and the hateful words my sisters spoke.

Their loss has been my gain. I am Rebecca Ann Starr Fitzroy, wife of Addison Jesse Starr Fitzroy, Viscount of Arlington, mother to Noelle Rose Starr Fitzroy, daughter-in-law to Leotie Starr Fitzroy, and soon to be mother of another Starr Fitzroy. I am loved. I am cherished. I am blessed. I am happy.

She paused to dip the pen in the inkwell. And then she wrote, *Ours has been a long and arduous journey, but sometimes the most difficult journeys lead to forever happiness.*

"We should have a bumper crop of foals in the spring." Jesse's voice startled her.

She closed the journal and locked the clasp. Oh, how she wanted to share her secret, but she would bide her time until absolutely certain there was a child growing inside her. Instead, she said, "Arlington is thriving with new life."

Noelle pointed at the ducks. "Poppy, wuk. Cak-caks."

Jesse chuckled as he lifted his daughter into his arms, then held out his hand to Rebecca. He drew her hand to his lips and slowly kissed the lean white knuckles while each gazed warmly and played within the depths of the other's eyes. Rebecca's gleamed as she stared at him from beneath lowered lids. Her body roused, wanting more than a kiss on the hand.

Jesse waggled his eyebrows. "You are looking very much like a temptress, milady."

She laughed with ebullient joy and linked her arm through his. "I will take that as a compliment, milord."

Arm in arm, they walked toward the house, replete in their forever-ness.

Thank you for purchasing
this publication of The Wild Rose Press, Inc.

If you enjoyed the story, we would appreciate your
letting others know by leaving a review.

For other wonderful stories,
please visit our on-line bookstore at
www.thewildrosepress.com.

For questions or more information
contact us at
info@thewildrosepress.com.

The Wild Rose Press, Inc.
www.thewildrosepress.com

Stay current with The Wild Rose Press, Inc.

Like us on Facebook

https://www.facebook.com/TheWildRosePress

And Follow us on Twitter
https://twitter.com/WildRosePress